KT-389-669

St Helens Libr

I DID IT FOR US

I
DID
IT
FOR
US

ALISON BRUCE

Constable • London

CONSTABLE

First published in Great Britain in 2018 by Constable

A CIP catalogue record for this book is available from the British Library.

ISBN: 978-1-47212-384-8

Typeset in Times New Roman by TW Type, Cornwall
Printed and bound in Great Britain by CPI Group (UK) Ltd, Croydon CR0 4YY

Papers used by Constable are from well-managed forests and other responsible sources.

Constable
An imprint of
Little, Brown Book Group
Carmelite House
50 Victoria Embankment
London EC4Y 0DZ

An Hachette UK Company
www.hachette.co.uk

www.littlebrown.co.uk

To Krystyna Green,

You made the entire Goodhew series possible and championed this book from the outset. This book is dedicated to you with my heart-felt thanks.

With love, Alison xx

PROLOGUE

I never *considered* suicide. I didn't sit on a bridge parapet or stare into the neck of a bottle of pills. I looked into the future and I considered every way I might turn. And I don't think I wanted to die. Not then.

But each choice I faced swelled with hopelessness and the only achievement by the end of each day was counting the hours that I'd squandered and being glad I wouldn't have to live them again. I had options, everyone does, but none that I could face; they filled me with nausea, the feeling of vertigo I remembered from childhood, when I'd climbed the rocks by the pier at Clevedon beach and was too scared to scramble back down.

My parents wouldn't help me this time though. They said they would, but their stiff body language and guarded expressions had said otherwise.

And through it all the only constant was the virus-like thought that told me to just let go, to take control one final time and surrender. To choose nothing over something. Wasn't that what I was doing anyway? To fall, to swallow, to just not bother breathing anymore.

I never considered suicide but in those darkest times it considered me. It courted me and acted like my only friend. I never sent it packing but I woke one day to find that it had tired of me and had slipped away. Probably to find someone else.

It took three days for my life to fall apart. That doesn't sound like a long time to wipe out a marriage, a career, family support, love, finances, security, sanity. I could have said that it took ten minutes but if I'd kept those ten minutes to myself then I wouldn't be where I am today.

Three days then to step from one life into another.

I'd driven along East Road in Cambridge countless times. I was aware of the building, curved and large with unimaginative cream brickwork and government-issue sliding doors. I was certain that it was a multi-storey car park when I'd first noticed. Later, I read the signage and registered the lion and unicorn crest over the entrance.

Dieu et Mon Droit.

God and My Right.

I never expected the building to mean anything to me.

I made myself visit a week before the trial. The doors slid open. A few feet inside stood a security desk and the frame of a walkthrough metal detector. A lone security guard stood nearby. He was the only person in view, a wiry and unsmiling man who stared at me until I spoke first.

'Am I allowed to look around?'

'It's a public building. Anyone can go in.'

I nodded and he checked my bag, then I stepped through the metal detector and he double checked by passing an electronic paddle through the air, inches from my body.

'Which way do I go?'

'Just follow the signs,' he said then walked away. I took the stairs and spent the next half an hour without seeing another soul.

The newness of the building was reinforced by fresh white walls and unscuffed beige floor tiles. Outside each of the three courts were

2

rows of grey metal seats bolted to the floor. The signage was midnight blue printed with sans serif lettering in a milky white font. The doors along the corridor were all pale beech wood.

No two items matched but each was repeated. Doors, signage, thermostats and smoke alarms. Again, again, again. The effect was uniformity but without statement.

It left me feeling strangely mute. I thanked the security guard as I left and my words came as a whisper.

DAY 1

We were at the court building in a side room.

I was being represented by Dominic Templeton and he faced me across a small table, which he was using as his makeshift office. I didn't choose him, he was allocated to me, but DI Briggs told me to trust him, to tell him everything I could. We never reached the position where I referred to this man as anything other than Mr Templeton. He was far better educated than me with my single A level and I felt reminded of this every time he spoke. I could hear myself trying to sound more formal, picking words that I normally wouldn't use, and I wondered why I didn't have the balls to be myself.

'Mrs Stirling?'

I'd tried 'Call me Emily' but he ignored me.

He tapped the paper between us. It was a photograph of the clothes I wore that night. They were spread out and arranged with the top and the skirt the approximate distance apart as they would have been when I wore them; exposing the skin from the top of my hips to a couple of inches below my bra.

'You have to be ready to respond to the accusation that you dressed in a provocative manner.'

We'd been through this discussion before and now, minutes before my testimony, he'd come back to it.

'It was a Halloween party.'

'Were all the other women dressed like this?'

'No. Why does that matter? I was there with my husband, why would I be wary of what I chose to wear?'

'So what you wore was acceptable, only because you were with Mr Stirling?'

'That's not what I meant.'

'As a lone woman would you have dressed in that way?'

I opened my mouth to speak but then changed my mind. Mr Templeton's attention was both critical and disappointed. 'You need to avoid opening yourself up to that kind of evaluation. Your choices will be scrutinised.'

'I have the right to dress as I choose. It doesn't equate to an invitation for sexual assault.'

'It shouldn't,' he corrected me, 'but there are incidences when it encourages inappropriate behaviour.'

'Inappropriate behaviour? That's rowdiness or stealing road cones, not this.'

He sat straight backed with his fingers woven together in front of him. He stared into his palms for several seconds before replying. 'But this isn't one of those cases. Andrew Tyler was a close family friend and his behaviour, it will be argued, was either out of character or not what you claim it to be.'

'Why are you going over this again now?'

'Your choice of clothes needs to be out of character too. The court must believe that you didn't dress in order to titillate or encourage the defendant.'

A court usher opened the door before I could reply. 'Please come through.'

I stood immediately. Dominic Templeton gathered his papers with less haste.

'You're not required yet, Mrs Stirling,' he told me. 'Don't you have someone who can wait with you?'

I had family there but they were already seated in the public gallery and my instant reaction was to try to hide my disorientation. 'I'd rather have some time on my own,' I lied.

He didn't react and said nothing more until he reached the door. The usher held it open and Mr Templeton looked back in my direction although his gaze didn't quite meet mine. 'Remember what we just discussed, Mrs Stirling. Tread carefully.'

I couldn't be myself in front of him and now I couldn't be myself in court either. Being myself was no longer good enough.

The usher walked in front of me and bowed to the court as he entered. I reminded myself that I was not on trial. And I stepped forward.

I didn't need to be hidden from public view or escorted in and out through a private entrance.

But I was.

There was a screen shielding me from Andy Tyler. From the time I made my initial statement I'd been referring to him by first name and last name together. It distanced him from the Andy who was my husband's best friend.

I knew about the screen, I wasn't sure whether I should 'bravely face him across the courtroom' or 'have to give evidence from behind a screen'. Like most people, my knowledge of courts and trials had come from newspapers and been tainted by TV drama. I'd agreed to the screen but hadn't understood that it would also shield me from the public gallery and that I wouldn't be able to see the faces of the people I needed the most.

From the witness box, I could see the judge, jury and both the defence and prosecution lawyers. The screen was concertinaed and made from tubular steel and pale blue fabric. It looked as though it belonged in a hospital corridor and blocked out everything else in the courtroom. I wondered who else was on the other side, the officials I couldn't see, expressions that I wanted to be able to read.

And hiding from Andrew Tyler suddenly felt like cowardice.

I beckoned towards Mr Templeton and he approached me, stony faced. He turned his head so that I could speak quietly in his ear. 'I don't want the screen after all.'

'It was brought for your benefit, Mrs Stirling.'

'Please remove it.'

I knew that in facing Tyler I wouldn't be able to stay partitioned off from everyone else but when the screen was wheeled away I only took a quick glance at the court. To my very left was a long bench

6

occupied by three people including the usher. None of them were looking towards me and it was only when my gaze was sweeping across a group of seats in a recessed area of the wall facing the judge that I saw my mum's pale face and realised that the public gallery was nothing more than two rows of chairs.

My attention rested on them for such a brief moment that I saw them all as an unmoving snapshot. Mum, then Ben with a small tight smile, Dad looking down at his lap. I paused for a moment at Jess; we'd always been able to read each other's expressions. But when her eyes met mine I couldn't tell what she was thinking. I gave a tiny shake of my head and moved on. Andy Tyler's parents were there too and my gaze hurried past them, avoiding the dock where Tyler waited and landing back on the judge.

Judge Geraint Williams looked about sixty. He had a close cropped grey beard and an expression cultivated to look enquiring. Until he spoke I thought he looked like a teacher, or perhaps one of those college tutors that it was okay to address by their first name. But with his first words those ideas vanished. The sound of his voice stirred an unsettled feeling in the pit of my stomach. His tone was without emotion. He talked of proof and demanded clarity over the most minor details.

I took the oath and was handed my own statement. I'd known this was coming.

Dominic Templeton stood. 'Please read your statement to the court, Mrs Stirling.'

I lifted the sheets from the table but my hands were shaking. I placed them back down and the only option was to read them with my head bowed. My voice was amplified but so was the way it trembled. I began.

My name is Emily Laurel Stirling. I live at the address overleaf. I am making this statement following an incident when I was attacked and raped by a man I know as Andrew Tyler. I'm a white female, age thirty, height five feet five, weight nine stone two pounds with light brown hair and blue eyes.

On the evening of Saturday 29 October 2016 my husband

7

Ben Stirling and I attended a Halloween party at Mr Tyler's house along with twelve other guests. Although I didn't know them all well, they were all people who I'd met on previous occasions. We arrived after 8 p.m. but before 8.15 p.m.

Mr Tyler lives approximately half a mile from our house and we drove to the party with the intention of drinking, walking home and picking our car up the following day.

My husband was wearing jeans and a T-shirt with a wool winter jacket and I was wearing a black skirt and top with a heavy cape. My husband's T-shirt depicted a skeleton and my outfit was also themed for Halloween because we had been told that the event was a fancy-dress party.

Mr Tyler lives alone and I have known him since 2012 when I met my future husband. He has been my husband's closest friend since they were at school together. Mr Tyler was the best man at our wedding but I only know him in that capacity and have never socialised with him without my husband being present.

The words were mostly mine but more stilted. I'd been led through the statement as I'd given it and expected to clarify every sentence. The resulting paragraphs sounded stiff and self-aware. I wished the nerves weren't so evident in my speech but they were all I could hear and I wondered whether I sounded as though I was lying. I tried to avoid either hesitating or rushing, and described the events of that night while fighting to keep my voice from shaking.

Progress was slow but no one questioned or challenged this. A court moves at its own pace. It was like a slow-moving mechanism. We stepped on and passed through the machinery.

Counsel for the defence was Rebecca Hobbs and I tried giving her a polite smile when she first addressed me. It wasn't returned.

'Mrs Stirling, how long have you been married?'

'Just over three years.'

'And how would you describe your relationship with your husband, Mr Stirling?'

'Good,' I glanced across at him and he pressed his lips into a tight smile. 'It's strong,' I corrected myself. 'We've been very close since we met.'

'So, would you say that it's an honest relationship?'

I nodded then reminded myself that they were waiting for the verbal response.

'Yes. Yes, I would.'

I made sure that I spoke clearly and that my tone was firm. My job involved public speaking and I knew how to communicate with a roomful of people: make eye contact with different parts of the audience, speak with conviction, make each point clear and concise. Be natural and let the audience warm to you. That was the hardest part.

Rebecca Hobbs continued, 'So two years ago when you told your husband, Mr Stirling, that his friend Andrew Tyler had . . .' She paused to refer to her notes as though my quote was alien to her. 'That he had "tried it on" with you, your aim was to be honest and open with your husband?'

'Yes.'

'And what did you expect to happen as a result of making this accusation to your husband?'

I hesitated. I couldn't remember what I expected at the time, but I could remember feeling stung when Ben had laughed and tried to brush it off. 'It was important he knew,' I replied.

'Did you expect something to change between Mr Stirling and Mr Tyler as a result?'

'I wanted my husband to be aware.'

Rebecca Hobbs flicked the paper in her hand in order to straighten it. It made a small cracking sound. She raised her voice slightly. 'Are you telling me that you wanted your husband to know that his friend was sexually attracted to you but that you were still happy to continue having the same contact with Mr Tyler? To have him as a visitor to your house? To accept lifts from him? To . . .'

'No,' I snapped, my tone too loud and harsh for the room, 'of course not.' I took a breath and tried to gather my thoughts. I glanced across at my mum and could tell that she'd heard the panic in my voice. 'I thought my husband might distance himself from Mr Tyler.'

'So, you wanted to end their friendship?'

This time it was Ben's gaze I met before replying. 'No, I didn't. I had to tell Ben but it put me in a difficult position. I didn't want to hurt him, but not telling him would have played on my conscience.'

'It must have hurt you when he didn't take you seriously.' She didn't pause for me to reply, 'Do you worry that he thought you'd made it up?'

'No.'

'In your opinion then, why did he refuse to act upon what you'd told him?'

I opened my mouth to speak but couldn't think of an answer that wouldn't reflect badly, either on one of us or on our marriage. The silence stretched out until any reply would have sounded like a fabrication.

'Mrs Stirling?'

'I don't know.'

'You hadn't given it any thought, then?'

I gathered myself enough this time and raised one hand in a 'stop' gesture. 'I thought about it and, although I don't know why my husband didn't distance himself from Andy Tyler, I assumed that it was because he trusted both of us and had no expectation that anything would actually occur.'

I felt relieved at my reply and glanced at the jury. Several of them seemed to be making notes. I hoped that was a good sign.

Rebecca Hobbs appeared satisfied with my response. 'So, in summary, you're glad that you confided in your husband, you feel that he believed your claim that Mr Tyler had made an advance towards you of a sexual nature and you understood why he chose not to act upon that information?'

My moment of feeling positive vanished and I felt my face redden. Surely everyone could hear the difference between what I'd explained and the way it had just been described. I doubted that I had the ability to challenge her so I agreed. We moved on.

'Which brings us to this latest incident. The alleged assault took place on the night of Saturday 29 October last year as you and your husband were attending a party to celebrate Halloween?'

'Yes.'

10

'Did you have any concerns about attending a party where you would come into contact with Mr Tyler?'

'No.'

'Why not?'

'It didn't cross my mind. I had no reason to think that the other comment hadn't just been a one-off. I'd decided it was in the past.'

'So, you didn't consider Mr Tyler when you chose what to wear that evening?'

'No, of course not.'

'You described your outfit as a black skirt and top.' She handed me a photograph of the clothes in question. It was taken just before they were bagged and passed to the police lab for analysis. 'Are these the items you wore on the night in question?'

'They are.'

'And the top is what I would describe as a basque, is that correct?'

'It's that style,' I agreed. Not for the first time, I shot a glance at Dominic Templeton, wondering when he planned to intervene. He remained expressionless.

'Would you describe this as your usual style of dress, Mrs Stirling?'

'No, it was Halloween.'

'I see. And which character were you trying to be?'

'No one in particular.'

'You bought your outfit from a fancy-dress stockist. Do you remember the name of the outfit?'

'I saw a photo I liked, I don't remember reading the packaging.'

'I see. It's actually called "Vamp or Vampire". The definition of vamp being a woman who aggressively seduces men. What made you choose such a provocative outfit?'

'I chose it because I liked it.'

'So you accept that it could be considered provocative?

'It was a bit daring by my standards.'

'It attracted attention, I believe.'

'Not everyone had bothered to dress up. I felt a bit awkward when we first arrived but when more guests turned up it was fine.'

'And how much contact did you have with Mr Tyler during the evening?

'He was talking to my husband early on and after a while I left them and went to the kitchen for another drink.'

'So you spoke to Mr Tyler?'

'I would've said "hi" or similar.'

'Do you remember what he said to either you or your husband at that point?'

'No, I don't remember him saying anything in particular.'

'I see.' Rebecca Hobbs tapped her index finger to her pursed lips as though my reply had thrown her off course and now she needed to reconsider her plan. 'And when did you next encounter Mr Tyler?'

'I was still in the kitchen when he came through. A few of us stood out there but I wasn't talking to anyone at that moment.'

'Why were you there then?'

'I was getting a drink.'

'And how long would you say this was after you first went to the kitchen?'

'It's difficult to say. Probably fifteen or twenty minutes.'

'So, you'd gone to the kitchen for *another* drink and you were there *again*?'

'Yes.'

'And by then this was . . . third . . . fourth drink? Or maybe more?'

'I don't remember.'

'I see. And what were you drinking that evening?'

'Wine, mostly I think.'

'Mostly?'

'I might have had a couple of shots later on.'

'Very well, we'll come back to that. But on this occasion, you'd returned to the kitchen for your third, possibly fourth drink and Mr Tyler entered the room?'

'That's correct.'

'And you spoke to him?'

'I did. I offered to pour him a drink as well but he picked up a bottle of beer.'

'And what was the subject of your conversation?'

'He asked if I thought Jess would be able to make it along later but I told him she was busy with work.'

12

'And this is the business that you ran together?'

I noticed the past tense but I didn't correct her.

'That's right.'

'What was his relationship with your friend, Jessica Foley?'

'They'd been dating for several weeks.'

'And what was his response when you told him that she wouldn't be there?'

'He told me I should have made sure she came along. The conversation was very light-hearted at that point.'

'So, he felt you should have brought her with you?'

'Yes. But we had a lot to do.'

'But you managed to make it to the party?'

'Yes, I did. I'd promised Ben that I would be there.'

'I see.'

'I smiled and I told him that Jess would have been there if she'd wanted it enough.'

'And what did you mean by that?'

'It wasn't meant to be insulting, it was banter.'

'Banter? Please explain.'

'I suppose I was teasing him that she might have better things to do.' I knew my choice of words had been poor and Rebecca Hobbs didn't miss a beat.

'You were teasing him. I see. Was that the end of the conversation?'

'Yes, it was.

'When did you next see him?'

'It was a while later – I don't know how long – when I went to the bathroom and he followed me up the stairs.'

'Please explain what happened next.'

'It's in my statement.'

'Yes, but in your own words.'

My gaze flickered from her to the jury to the public gallery. Those who looked at me were expressionless, the rest looked away, invariably downwards as though hanging their heads was the order of the day.

'I went into the bathroom and made sure that the door was properly locked, not because of him . . .'

'Mr Tyler?'

'That's right, not because of Mr Tyler but because that's something I always check. And then I went to the toilet, washed my hands and left.'

'And how long did this take?'

'A few minutes I guess – longer than usual. It's always awkward in somewhere strange.'

'In what way?'

'I'm always self-conscious, I don't want someone hearing me pee, or hearing how much toilet paper I use,' I tried to sound light-hearted, to hide my discomfort with a joke. Maybe being overheard in the bathroom doesn't bother most people but it has always embarrassed me and the whole truth was that I couldn't make myself go at all knowing that he was standing outside the door and overhearing everything. And maybe the fact that I was drunk by then magnified my inhibitions rather than defeated them. I had decided to leave it until we reached home. I doubted we'd be staying much longer. 'When I opened the door, he was still there.'

'Please, go on.'

'I made a comment, "all yours" or something. I don't remember but I know he looked at me strangely.' I closed my eyes to help me describe it. 'He looked in my direction but he didn't seem focused on me. He seemed angry and distracted. He pushed his way in before I'd had a chance to step on to the landing. It seemed rude. I think I said, "Oi," but then I realised that he'd grabbed hold of me and was pulling me back into the bathroom with him.'

'And how did you respond?'

'I asked him what he was doing.'

'How?'

'I'm sorry?'

'In what manner did you ask him? What tone did you use? How loudly did you speak to him?'

'I said, "What are you doing?" My voice would have been raised to some extent because I blurted the words out as he dragged me.'

'No one reported hearing you call out. Is it possible that you weren't as vocal as you thought you were?'

'It was a party. It was noisy downstairs.'

'I see.' It was the fourth time she'd used those words and I hated them already.

'He shut the door behind us and, although I could tell he was agitated, I didn't immediately feel threatened. My first thought was to try and make sense of what he was saying, as though there might be a legitimate reason for him wanting to talk to me like that. But I could tell straightaway that he was angry about something and I was immediately annoyed because he'd been quite rough as he'd grabbed me.'

'But you didn't call out for help at this point?'

'No, I didn't. I asked him what the hell he thought he was doing and he said he could say the same for me and I didn't have a clue what he was talking about. I went to open the door again. I said, "We don't need to be in here to have this conversation," but he held me back and reached across and slid the lock.

'He asked what I was playing at with Jess. I didn't know what he meant. "You think I'm not good enough for her, don't you?" he said.

'I shook my head and frowned. "No, I didn't say that," I told him.

'Then he said I'd talked her out of coming.

'Again, I shook my head when he said that. If Jess could have been there she would have been. There'd always been mild flirtation between Jess and Tyler but by the time of the party they'd been together for a few weeks and I knew she was disappointed to miss it.'

'But you didn't explain this?'

'No. I was feeling frustrated by then, just angry at him for demanding my attention like that. So, I repeated what I said earlier, that if she had wanted to be there enough, she would have made the effort.

'Then he broke out into some rant about me controlling Jess and me controlling Ben. I don't know where it all came from. It was like he wasn't himself by then. We were arguing, not shouting, just like, loud angry whispers. You don't remember word-for-word everything you say when you've been arguing like that. Suddenly it twisted round and it was all about me disrespecting him and him feeling that I was looking down on him and needing to be taught a lesson. I remember saying, "This is ridiculous," and turning away, reaching out for the door again. That seemed to be when he snapped. The next thing I knew, I was on the floor. I banged my temple on the side of the toilet and I don't understand how it happened so quickly because suddenly his trousers were undone, my skirt was up around my hips and he just pulled my knickers to one side. I just remember staring into his face, shaking my head but I couldn't speak.'

'So, you didn't actually say no?'

'No.'

'You didn't shout out? Call for help?'

'I was too shocked.'

'But you fought back? You struggled to get away, I suppose?'

I looked down at my hands and shook my head. 'No. No I didn't.'

'Which would explain,' Rebecca Hobbs spoke in a firm and very patient voice, 'it would explain why, apart from a small bruise to your forehead, that there were no injuries when you were examined. No bruising consistent with rape. No abrasions consistent with a struggle.'

She left it for what felt like a full minute before moving on and in that time, she stood in front of me, her head cocked slightly to one side and a small smile on her lips. I think she was waiting to see whether I began to scratch around for excuses, maybe talk uncontrollably. The only reason I didn't was because I could think of absolutely nothing to say.

Finally, she spoke.

'How long did you stay quiet, Mrs Stirling?'

'Until it was over.'

'Which was approximately when?'

'One a.m.'

'And you immediately told your husband what had happened?'

'No. No, I didn't.'

'You waited until you arrived home?'

'No, I told him on Monday.'

'You waited until Monday 31 October? Why the delay?'

'I wasn't sure what to do. I think I was in shock, trying to process it.' Process, I realised, was the wrong word, it sounded too functional, too mechanical. 'I wasn't sure what to do.'

'So, you hadn't made up your mind whether to share this important information with your husband?'

'I knew I had to tell him. I think I was shocked.'

'So you say, but I'd like to examine whether something that happened on Sunday 30 October was the real reason you decided to speak to Mr Stirling.'

I shrugged. Nodded. Waited. Then, with undeniable certainty, I saw it coming.

'Where did your husband go on that Sunday evening?'

'To play pool.'

'And who accompanied him?'

'Andrew Tyler.'

'How did you feel about your husband spending the evening with Mr Tyler?'

'Normally I wouldn't have minded.'

'But on this occasion, you did?'

'Of course I did.'

'Had this night of theirs been planned?'

'They play pool every couple of weeks. I don't remember that night being planned but it wasn't out of the ordinary.'

'You say you don't remember it being planned. In fact, it created tension between you and your husband, didn't it?'

'Well, of course, given what had happened.'

'Given what had allegedly happened. Isn't it just that, after a weekend of partying and spending time with his best friend, you were annoyed at your husband wanting to go out for another evening?'

'I don't remember.'

'You don't remember? In your previous statement, you said the two of you "had words".'

'We did.'

'Ah, so you *do* remember?'

'I'm sorry, I misunderstood the question.'

Of course, I hadn't misunderstood anything. I don't even know why I said that but there seemed to have been some sort of disconnect between my thoughts and my mouth. I was hurrying to speak and not totally processing the things she was saying to me. It didn't make sense. I'd done the hardest part, hadn't I? But now I seemed to be stumbling over the most inane questions. I tried to regain control.

'There was nothing else on my mind apart from what had happened.'

'You mean at the party?' Rebecca Hobbs prompted, as if I might have been referring to something else entirely.

'Yes, obviously.'

'So, your husband was going out for the evening with his best friend and you hadn't told him at that point that this same best friend had allegedly assaulted his wife. Is that correct?'

'It is,' I nodded.

'I fail to understand why you hadn't had that conversation with him before that moment.'

'I should have done.'

'Or did you just decide to accuse Mr Tyler out of spite? Out of jealousy because of the time he was spending with your husband?'

'Of course not!'

'Then tell me, was it finally the idea of the two of them going out for the evening that prompted you to make this accusation?'

And finally, Dominic Templeton objected. It was upheld and Rebecca Hobbs rephrased but her original words were still in my head.

'I knew I had to tell Ben. I didn't want to hurt him but he needed to know.'

'So, in the end it wasn't shock that affected the decision to tell Mr Stirling but a cold analysis of your situation?'

'I told him because he needed to know. I didn't mean to keep it from him. I made a mistake.'

Rebecca Hobbs looked satisfied. 'The mistake of attempting to destroy your husband's relationship with his best friend?'

I shook my head but it was too late to respond. She had no more questions and I was led from the witness box.

When the afternoon session ended it was abruptly; the judge decided that it was too late to begin new testimony and everyone was excused until the morning. Dominic Templeton waited until he saw Ben and my parents emerging from the court before leaving me. He made no comment, but I felt like a child being handed from the care of one adult to the next. The four of us headed towards the exit in silence and the first person to speak was Mum, she nudged my arm and I followed her gaze towards the security guard. Jess waited just beyond him.

'I'll catch you up,' I told Ben and the three of them walked on without me.

I wasn't sure that Jess was waiting for me but instincts told me she was. She glanced beyond me before offering a weak smile, 'Can we go somewhere?'

The court stood in a stretch of East Road dominated by commercial buildings and student accommodation. 'Where?'

She was already moving towards the exit. 'I don't care, but not in here.'

It wasn't cold outside. The sky was a uniform pale grey but with no hint of rain. So we walked, eventually making a circuit through the unfamiliar back streets.

'I know this is hard for you,' I began but my words fizzled out. We'd continued to work together through the months since Andy's arrest. We'd existed in an unreal bubble where the depth of our friendship and the pressure of the business had kept us functioning. I'd continued to come to work and Jess had continued to see him. Neither of us discussed the other's decisions.

By the time she spoke her voice was thick with emotion. 'It wasn't real until today. It only hit me when I entered the public gallery and saw your family. And his.'

I pushed my hands into my jacket pockets. 'We both knew it was coming.'

'You don't talk about it and neither does he. I've been worried but it hadn't sunk in.' She stopped walking and turned to me. 'I thought that, at the last minute, it wouldn't go ahead . . .' She paused and seemed to be trying to read my expression. 'You know this trial will hurt a lot of people don't you, Em?'

I stopped in my tracks, 'Like Andy? I can't feel guilty about that.'

Jess reached out and clutched at my hand, 'Not just Andy. There's his family. And your family.' She took a breath and swallowed. 'And you, Em. I'm scared for you and I think you should stop it.'

I shook my head, 'Stop what?'

'Stop the trial. Pull out, I mean.'

I tried to step back but she kept hold of my hand and actually moved closer to me. 'Emily, this is hard for me. I care about you and about Andy and it was horrible in there today.'

I pulled my hand away. 'You wouldn't be going out with him if you believed me.'

For the first few days after Andy's arrest this conversation had run on a loop. It had made working together close to impossible but, somehow, Jess had remained loyal to us both. I had never been sure that she did believe me, but on the other hand she hadn't been confident enough about his story to ditch me either.

'I'm trying to do the right thing, Em.'

'That's all you keep saying. What's going to happen when the verdict comes in? Will you choose sides then?'

'That's not it, I want the truth to come out and I want there to be . . .' She paused and flung her hands into the air in frustration.

'What?'

'I want an explanation that means I don't lose either of you.'

'There isn't one, Jess. This isn't going to work out to your convenience.' I broke off and started to walk away but after just a few yards I turned back to her. The thing was, we were like sisters and about twenty years past the point of just walking away from our friendship. I hugged her and whispered, 'He's lying to you.'

I felt her tense.

'I've been a mess in the past, Jess, but not this time. Please leave him.'

'Please drop the case,' she whispered in reply. She hugged me tighter.

'And what if I can't?'

'I love you, Em.'

I should have told her I loved her too. Instead I thought about what she always said in a crisis: *hope for the best, prepare for the worst.*

DAY 2

I should have tackled Dominic Templeton at the end of the first day but instead I left as quickly as I could. The hours in the witness box had left me shaken. Although Ben and I didn't speak much during the evening we sat together on the sofa, and he kept his arm wrapped around me.

By morning I'd gathered my thoughts and began challenging Templeton immediately. 'You left me totally unsupported out there yesterday. Why didn't you object to the way I was being questioned?'

'I did when it was necessary.'

'Once?'

'You were holding your own, Mrs Stirling. The jurors won't like it if it looks as though we are trying to avoid certain lines of questioning.'

'She was feeding them with negative ideas about me. She was implying that I lied about everything.'

He remained unperturbed. 'Of course she was, she's representing Mr Tyler and his entire case is based on that argument. You know that. I'm not sure why you're surprised that she took that line.'

I reminded myself that he was hardened to this and I wasn't.

I pressed my lips together to hide my clenched teeth, glad that his attention had returned to his paperwork. I didn't know which documents he was studying and I wasn't going to ask. I didn't understand the technical aspects of the court procedures or the laws and precedents he might have quoted at me. I already felt vulnerable, I didn't need to feel ignorant too.

The silence dragged out for a while and I took my mobile from my pocket. I checked but there were no new texts.

'You don't need to be here,' he said. He spoke without warning and his tone was noticeably softer. 'And people you expect to come often won't. Some aren't cut out to hear the details of any court case.'

Suddenly Dominic seemed human after all.

'It's my best friend, Jess. I haven't seen her here this morning.'

'Did she say she would come?'

'She said she'd try. We work together and without me there she's struggling to keep up.'

'People find a way if they really want to attend.' It didn't feel as though there was unkindness in the comment. 'Have you spoken to her since?'

'I spoke to her yesterday, then I called her last night but she didn't pick up. I thought she might text me.'

'Don't let yourself dwell on it. These are the kind of details that you mop up afterwards. Have you thought about today? Do you still want to sit in court?'

Now I'd finished giving evidence I could sit with the others in the public gallery. My family would be there, as would Andy Tyler's.

'I need to,' I told him.

His expression hardened again. He rose and began to gather his papers. 'Remember, you have no role in court today. You may leave at any point but while you are in there, you are just an observer.'

When Andrew Tyler took the oath, his voice was clear and calm and everything about him displayed just the right levels of respect and trepidation. I'd never seen him look so smart either, certainly not since mine and Ben's wedding. Andrew was wearing a new suit on both occasions but this time it was slightly more subdued. He'd had his hair cut and everything about him seemed well thought out.

When Rebecca Hobbs addressed him, I noticed that the suspicious tone had dropped from her voice and, perhaps I was imagining it, but to me, she sounded confident on her client's behalf. She took him through his statement, step-by-step, up until the moment where he was about to enter the bathroom and I was trying to leave.

'So, Mr Tyler, at the moment Mrs Stirling came out of the bathroom, what were your thoughts?'

He looked momentarily baffled at the question, as if there could only be one answer.

'I just wanted the loo,' he said.

'Okay. So, you had no interest in stopping to chat to Mrs Stirling?'

'No. Obviously, we had the normal polite exchange.'

'Which was?'

'Perhaps something along the lines of "There you go" and me thanking her. I don't really remember.'

'Because you were drunk?'

'No. I don't really remember because those are the type of passing comments you make all the time. But it was the first time that evening that I'd seen her by herself. I remember asking how she was and she told me her work was busy but, she said, not as busy as Ben's.' He ran his hand through his hair. I knew it was his sign of discomfort. 'We both know Ben's a bit of a workaholic,' he continued. 'One of those people who goes above and beyond to get the job done. So, I told her, "Tell him to take it easy," and she asked me if I'd speak to him, tell him to take a day off or something. And then we chatted for a few more minutes.'

'About what?'

'Still about Ben as far as I can remember. And I told her he was a lucky man.'

'Meaning what?'

'I thought the way she was concerned for him, the way she obviously cared about his workload, about their life together. It was just a comment.'

'And how did she respond?'

'She told me I could tell him that too.'

'I see. Did you conclude from this that there was some friction in their relationship?'

'Not initially, no.'

I watched the exchange with growing unease. Yes, there had

been a conversation, but not at the party. It had been a couple of weeks before, a passing conversation as the kettle boiled. I had commented that Ben was working too hard, that he needed a break. Andy had given me that 'Ben's a lucky man' line but I don't think I'd replied.

And none of that conversation had been repeated at the party either.

But I've always known that the best lies are grounded in truth and maybe it was the seed of that real conversation that made him sound so genuine.

'Tell me what happened next.'

'Nothing.'

'So, you didn't pull her into the room with you?'

'No. We stood in the doorway talking.'

'In the open doorway?'

'Absolutely.'

'Did anything about Mrs Stirling seem unusual to you, Mr Tyler?

'Such as?'

'Did she seem unusually agitated or drunk or—' Templeton cut her short but I could tell that it was only what Rebecca Hobbs had expected him to do. She spoke again, 'How did Mrs Stirling seem to you, Mr Tyler?'

'Agitated and drunk actually. I had the feeling that she was upset with Ben, that given a chance she would start confiding in me but I didn't want her to.'

'Can you tell me why not?'

'I've been Ben's best friend since school. I didn't want to be asked to side against him, did I?'

'And what happened after that?'

'Nothing really, I told her not to worry. I went in the bathroom and I don't remember seeing her throughout the rest of the evening until she and Ben were leaving.'

'So, the last time you saw Mr and Mrs Stirling was as they left your house?'

'That's correct. I don't know the time.'

'That's fine. Tell me about that moment.'

24

Tyler shrugged. 'Nothing to tell, I hugged Ben and kissed Em –
Mrs Stirling – on the cheek.'

'And when did you first hear of the allegation against you.'

'On Monday. Ben rang me.' Tyler's gaze dropped and he hesitated
for what felt like a long time but Hobbs didn't hurry him. 'I didn't
understand what he was saying at first.' He looked up and towards
me. He didn't make eye contact though, he seemed too unfocused for
that and his gaze drifted on towards the jury. 'It didn't make sense.'

'Do you remember Mr Stirling's first words to you?'

Tyler nodded. 'He said he was really sorry, but I needed to hear it
from him first.'

I waited for Rebecca Hobbs's firm little smile and the words *I see.*
She didn't seem to need either and even I could see that Andrew Tyler
had done well.

From the time we left the court until seven o'clock dragged and, by then, I couldn't wait any longer for Jess to phone me or text me. I said I was going to the shop and left Ben at home.

First of all, I drove to Jess's. She lived in a house on the edge of Cambridge. But her car wasn't there and there was no sign of any life. It suddenly made sense to me that she must have been working late.

We were at capacity, simultaneously organising several corporate events, and it always seemed so difficult for us to manage our time for those. The amount of work became endless so I thought I suddenly understood why she'd been too preoccupied to contact me.

Well, that's the excuse I gave myself anyway.

In truth, we'd been friends for such a long time that I must have known that there was something else keeping her away. The Jess I knew would always find a minute to get in touch, just like I would for her. But right then that wasn't how I was looking at things; I just grasped at the idea that she'd been so busy with me out of the office that she was probably feeling terribly guilty for not being with me in court.

So I decided to drive out to the unit where we worked.

Jess started the business with help from her dad. At first, all she could afford was a converted farm unit and initially it was just the two of us working together. We'd grown a bit since then and from time to time we'd use contract staff – a whole herd of them for big events, but at that moment it was back down to just me and Jess, and the two of us doing the work of four.

It was south of Cambridge, halfway between our house in Foxton and the city and I drove out there knowing that I'd already been away too long for just a trip to the shops. I decided to text Ben once I'd located Jess.

When I arrived at work, she wasn't there either. The place was locked up. But even then I didn't dismiss the idea that she was still snowed under with work, just somewhere else. I couldn't just leave it, though. I suppose I could have texted her again but I felt that little niggle of doubt so I drove back to her house and waited. After a while I texted Ben:

Don't worry, but I'll be a while.

From memory, I think it was about half-past nine when she came back. I caught sight of her black Jaguar pulling into the street but I waited until she pulled into her driveway before I stepped out of my car. Thinking back though, she must have seen me. You recognise your mate's car, even if you are not trying to look for it, don't you?

Her key was at the ready and she was about to unlock the front door when I called across to her and I could see, as she turned, that it was with reluctance.

'Is everything okay, Jess?' I asked. 'I don't know if you've missed them but I've tried to phone and text you. I thought you'd be in court today.'

She pinched her bottom lip with her teeth and it took a second for her eyes to meet mine and even then I wasn't sure whether she was looking at me properly. I thought she was doing that thing when you concentrate on the space between somebody's eyebrows, when you are conscious of trying to look them in the eye but can't quite do it.

'I'm sorry,' Jess said. 'I've been having to do everything by myself and . . . I haven't had a minute.'

As much as I'd have liked to, I didn't believe her; there was too much awkwardness in her expression.

'What have I done?' I asked her.

She shook her head, 'It doesn't matter.'

'No, come on, Jess, we need to talk,'

'It would be better to wait until it's over, the court case I mean.'

'What difference will that make?' I asked and she just looked at me. 'Can I come in?' She didn't say no, but I could tell that she wasn't enthusiastic either. Funny, when for years we'd had the sort of relationship where we didn't even knock – we'd just open the door and call the other one's name. I knew where to find her spare key, and it

27

had been okay to let myself in and put the kettle on. That wasn't the case today. I could feel it.

Something had broken.

I stood in the middle of her front-room carpet. It didn't even occur to me to sit down without being invited.

'I don't understand what's going on,' I said.

I think she would have avoided answering if she could but at the same time she couldn't just have me standing there all evening, waiting.

'My dad's unhappy about the impact on the business.' She stared down at the carpet.

'What impact?'

'Clients. They know what's going on.'

'You've told them?'

'No, not really.' She shifted her weight and moved a step away from me. 'I've explained that you're away but the business has been built up from my dad's friends, my dad's contacts, and this case involves us and our friends. The newspapers might not report your name, Em, but people who know us know what's going on and it's causing a problem.'

I crossed my arms and I could feel the tension making my back rod-straight. My jaw was set and my lips pressed hard together. Seconds passed before I could force any words out. 'I haven't caused this problem.'

Jess arched an eyebrow and the corners of her mouth turned down in distaste. 'I asked you to drop it, Em. All these months I've been hanging on for it to come straight but, after being in court yesterday, I know that I can't take any more. And that's just me. What is this doing to your family?'

'Jess, this court case isn't happening because *I've* done something wrong.'

'You said he tried it on with you? Two years ago?'

I nodded.

'You never mentioned it to me.'

'Because you liked him. I didn't want to upset you.'

She shook her head. 'I don't believe you wouldn't have said.' Her

28

voice became weary. 'How did you think you could go through with this and not cause fallout at every angle? I don't even know what went on in court today, but I can bet this isn't doing you any favours.'

'It was tougher than I expected,' I admitted.

I saw the flicker of resentment on her face but she blinked it away.

'Hang on, you think I've lied? That I've accused him out of spite or something?'

'That's not what I meant.'

'Isn't it?' And within seconds we were staring at one another, locked onto one another with mutual disbelief and matching anger. 'You don't believe me, do you, Jess?' I reached out and tugged on her sleeve. 'I know we've been ignoring it all but at the very least I thought you believed me. How long have we known each other?'

She shook me away. 'Long enough for me to have seen the after effects of you having bad sex with people you don't even know. Lying to play one boyfriend against another or playing games to take petty revenge.'

'When we were teenagers, Jess. And how much better were you . . .'

She just cut through me. 'And now you're dragging Ben and your family and his family and, if I'm not careful, my family, all through this. I don't know how to make this clearer; you're being naive and you must stop this right now.'

I felt as though I was standing on the cliff top and part of it had just crumbled away, that I'd been left on the edge with no idea where it would be safe to stand. The only thing I could think to say to her was, 'I hate you'. But I didn't. I stayed silent because I didn't hate her, I loved her. She'd been my best friend, almost forever, and, even then, I didn't want to say anything that we couldn't come back from.

I turned away, fumbling with the door latch and stumbling out on to the street. She called after me. But, I didn't stop; it was time to go home.

DAY 3

Mum and Dad were in the third-floor waiting area when I arrived at court. The long windows and rows of bolted-down seats reminded me of a departure lounge, except that the doors led to Courts 2 and 3 rather than a holiday.

I stopped briefly, gave Dad a hug. He kissed me on the cheek. And then Mum. Her hug lasted a little longer and she whispered, 'Are you all right?'

'Yeah, I'm fine, Mum,' I replied. I wasn't sure if I felt it at that point.

'Look, I need to go and meet Dominic Templeton. I'll be through in a minute.'

They both nodded and I found Dominic in the same room as he'd been in the day before.

He looked up as I entered and it felt odd to have his full attention.

'They have a new witness,' he said.

And by *they*, I knew he meant the defence.

'Who?'

'A guy called Clive Kerkes.'

I shook my head, pulled a face that was somewhere between confusion and I don't have a clue.

'Kerkes?'

'Yes, K, E, R, K, E, S,' he said. 'Do you know him?'

'I don't believe so.'

'Apparently he knows you.'

'Oh.'

I tried to think. I couldn't remember that I'd ever met anyone called Clive.

'What have they told you?' I asked.

'He claims to have gone out with you. He claims that . . . gone out with you might be a loose term. He claims to have spent some intimate time with you.'

I frowned and chewed my lip. Of course, I could see what he was implying but the name still didn't mean anything to me.

'Where's he from?'

'He's from Cambridge. He was studying here and he says that he met you on a night about five years ago.'

I wracked my brains. Five years ago, I was going out with Ben.

'That doesn't make sense,' I insisted.

Dominic referred to his notes. 'He's claiming it was December 2011.'

So, just before I met Ben; that made more sense. I rubbed my lip with my knuckle as I puzzled.

'What else does he say? Where did I supposedly meet him?'

'You met him in a pub in the centre of town. The . . . let me look . . .' He scanned the page and about two-thirds of the way down found what he was looking for. 'In the Eagle on Bene't Street.'

I knew where he meant immediately. Everybody knows the Eagle. It was probably Cambridge's most famous pub. It was where Crick and Watson shared their news of the discovery of DNA and where the signatures of Second World War airmen were still visible on the ceiling. It was always busy, always crammed with students and locals, tourists, theatregoers, eaters and drinkers.

I remembered the night as soon as he said that. I'd been working in an office in town and we'd all gone out for pre-Christmas drinks and something to eat and I'd ended up chatting to this guy. I'd forgotten his name was Clive and I wondered how they'd tracked him down.

Dominic Templeton looked at me. 'I've already requested that the defence doesn't present this witness and I will object again, but they're arguing that it's relevant.'

31

I could see by his expression that he was concerned.

'How serious is this?' I asked.

He shrugged. 'I don't know. It depends what comes out. What is he likely to say?'

'What do you think? I was single. It was Christmas. I didn't have anyone to answer to except myself and I didn't ever expect it to become some kind of personal assassination.'

He shook his head. 'But that's exactly what it is. They will intend to show that you have a reckless attitude towards sex or that you are untrustworthy. Perhaps both. They will want to call into question your set of values.'

'But this shouldn't be anything to do with the case. It's supposed to be Tyler who is on trial, not me.' And as I said it, I realised, as Jess had said, just how naive I sounded. And how many times I had read in the press of a rape victim's morality being called into question.

'I don't care actually,' I said. 'I don't care what this Clive Kerkes says. What happened with Tyler didn't happen because of an encounter from half a decade ago. The jury will see that.'

Dominic Templeton leant back in his seat, his arms still stretched in front of him, his palms flat on the piece of paper that briefed him about the new witness.

'We'll do our best,' he said and nodded slowly. He looked at me and I wondered what he was thinking. 'He's trained as a doctor. That's not great.'

It wasn't good at all; it helped to make Clive Kerkes a particularly credible witness.

I stared into my lap as he made his statement. I certainly didn't want to be seen to be gazing at him. And I didn't want Ben to watch me staring at somebody I'd slept with and wondering what was going on in my head.

I felt my face redden as Kerkes spoke. It wasn't through shame at what I'd done but through embarrassment because it was being revealed in an open court and I should have had the right to keep it private. I doubted that those jurors were seeing it that way though.

Kerkes had a strong voice. Calm. He was probably a good doctor; that's the impression he gave and, in a situation like that, an impression is everything.

'I've only met Emily Stirling once. Emily Jenkins as she was then, although I never knew her last name. "Em" she called herself because I asked whether that was her name or an initial. Yes, "Em".

'We were both in the Eagle. I'd gone with a bunch of medical students and she was there with some friends I think, or work colleagues. We were both at the bar to buy drinks and that's when we started talking.

'She made a jokey comment when I said I was medical student. Something about playing doctors and nurses. That's what people do. And medical students have this reputation for being a bit bawdy, I suppose. Our group certainly was.

'It was a pleasant enough conversation and then later, when I went for drinks, she was there again. I don't know actually whether it was a coincidence or not but that's what I thought at the time. There she was and there I was, so we had that moment of recognition and it felt as though we knew each other better than we did. And there's that Christmas-party spirit where everybody just gels so I asked her if she fancied a drink later and she said she did, so we hung out in town for a bit after everybody else had left.

'I invited her back to my flat. She said we didn't need to go back – we could do it somewhere else. I genuinely hadn't made the assumption that just because she was coming back to my flat, there would be sex. But she'd made the assumption that the whole point was sex. I don't know whether she thought we'd do it in the car or down some alley or other. That wasn't for me, but she was certainly keen and I was more than happy for us to go back to mine.

'By then I was in my final year and we were in a house share. When we arrived back some of the guys were up and still having a drink and just kind of hanging out together. I took her into the kitchen first and we had a chat for a few minutes, but she was focused on moving upstairs, if you know what I mean.'

'Please explain, Mr Kerkes.'

'She was keen to have sex.'

33

There had been other moments when Rebecca Hobbs could have stopped him and asked for clarification but none would have been more timely than this.

'The atmosphere in your house was quite social?'

'Yes.'

'Almost party-like?'

'Almost.'

'Please continue.'

'Perhaps I should have seen it as a warning sign, but she had her hands all over me in front of my friends; with hindsight, it was exhibitionism. I think she wanted to be seen to be sexy, if that makes sense. Anyhow, we went up to my room and it was late. She didn't get completely undressed. Neither of us did. We just pulled off the clothes that were necessary and had sex there on top of the bedcovers. That's how I fell asleep, still wearing my shirt and nothing from the waist down.'

Kerkes took a sip of water and looked across at the jury, his gaze steady.

'Something disturbed me, I don't know, an hour or so later and she'd gone. But I could hear some noise downstairs. I wanted to make sure she was okay, you know. I thought perhaps she was getting a drink or even being sick or something. We'd both had a fair amount of alcohol. The stairs led directly into the front room. I was halfway down when I saw her on her hands and knees on the carpet with my flatmate Toby. They were having sex. And I swore at her. I swore at both of them and I went back to my room and slammed the door and that's the last I saw of her until today.

'When I was asked to testify, I decided that it was the right thing to do. In my opinion, hers was not the behaviour of any person, male or female, with a decent set of morals. I was left feeling that I'd encountered somebody who was deceitful and had no conscience whatsoever.'

Kerkes's evidence and cross examination took a painfully long time. Eventually, when he was dismissed, the court took a break. I followed my parents and Ben outside.

While we'd sat in the court I'd been desperate to speak to Ben, to look at him to see if his expression gave away anything. Did it really matter what either of us had done before we met? Logically I didn't think so, but how you react emotionally is a different story. But before I had the chance to talk to him I saw my dad walk away and my mum hurrying to follow. I called out to her.

She stopped briefly, turned towards me and just said, 'I need to be with your dad.'

'I'm sorry,' I said.

She shook her head. 'Not now, Emily, not now,' and her body was already half turned away. I knew she wanted to catch him, but I persisted.

'What did he say?' I asked.

'That he can't take it anymore. I'll speak to him,' she said.

Mum was usually tactile. She'd never miss a chance to hug me or squeeze my hand or kiss me on the cheek. This time there was nothing. I watched until the doors swung closed behind her and then I turned back to see that Ben was standing at the window, looking down on to the traffic of East Road. I walked across to him, aware that the gaze of every single person in the waiting area seemed to be following me.

Ben and I stood shoulder to shoulder. 'I'm sorry you had to hear that,' I whispered.

'It was uncomfortable listening,' he acknowledged.

'I can imagine,' I replied, and heard myself apologising again.

'Was it true?' he asked.

What could I say? That I was so drunk that I didn't really remember? That I had a vague recollection of two men in one night? That if I thought long enough about it, the intense shame I'd felt the next morning would probably return, absolutely undimmed by the intervening years?

No one wants to relive their worst mistakes or most humiliating moments, or the times they've said something hurtful or inappropriate without thinking. And this was beyond that. I couldn't undo what had happened all those years ago.

He waited for an answer.

'Yes, it is,' I said finally. 'But that's not who I am now. You know that, don't you?'

Ben was a logical person. He was always the same; logic first, feelings second.

I'd always loved that about him. There was no big drama or over-reaction, not usually. But I also knew that sometimes it took him longer to process his emotions. Arguments between us could be frustratingly brief as he cut short his emotions with reasoning. Then days later, he might comment on how something I'd said or done had actually hurt him.

I'd always been the other way around; more emotional, more spontaneous and once it was over it was over, at least as far as I was concerned.

So, although I could see that Ben was being logical when he said that it was before we met, he still had to process the whole feeling of hearing his wife's sexual history being replayed in the court room. Of picturing his wife behaving in that way.

And it was in that starkly lit space, with us staring down at the mundane queue of traffic below, that I wondered whether Ben and I would ever have a proper sex life again. Whether he'd still look at me in the way he always had, with a kind of quiet admiration and deep affection.

Maybe I knew the answer already.

He put his arm around me but it wasn't hard to see the sadness in his eyes and the slightly frozen, distant expression fixed on his face.

The embrace felt uncomfortable.

'I need the bathroom,' he said at last and left me standing with my back to the window, staring at the few people who remained in the waiting area. None of them were there for me and the ones who were had gone.

I didn't notice DI Briggs until he was almost standing next to me.

'Not your best morning then?' he said.

I managed a half smile at his impressive understatement.

'You could say that. It's not looking good, is it?'

He was cautious. 'It can be difficult to tell. You'll just have to wait and see.'

36

I stared hard at him, trying to see if there was some hint in his expression that would tell me whether he was just being diplomatic. Whether he really knew the answer already.

'It's nearly over, isn't it?'

He pushed his heavy-framed glasses tighter against the bridge of his nose. 'The court case is,' he said.

I knew what he meant. I could feel what he meant. There were parts of this that I felt would never be over.

'I've come to hear the summing up,' he told me. 'Will you be coming back in?'

I saw Ben walking towards us. 'I don't think I can,' I whispered quickly. 'I don't think I can face any more.'

'That happens,' said Briggs. 'You might wish you had, though.'

'Will it look bad if I don't?' I managed to ask him just before Ben was within earshot.

Briggs shook his head. 'At this point I doubt it will make any difference.'

I felt a wave of relief.

'I've decided not to go back in,' I told Ben.

He frowned. 'Why?'

'I can't face it.' I tried to reach out to touch his arm but the gesture was awkward. 'That was the last straw this morning.'

'I don't think you can bail out now.'

I shot a quick look at Briggs, hoping for a bit of support but ended up repeating myself. 'I can't face any more.'

'Well, some of us haven't had much choice,' Ben muttered. He seemed oblivious to Briggs. 'I'm going back in. I have to get to the end of this,' he said.

So I stood there for a second, completely torn, feeling the pressure to go and sit back in that court room again but also feeling like my feet were bolted to the floor.

In the end, I just shook my head. He made three or four attempts to talk me round but I wouldn't budge. When everybody else had gone inside and the doors were about to close, Ben finally gave up and followed them.

Briggs was the last to leave. Smiling didn't seem to come easily to him but now his heavy features were even more solemn. 'I'll phone you,' he said. 'I'll let you know. But you might want to be somewhere private. If your family aren't here, go and see them, because whichever way this goes, the press will be after a comment. I'll speak to the journalists and hopefully that will be enough. But you certainly don't want to be standing here when it happens.'

Then he left too and it was just me and what felt like an empty building.

FRIDAY 24 FEBRUARY, 2017

Have you ever read a case in the paper? Quite often the headline is the verdict.

MAN FOUND GUILTY OF . . .

WOMAN SENTENCED TO . . . etc., etc.

The verdict is like the punchline, the final turn in the story. It's the denouement, where the twist is revealed. It's the bit you read at the top of the article and then the details of the case follow.

Most of the newspapers had variations on the one headline that stuck in my head more than the others.

JEALOUS WIFE TRIES TO DESTROY HUSBAND'S BEST FRIEND

Those were a few of the judge's words.

All the way through the case, he hadn't been the over-bearing authoritarian figure that I'd expected. He'd had a firm tone but he'd been mostly softly spoken. He'd tilt his head and listen to the evidence and seemed to think carefully before he spoke.

If I hadn't been me, I would have trusted his comments. But as I was me, all I could do was listen to them with growing horror.

Andrew Tyler was found not guilty and, according to that same news article, applause broke out in the public gallery. In summing up, Judge Geraint Williams said that the defendant, through no fault of his own, had been subject to malicious accusations. That there was no evidence that he had committed rape. That the case was marked by Mrs Stirling's attempt to discredit a man who had always been a good friend to Mr Stirling. That the police should not have brought a case that was clearly one person's attempt to ruin Andrew Tyler's reputation and his life.

I was the woman who could not be named for legal reasons but anonymity for rape victims goes only so far.

My family knew, my friends knew, the press knew and, while my name didn't appear in the papers, salacious gossip spreads quickly.

It felt as though the anonymity only held water for people I didn't know anyway. It seemed like every acquaintance knew something of the case and it would only take the slightest bit of curiosity to pull up the article and find out what a vindictive bitch I had been.

I moved back to my parents' the following week. It seemed that Ben needed time to think. I had too much time to think. I no longer had a job, for one thing.

Luckily Dad worked, so the stiff conversations between us occurred only in the evenings in an awkward hour over dinner and just afterwards.

Mum was the way Mum had always been, I suppose. Except I could tell that the case had left her crushed.

I didn't know how to describe that for a while and then I came up with the idea that she was in mourning, and that seemed to fit.

I didn't ask her and I didn't dwell on whether she was mourning over what I'd lost or what she'd lost or a whole combination of things.

I'd only been back at home for a few days when the anonymous letters began arriving, addressed to me and filled with hate.

TUESDAY 28 FEBRUARY, 2017

The first came in a white envelope. One of those long thin ones without a window that could be a bill or just as easily something private. It was decent quality, I noticed that. It had that kind of grainy, cloth-like texture to it. It was one of the first letters that I'd received at my mum's, without it having been redirected from our old house.

My name and address were handwritten in blue pen. The writing was neat, regularly spaced. I didn't think it at the time but afterwards I wondered whether it was artificially neat, as though somebody had spent a long time carefully forming the letters.

But anyway, I was in the kitchen when I opened it, leaning against the freezer while Mum was boiling the kettle. She had sorted through her post and passed me two items: a forwarded reminder about an optician's appointment and this one.

I was chatting as I tore the long edge, not really paying attention to it I suppose. I remember being curious, but no big deal. I slid my finger along and pulled out what I thought was some kind of greeting card. It was heavy stock but just a plain white sheet, folded in half. Whatever I was saying, I forgot immediately. My words stopped mid-sentence and my mum stopped mid-pour of the kettle.

'What's wrong?' she asked.

I pushed it back in the envelope but I already knew I'd been far too slow to get away with pretending that it was just junk mail.

'It's rubbish,' I assured her, 'absolute rubbish.'

'Can I see it?'

'Really, Mum, it's just somebody trying to be funny,'

She finished pouring the drinks and handed mine across to me.

'Is it some kind of hate mail?' she asked me.

'Nothing that matters,' I told her.

'It does matter though,' she said. 'There are always people who kick other people when they're down. Doesn't mean you need to put up with it.'

'It's just one letter.'

'Can I see it then?'

I shook my head but she persisted.

'If you don't show me what's in it I'll be imagining far worse.'

I could have bet that she wouldn't. She probably thought it was one of those classic bits of spinster hate mail, calling me a trollop or something similar. But no, it was more personal than that.

I folded it in half and slid it resolutely in my pocket. It would stay there for only as long as I was talking to my mum.

I waited until she'd gone out. I didn't even dare go to my room and open it with her in the house, in case she came in unexpectedly. You see, it wasn't just words. There was a picture too.

Somebody had taken the time to draw my face. Its style was juvenile, me with my head tilted back and my eyes half closed. My hair was furled back, touching the top of my collar bone just the way it really does and my shirt open at the neck revealing a flash of cleavage. But in this picture my mouth was open and there was an erect penis drawn close to my lips. Yes, the picture was juvenile but the skill it took to draw it wasn't and it was that more than the words that I found unnerving. The message itself was simple:

Em . . . Emmy . . . Emily

Do you know what you've done?

Do you know the people you've damaged
and do you really care?

42

Or is it just about you and what you want?

But who's going to want to fuck you now?

I refolded it and this time I left it in my bag. I tucked it underneath the stiff piece of lining that lay at the bottom.

Part of me wanted to throw it away but I knew I mustn't.

I didn't want to walk around with it, but I wasn't going to leave it at home either. I couldn't risk that somebody I cared about would see it.

I placed my bag back on the floor and noticed how a single envelope made it feel heavier. It was only in there about thirty seconds before I took it out again in an attempt to read the postmark. I'm not sure that anybody gets readable postmarks these days. And this one was a blur. It might have read Cambridge but I couldn't really tell. There was no clue in the handwriting, although I would have guessed that it was female. The capital letters were slightly rounded, the Ls had loops and so did the Ts but then again, not every man pushes aggressive imagery into his handwriting style and quite clearly not every anonymous letter writer gouges at the paper or writes with an openly maniacal hand.

I put it away again, determined that I would show it to nobody. Let's face it, what was I likely to achieve? The police didn't believe me and I really didn't want to cause more upset to anybody close to me. But neither hiding it nor refusing to deal with it stopped me wondering who would have sent it.

It could have been anyone. I reckoned our whole street knew about the case. I could imagine my dad at work saying, 'Yeah, she's been having a bit of a difficult time.' And then having time off to go to court on the same days as there was a high-profile case in the paper featuring a thirty-year-old married woman. Joining the dots wouldn't have been so hard. And Mum worked part time at the school. I'm an ex-pupil. That would have been more interesting than the next Ofsted report.

Except it wasn't.

Nobody was really interested. They just wanted to see somebody else's life imploding, to take the heat off their own.

My little brother, he was off at uni. Even he knew. No doubt he told people, too, not that it made any difference. The point was that everybody in my parents' house knew. Everybody in their street knew, too. Everybody in the whole bloody village might as well have known. And whoever sent that was somebody who knew what happened, who knew that I'd gone back home and had read enough about the case to form their own oh-so-accurate opinion.

SATURDAY 4 MARCH, 2017

In the days afterwards, I wasn't exactly hanging around waiting for the post but one eye, one ear, they were always open. A bit like a dog that pretends to be asleep by the hearth. You can see its ear twitch, and with the first clang of a gate, it's up and barking at the window in one smooth move. That was me – not the barking, but meeting the postman at the door and grabbing the mail before Mum had a chance.

It was four days later when the second one arrived.

If I was into erotic art I probably would have been flattered, I thought, with an unexpected flash of black humour.

I opened the envelope from the end this time, slid the card out. The picture was the same, a photocopy of the last one I think. The message just read:

Thinking of you.

I slid it back into its envelope and then put it with the other one in the bottom of my bag.

I suppose I could have gone to the police but, once again, I didn't. What would have been the point?

That second time I was more annoyed than shaken. And in turn, angry again when I thought how much it would hurt Mum if she found out. In the end, I couldn't think of anything I could do apart from move away. The idea had been stirring at the back of my mind for a few days by then and I couldn't help but think it would be good for everyone, not just for me.

More letters arrived and I wasn't sure that I didn't deserve them. I kept them all in my bag and took them with me eight weeks later, by which time Ben had bought me out and the time had come for me to start again.

THURSDAY 27 APRIL, 2017

The house stood before me. A draught-free and muffled version of the mansion it had been in its heyday. Somewhere up there on the first floor was the apartment I'd come to view.

I looked at the letting agent, 'Why doesn't anyone want it?'

'It's only been available for a week.' He had a lank strand of hair that kept dropping across his forehead as though it couldn't decide whether it really wanted to be a fringe. He pushed it away again. 'Mill House is very desirable.'

I corrected him. 'It has been available nearly three weeks and flats elsewhere have been rented out before I've had the chance to view.'

'It's not the price,' he assured me.

When wasn't it the price? I thought. 'What then?' I asked.

'Single people, like yourself, often prefer the town. They want to be close to work or live in something more modern.' He didn't have my history; he had my maiden name and my first name shortened to Emma. 'We do have two newer flats coming onto the market today.' He sounded hopeful. I ignored him.

'And?'

'I'm sorry?' He looked perplexed and his eyebrows flickered, a frown furrowed his forehead. He looked like a man who would rather be smiling and nodding.

I looked up at the house. The frontage wasn't ornate but there was something appealing in the three rows of uniformed sash windows. It was Regency or so I guessed. I gave him a prod. 'What else is putting people off?'

'I don't know, perhaps it's too isolated for some tastes.' He stepped forwards and I followed, 'I'll show you. It's what *you* think that's important.' And he led the way, more confident now he had used one of his stock phrases.

He didn't know that it had been a long time since what I thought had had any bearing on my life and that, if I'd had any choice, I would have been living a different existence to this one. But that, as I reminded myself frequently, was irrelevant and as remote as turning on the TV and stepping into any other fictional world.

I expected to enter through the front entrance but instead he led me around the side of the building. 'The flat is accessible through the main door,' he told me, 'but this route is more direct, prettier I think, as you'll see the gardens.'

We turned the corner again and immediately I saw how the rear gardens had once been a major feature. We were standing on what might have been the croquet lawn and I could just make out the shape of crumbling brickwork beneath a leylandii hedge and the step down to what should have been the next tier of lawn. I imagined the old view had included a ha-ha and cattle grazing in a water meadow. All that remained was a rectangle of grass with clumps of faded shrubs in the corners nearest the house.

Two black metal fire escapes, one on each side of the rear wall, dominated the property.

He must have seen my disappointment. 'From the apartment, there is a view beyond the hedge,' he said.

And so it had become an apartment rather than a humble flat. 'Who cuts the grass?'

'It's done fortnightly in the summer, included in the price.'

That hadn't been my question but I let it slide. I looked up to the first floor. 'Which windows?'

He pointed to the right-hand end, 'The first two. Shall we look inside?'

When Ben and I bought our house, it was new. Both my parents and his parents loaned us money and we scraped enough together for the deposit. Then we overspent on the carpets. I suppose we had this unspoken idea that we'd make the place perfect so we bought the carpets and then didn't have enough to buy decent furniture. We spent the first year with the only luxury being the smell of freshly laid Wilton.

The back stairs up to the flat at Mill House were bare tiles. It had been a long time since this place had been given new flooring of any sort. At each internal doorway, the carpet had thinned, with cardboard-coloured backing showing through the worn pile. The place smelled slightly damp.

'It's hardly plush,' I said to the estate agent.

He pushed back the rebel strand of hair. 'But it's hardly the most expensive one here either. You could easily be paying another couple of hundred for this.'

He opened the door. When the house had been in its heyday, this would have been where the least desirable rooms would have been located, overlooking the kitchen garden and at the side of the house.

Yes, there was a view to the front and the back, but it was most convenient to look out of the side window and, when the conversion had taken place, this had probably been the last part of the house that had been given any attention. And the part of the house that had suffered when, it seemed, their budget had run out. Still, if I stood at the kitchen sink I could look out of the front window and if I sat on the end of the bed, I could look out the back.

In the sitting-room area, the view was to the side and the back across the fields and a pretty blank canvas. The bottom fifth of the panorama was plain farmland with barely a tree breaking the view, the top four-fifths, the sky. And today it was solid grey. No gradation in colour from top to bottom and, at night, I had no doubt that the view would be of almost total blackness.

'I'll take it,' I told him, and paid six months' rent up front.

FRIDAY 5 MAY, 2017

I'd lived my whole life in Foxton. That didn't sound spectacular but I'd never considered living anywhere else, and when Ben and I decided to buy a house together we never looked further and moved just a couple of streets away on the new estate built near the centre of the village.

Foxton is what I had always thought of as a normal place to live. You could drive in and understand the layout. It is obvious where to find the heart of the village just by looking at it. And the scenery around it seems normal too, with old orchards and big farms and undulating hillside, as they say in geography class. You could pick up the village and drop it into many other counties and it would seem at home. And it has a train station. It is only an hour into London or fifteen minutes into Cambridge.

Wicken is radically different. It attracts tourists in the summer, or so I was told. Some in the winter, too; the types who like to walk across the Fen. The road through Wicken weaves through farmland, joining one A-road to another, and the village is spread out along it. Some of the houses are old and quaint but I don't think that's deliberate. I think they were part of what was left behind when the rest of the world moved on.

To me, Wicken was bleak. It was just over half the size of Foxton. A batch of houses sprinkled along the side of the road, the whole thing lost in the middle of Fenland expanse.

From my window, all I could see was flatness. Earth the colour of coffee grounds and the black skeletons of hedgerows and trees. In the evening, I could see the lights of Cambridge glow but during the daytime the monotony of the sky and the monotony of the ground met at what seemed like an infinite point. On a grey day, I couldn't even see where one merged into the other. On days like that I looked out of the window and it seemed that Cambridge may as well have been a hundred miles away.

There were three floors and my flat was on the first. As you faced the house it was on the left-hand side. The building was symmetrical and nothing but right angles and rectangles, designed by somebody with a great love for rulers and set squares.

My flat might have been less desirable than the others but the extra staircase was its one quirk. It was a single steep flight that ran down to the rear door. I guessed, though I didn't know, that I lived in some kind of former staff quarters. This staircase was narrow, so narrow in fact that if I carried something, I'd have to be careful that my elbows didn't graze the walls. But it meant that I could slip out to what had been the kitchen garden without having to trail through the rest of the house.

As far as settling in was concerned, I moved on 2 May, straight after the bank holiday, and used the same entrance as everybody else. The front door, located symmetrically in the middle of the building.

I didn't hire a removal van. I'd left most of my furniture behind. Ben and I had gone through the usual scrabble of picking over who owned what. None of that was important. It was just part of the sub-text of betrayal and disappointment and loss.

There were a couple of larger pieces of furniture that I'd fought hard for but, in the end, I just walked away. I didn't really want them for myself, I realised. I wanted to take them to make some sort of point but I don't suppose I had a point worth making. And there they would have sat, wherever I was living, and just been a reminder of a past that I needed to escape.

Having said all that, I didn't really let it go.

I used my own car to move clothes and bedding, books and a new microwave, and the bones of what was needed for a new life. I did it in multiple trips across three or four days, packing the back seat, the front seat and the boot with heavy cardboard boxes that had originally contained fruit. I was carrying a stack of three of these through the front door when an elderly man appeared from inside and offered to help.

'I'm Frank,' he said, and the expectation hung in the air as he waited for me to respond.

'I'm Emily.'

I silently scolded myself. I'd failed to become Emma. 'Emily Jenkins.'

It was easy to slip back to my maiden name. It would have been harder to change my Christian name.

Emily Jenkins, I repeated silently to myself.

That was the first moment I'd officially used my former name and, to my surprise, it felt okay.

Frank was well into his seventies. He wore dark-blue trousers, a long-sleeved white shirt and a knitted waistcoat. I wondered if he was ex-military. He had that kind of well-pressed and well-organised air about him, but I didn't ask any personal questions.

He worked hard on starting the conversation, though, and eventually I relented and I had my first chat with a neighbour.

'I lived here before,' he said, 'before it was done up. It was still flats then, but a very roughshod conversion. They've done a better job of it now. Mine's the ground floor on the opposite side. I'm sure you'll meet the others at some point, but none of them have been here quite as long as I have.

'One flat's empty, that's the one below you. I've heard that someone's moving in next week. It's taken a while to fill these places. But three other flats are all occupied now. Are you by yourself?'

'I am.'

'Good. The last thing we need is rowdiness in this building. Above you is Mrs Carson, she's a widow. She's pleasant enough but you don't want to be playing lively music – that will grate on her. The flat above me is unoccupied most of the time but above that are Mr and Mrs Watts. They're younger than the rest, older than you but younger than the rest. How old are you?'

'Thirty,' I replied.

'You look younger than thirty.'

There was no hint that he was trying to be charming. I smiled.

'So, you don't have a husband then?' he said.

'I'm getting divorced,' I told him.

'Oh,' he said, 'say no more.'

'Do you live on your own?'

'I do. Have done for eleven years. I prefer it that way. You reach a certain age when you don't want to be doing all that considering somebody else. I don't mean that for you, of course. But in thirty years' time you might feel that way.'

Thirty years. I couldn't imagine where life was going to lead me in that time.

'Do you have family in Wicken?' he asked.

'No. I'm from the other side of Cambridge and I decided I wanted a fresh start.' And as soon as I said this I felt as though I'd opened up too much. I backed away, 'Anyway, nice to meet you.'

And I hurried off and then to and fro with box after box until they were in a stack in the middle of my new front room.

I added the final box to the pile and locked the door behind me. I found enough toiletries to shower and, although they were my things spread round the bathroom, I still had that feeling that I was in somebody else's space. I didn't relax and I dressed before leaving the bathroom.

One of my dining-room chairs was next to the wall. I made a cup of tea and sat in it for a while, staring at my small stack of boxes and feeling no desire to unpack any of them. For the past few weeks, moving house had been my end goal and, now it was done, I had nothing left.

I found my duvet, but no covers and no pillow. I plugged my mobile in next to the bed and curled up under the duvet, resting my head on a rolled-up sweatshirt, with its sleeve close to my nose. It smelt of home and helped me relax as I finally drifted off to sleep.

SATURDAY 6 MAY, 2017

I woke the following morning, momentarily confused about where I was and even unsure of the day. As I gradually surfaced, I realised that it had to be early still. There was virtually no daylight seeping into the room and the air had that pre-dawn chill. I wondered if it was cold enough to be able to see my breath but I didn't try. I just pulled the duvet over my head and lay there a while longer, trying to make a plan for the day.

Since the trial there had been days when I hadn't left my mum and dad's house. I knew that wasn't healthy. I suppose it would have been okay if I'd been in a good place mentally, but I'd been sitting at home all day and letting the rest of the world drift by. It didn't make sense and I'd promised myself it was something I wouldn't do once I'd moved in.

I made a mental note of all the things I wanted to achieve in the day. Listing them in my head made me feel as though I was organised. I didn't want to set myself up to fail so I kept the day's list short. Get up. Unpack food. Take a walk. I couldn't think of much else to add.

When Ben and I had moved into our old house, my parents and his parents had come around. The unpacking had been a day of snacking and chatting and squeals of 'Oh, you wouldn't believe what I just found in this box.'

This time I just lay there. Yeah, you're right. I did feel sorry for myself.

In the end, I went back to sleep. I crawled out of bed mid-afternoon, listless, feeling a little queasy.

I ate Weetabix at teatime. I realised I was running out of milk, that there'd be nothing for tomorrow. I planned to go to the shop. I thought about digging out my coat. I did none of those things. Those simple nondescript things were too much for me. I returned to bed and slept through until half past ten the following morning.

It was a stray cat that finally made me drive to the shop.

The lease was strictly no pets and this was the only house for half a mile. So, when I looked out of the rear window and saw the scrawny black and white cat down by the hedge, I guessed it had no home.

I found a can of tuna and left it on the ground by the back door. I didn't see the cat come back but a little later when I checked, the can was empty and overturned. Feeding a stray, I reasoned, was not the same as having a pet and before I'd had time to think about going back upstairs, to make lists, to become listless, I was in the car and heading to the Co-op that stood three miles away in the centre of the next village.

Once there, I moved slowly from aisle to aisle and stocked up on enough to keep me going, as well as a small box of dried cat food.

On the one hand, a supermarket was the most mundane place in the world. But on the other, it was real life. Food and the other things I needed for day to day, all lit under relentless false daylight.

I came back with my box of groceries, feeling as though I'd had a breath of the real world, and I didn't sit back down again. I went through the boxes one at a time, unpacking anything that I would use. Anything for the bathroom or the kitchen, any items that were actually going to be of day-to-day value.

Every time I hit a box that contained something that could be classed as sentimental I'd fold the flap shut and slide it against the wall. I finished at about 3 a.m., with about a third of the boxes still unopened. And they would remain unopened and pushed against the wall while the other two-thirds turned the empty shell of a flat into my new home.

It wasn't that I'd suddenly become more upbeat. I think I'd suddenly found determination from somewhere.

It was a kind of seed of anger, and not just anger at Andrew Tyler. Anger at myself because, as much as I hated to admit it, I had rocked the boat. I had been the starting point of everything that had made my old life unravel.

So, I kept going well into the night and eventually crashed asleep on my now newly made bed. And when I awoke in the morning it was late but still dull in the bedroom. North facing, I realised, so it would be bleak in the winter and cool in the summer.

But I didn't care about that. I didn't care about anything that was a disappointment or anything that might have been an opportunity. I'd just reached the point when I had a day in front of me and I could cope with it, knowing that I wouldn't be crawling under the covers. That I could go outside and not be recognised or stared at, that I wouldn't need to feel that I had to continually apologise for myself.

It was three months, one week and four days since the trial and it was the first day that the ground felt solid under my feet. I didn't know if it would stay that way, but one step at a time was fine by me.

WEDNESDAY 17 MAY, 2017

My bedroom and the sitting room both faced down on to the car park. With six apartments in one building, the developers had needed somewhere to put the cars and the decision had been to throw down tonnes of gravel on to an area at the side of the house. I quickly realised that I would hear the grinding and grit-spitting of every person coming or leaving by car.

From both rooms, I could stand at the window and look down at the cars: two BMWs, an Audi and a Mazda MX-5, so all but mine were upmarket. The two BMWs had consecutively numbered plates so I guessed they belonged to Mr and Mrs Watts. I hadn't set eyes on the other neighbours and at the rate I was going I would recognise the cars sooner than I would recognise their owners.

The Mazda belonged to Frank. That was the first one I worked out.

He looked like a man who would have driven something small and sensible, ideal for going out on Sundays. But every weekday morning he seemed to be up and out as early as the rest of them. By 9 a.m. he'd return with his morning paper, and until then I'd be looking down at the roof of just my car. The ten-year-old, second-hand Ford Focus that I'd hung on to for the last four years.

Just before lunch I heard the churn of the gravel outside the window and wandered across to take a look, thinking perhaps I might catch sight of one of the other occupants of the building and maybe engineer a meeting in the hallway.

It wasn't that I was particularly hankering after company but it seemed sensible to at least be able to recognise the people I lived with. The new arrival was a vehicle I hadn't seen before. A black Tesla, and a man who looked to be in his early thirties stepped out and walked to the edge of the car park. I dropped back from the window and watched as, hands on hips, he slowly took a 360-degree view of the property. He looked up at the building and for a second I thought he was staring at my window but his gaze passed by and he seemed to be studying the roof. Then his attention dropped back down to the ground floor.

I moved closer to the glass and could just catch sight of him as he cupped his hands to the pane and squinted through the windows of the empty flat below mine.

He moved towards the front of the building and I shadowed him from the inside and looked down from the kitchen window as he surveyed the front of the ground-floor flat. It took me a moment to decide what to do. I was in no hurry to meet anybody who didn't actually live here, but then again, if he was about to move in downstairs, the sooner I had the measure of him, the better.

I was already wearing a jumper. I slipped on my trainers and grabbed my jacket, pushing my arms into the sleeves as I hurried down the stairs. When I opened the outside door, he was, as I'd hoped, still loitering near the front.

'Oh,' I said, feigning surprise. 'Can I help you?'

He was slow to answer but not as though he was struggling to find what to say, more that he was the laid-back sort of person who didn't hurry to answer anything much.

He stepped towards me. 'Hi,' he said, and offered the sort of broad smile that was too warm to be intended as purely casual.

He held out his hand. I hesitated, took half a step backwards.

'Matt Edwards,' he said.

He wore a suit. When I think of men in suits, they either look stuffy or a little too slimy. He looked neither. Everything about him was understated. Either expensive or he had a good eye for style.

His hair was short and dark and although his smile looked sincere, I spotted a mischievous glint in his eye. Whoever Matt Edwards was, he was attractive all right, but I reckoned he knew it too. My stomach tightened. Right there and then he reminded me of Andy. It wasn't a look, but a type.

I nodded and gave a cold smile. I didn't bother to introduce myself.

'What's funny?' he asked.

I shook my head, sorry I'd been misinterpreted.

'I was just on my way out. There's usually someone around,' I lied, wondering whether he was either an estate agent or someone casing the place. 'Who were you looking for?'

'I wasn't,' he said. 'I knew it was empty and I thought I'd check it out. But not for me,' he added quickly. 'I wanted to see whether it was ready yet.'

I swept my hand in the direction of the building. 'Help yourself,' I said, then realised that my choice was either to go out or make a lame excuse to go back in. I hadn't even brought my car keys down with me so I locked the front door and headed towards the centre of Wicken, close to a mile up the road.

I trudged along the grass verge, seeing the ridiculousness of the situation I'd put myself in. I walked for ten minutes and began to study the countryside. I didn't even realise I was doing this until a car pulled up alongside. I'd been absorbed in the dips and turns of a pair of birds, the way they moved, one moment as though they were giving chase and the next in harmony.

The low murmur of the car and the moving of the electric window were both barely audible but they were enough for me to turn around and I found myself looking down into Matt Edward's smiling face.

'I'm done,' he grinned. 'You can go back home now.'

I scratched around for a quick reply but my head was empty. I felt myself wordlessly open and shut my mouth but by then he'd pulled away. I kept walking in the same direction until he drove out of sight, and then I turned and headed back home.

I couldn't help it but I thought of him and that negligible encounter until I arrived back in my flat. I made a drink and stood looking out of the window. The man was a flirt, a player. I could tell that straightaway but for a split second, before I'd seen the Andy in him, I'd found him attractive. That attraction had turned to revulsion in

59

a single moment but it had been a long time since I'd felt that about any man.

I wondered whether those emotions or hormones, or whatever they were, had been permanently snuffed out.

The last time I'd tried having sex was with Ben. I'd worked hard to keep my mind empty but the more aroused he became, the more it repelled me. As the tension in my head increased I fought the urge to tell him to stop. I bit down on the inside of my lip; I had no right to tell him that I didn't want it when I'd never said it to Andy. Or had I? I didn't even know by then.

I became rigid under Ben and with every thrust I told myself to stay quiet until my thoughts began to scream at me, until I found myself writhing and pushing him away. I know we were both awake a long time after that, both pretending to sleep. Both lying there, facing opposite walls and probably contemplating our futures.

Sex felt like something I'd done in another life. But suddenly I found myself standing in my new flat, trying to start again and fighting the unexpected flush left by an imagined flirtation.

The feeling sickened me.

I threw my tea down the sink, rinsed out my mug and then, without planning it and for no apparent reason, I smashed it against the opposite wall and left the broken pieces on the floor until bedtime.

TUESDAY 13 JUNE, 2017

I thought no one knew my new address apart from Mum and Dad so I was surprised when, with the feeling of sinking inevitability, I received my first piece of junk mail. It was the second week of June by then and no one avoids mailshots forever. This was nothing special, just an advert for blinds or curtains, made to measure, and then another for a water softener. Things I was never going to spend money on here. The other items that came in the post had been redirected on by Mum. She'd stuck a white label on the front of each and had handwritten my new address.

It was the nudge I needed to contact her.

The trips backwards and forwards to my parents' home had fizzled out and it had been over a week since I'd seen or spoken to her.

I had decided not to have a landline installed at the flat, just to use my mobile. Although the reception around the village was patchy, I didn't think I'd be making that many calls anyway. Mum had called me once and I'd picked up a voicemail about half an hour afterwards.

I hadn't replied and she'd left me alone. Mum and I were similar in a way. We both understood when the other needed space and although my teenage years of stomping out of the house or stomping up to my room and wanting to be left alone had long since passed, I could tell she was waiting for me to get in touch and would have left it a long time before she bothered me again.

But there was something poignant about the image of her carefully addressing those labels. She'd probably written a whole sheet of them, peeling them off and sticking them squarely, one by one, onto items of post and forwarding them on to me without giving in to the temptation to add a little comment of her own.

I picked up the phone to call her but, in the end, I decided to go to Foxton and just turn up. I don't know why I thought this was the right thing to do but I wonder if I wanted to see her reaction when I arrived, what her exact expression would be as she opened the door and saw that it was me. If I phoned first, she'd have had a good half an hour to prepare.

On the drive over I wondered about this. I wondered if I really thought she'd be disappointed to see me and would need to put on a front. But when I knocked at the door and she opened it, I immediately saw the relief in her expression and her resisting the urge to hug me.

We sat in the kitchen while she made the tea. Dad was out and it was just the two of us in the house. My parents, I suppose, are a little bit old-fashioned; the kitchen is Mum's domain.

Several items of post were on the table. She noticed me glance at them. 'They're from this morning,' she said. 'I haven't had time to re-address them yet.'

I picked them up but there was nothing of interest: a bank statement, a reminder of a dental appointment. 'I should make a note of these people. Turn it into a list of the ones who need my change of address. You haven't told anyone where I live, have you?' I asked her.

She shook her head. 'No, of course not.'

'Absolutely no one?'

'Absolutely.'

'I've just started receiving junk mail.'

'Well, the letting agent knows where you are. The council tax, water rates, fuel companies, they'll all need to know your address. Perhaps they sell on their information. But don't worry, it hasn't come from me. So, what's it like?'

'The flat?'

'Uh-huh.'

'It's funny, it's in this building that was once quite a grand house I suppose. They've divided it into six flats and my one's the equivalent of the runt of the litter. I think it was servants' quarters once.'

'I thought it was on the first floor?'

'Yes, it is, but it has this little narrow staircase where you go down to the kitchen garden and it would have been connected to the original kitchen, and it's obviously less desirable than the rest. The rooms face north. The bathroom is at the back of the house. I don't know how old that is but it's obviously been a bathroom for a very long time. Did they have bathrooms in Victorian England?'

Mum smiled. 'Course they did. Those stairs would have been for the staff to come up. Those rooms were probably an elderly person's bedroom, or a child's. Maybe they were all one room once. It's interesting, though.' She'd always liked history and she would have been interested if she'd visited but I wasn't ready to invite her yet.

'How's Dad?' I asked.

'He's fine. Fine. He does miss you, you know.'

I moved the conversation along.

'I think maybe I should look for a job.'

'Doing what?'

'Anything really. Something local, something where I can be anonymous, I suppose. I'm not being ambitious right now. Certainly don't want to be heading into Cambridge again, not for work.'

There was a long pause and I wondered about asking after Ben and after Jess, but I couldn't bring myself to say anything. I would have been admitting that I still cared and I needed to stay away from that conversation.

'Have you heard from Charlie?' I asked.

Talking about my brother kept me on safer ground.

Mum screwed up her nose a little. 'Yes, Charlie's being Charlie. Late with essays. No doubt late with his bedtimes too. Doing the classic "burning the candle at both ends" first-year student challenge.'

'Oh, he'll be all right,' I told her.

Charlie always seemed to boulder through anything without coming unstuck. I'd always marvelled at the way he could bound through life and just cheerfully brush himself off and carry on when things went wrong. I'd always tried so hard to be seen to be doing things right, and look what that had achieved.

I was with Mum for an hour and then I knew it was time to leave. Not because she didn't make me welcome. She made me too welcome and everything I could touch and smell and see in that house was comforting and made me want to stay. But I didn't have to remind myself that it was my old life.

She was holding a tea cloth as she walked me to the door. She leant on the frame, ready to wave me off. I knew she would stand at the doorway until I was out of sight. It was the way she was with every visitor. I wanted to tell her how lonely I was. I wanted to cry on her shoulder or curl up with my head on her lap. I wanted to ask her to come to visit me but I wasn't ready for any of that.

I was half in my car when she called out again. She reached behind her to the telephone table that stood in the hallway and then waved an envelope at me.

'I forgot about this one. It came through the letterbox last night.'

The envelope was white and a standard size but I instinctively knew that it had come from the same pack as the last letter I had received. I found myself trying hard to look casual and wondering what casual looked like. Was my smile a little too broad? Was my gaze a little too fixed on her?

I knew I'd messed up when she asked me what was wrong.

I shook my head. 'Doesn't matter. Nothing.'

I pretended to look at the writing. I didn't want her worrying about me.

'I wondered if it might be from Ben,' I lied and folded it in my hands, determined not to look at it until I was out of sight.

Mum looked uncomfortable. 'Have you heard from him at all?'

I shook my head and I drove away with him and the letter fighting for attention in my thoughts.

* * *

Maybe it was deliberate and maybe not but I found myself driving towards our old house. After a couple of minutes, I pulled over to the side of the road. I couldn't wait any longer.

I checked the envelope. It was identical to before and I suspected that by turning it over in my hand I'd obliterated any possibility of using fingerprints to find out who might have sent it. The fact that somebody held this in their hands with the intention of posting it to me and using it to hurt me made me feel as though I was holding something dirty.

It contained one A4 sheet. Lined paper, ripped from a large notebook.

There was no picture this time and the message was brief:

I know you moved out and I know where you've gone. You can't change address and just rub out what you've done.

You'll see.
You deserve to suffer.

I folded it away, slid it back into the envelope. My fingers seemed fast and accurate but when I tried to drive my coordination seemed a little off and I clipped the kerb as I pulled away, swinging abruptly into the traffic and making a car hoot its horn.

And, what the hell, I decided to drive past mine and Ben's old house. It was the first time I'd been there since I moved out.

I drove towards the house. If anyone had asked I could have said that I'd driven that way out of habit, that I'd had my mind on other things and hadn't considered where I was headed. It would have been a ridiculous excuse. It seemed like forever since I had done anything without being acutely aware of how my actions might be perceived. I had this tabloid voiceover that ran in my head: *Rape Liar Stalks Ex – She Ruined My Life Now Won't Let Go*, followed up with a photo story in *Take a Tragedy* or some similar piece of waiting-room fodder.

In any case, no one would have asked me why I'd driven down that road. People who knew me had made their own assumptions about how my mind worked. They'd been more than happy to believe what they liked without having to put themselves through the embarrassment of speaking to me.

I kept telling myself that the route wasn't unreasonable. But I knew it was. I couldn't even kid myself that driving down Edis Way and past our old house was a valid shortcut; it took me nowhere. I could have visited Mum and never come within a mile.

So, I gave in to myself, although I don't know why. It was a home and a life that wouldn't ever be mine again. Why did I need to know if Ben had mowed the grass, left the lights on or changed his car?

As it was, it looked exactly as it always had when I'd come home from work, as though I could unlock the door and still belong there. It wasn't a life I'd chosen to leave and perhaps that's why it still felt as though I had a right.

I didn't slow. I promised myself that I would never go back again. There was nothing it could achieve. I promised myself but knew immediately that I was lying.

Despite what I said to Mum about job hunting, I had no real intention. I had no plans for anything that evening. I told myself several times that I needed to eat but by nine o'clock I still hadn't roused myself from the armchair.

The television was on but muted and it was the only light in the room. My current existence felt like a kind of limbo. I could see glimpses of the outside world but I sat there, detached from it.

It wasn't a good place to be. I switched over to the news, turned up the volume and tried to relate to the stories that flashed up on the screen. But I only ended up wondering how I could have spent the last weeks so oblivious to everything that was happening in the rest of the world.

Then there was footage from an earthquake. I didn't focus on the newsreader's words but in the background there was footage of people digging through the rubble and dust with their bare hands, brick by brick, frantically trying to reach any survivors.

That's all I could do, I realised. Just do what I could and hope that there was something worth digging for.

I switched off the television. I'd had moments like that; glimpses of something more positive. Mostly, they had quickly evaporated and I knew this too might be gone by tomorrow but right then it made sense to me that I should try to do any little thing I could.

I dug out the anonymous notes and spread them out on the floor, each next to its envelope.

They stared back at me. I don't know what I hoped to see but I willed them to show me something.

It was obvious that each of the notes had been written by the same person but I knew from my experience in court that my gut instinct wasn't enough. I still had the voices of lawyers reverberating in my memory and, aside from forensic proof, they would have handwriting experts to compare the rows of neatly blocked letters. I didn't have any of their resources and no scientific proof.

The writing was that kind that you use when you are filling forms. I don't know if they still exist but there used to be forms where you filled in the letters, one per square, and it made everybody's writing of uniform height and uniform spacing and one person's capital A looked much like another's. And I suppose a biro is a biro. Some of the notes were written in blue and others in black.

It was the content that made me sure.

Yes, the envelopes were of the same stock but the strongest similarity from one letter to the next was the level of spite. Maybe I was wrong, but it seemed to me that this had female written all over it.

My first guess was that it had come from somebody in Andy's family. I'd known his parents and his sister – vaguely at least – for years. They always seemed pleasant enough people, but I hadn't crossed them back then.

His mum never struck me as an imaginative woman. I think if she felt that angry she'd just come around and shout or try to punch me.

There was Andy's sister, of course, and I'd seen a few of her posts on Facebook, talking about her family's hard year, about how depressed she'd been feeling. About how some people you thought were friends really weren't.

I'd never been friends with her. We'd had drinks a couple of times, shared pleasantries while sitting among a bunch of other people. People who harp on about how they were once better friends than they actually were are as deceitful as those who stand by you one minute and then vanish the next.

No, it wasn't Beth.

And I didn't think any of Andy's ex-girlfriends felt that strongly. Maybe I was wrong but I'd never known him to be in a relationship for more than a couple of months at a time. He drifted in and out, enjoyed casual flings and flirtations. I'm sure he'd hurt plenty of girls in the past and I really didn't think he'd stirred up enough loyalty in any of them to come back at me with something like this.

But Andy wasn't the only one who'd been damaged really. We all had. My little misadventure with the police had screwed up a lot of lives.

I sat cross-legged on the floor and stared at the letters for some time before I acknowledged the truth; the sender was far more likely to be somebody closer to me than Andy's parents or his sister Beth. This was someone who was either close to somebody who'd been hurt by this or had been hurt themselves.

I wish I'd kept Christmas cards. I could have compared the writing. All the characters of 'Merry Christmas' were in these letters somewhere.

I made myself a drink and returned to the floor with the coffee and three biscuits on the saucer. I sat dunking cookies and waiting for inspiration. I found my mobile and used the camera to zoom in on the postmarks but they gave away nothing. Cambridge. Everything in my life started and ended in Cambridge.

One of the one hundred and twenty thousand people who lived there had sent me some letters. It didn't exactly narrow it down much.

I reckoned the envelopes and the paper were a mainstream supermarket brand. It wasn't Ben's parents, then, that was for sure. They wouldn't have been seen dead anywhere less than Waitrose.

If they'd sent me hate mail it would have been written in fountain pen and on paper that had come from John Lewis. I was being cruel. No, I wasn't actually, I was being accurate and didn't mean it as bitterly as it sounded.

Yes, they'd told me they loved me, thought of me as a daughter.

But when it came to the crunch, they were going to side with him, weren't they?

I picked up the first of the letters. The drawings were the biggest giveaway. Only so many people can produce work like that. But as I thought this, I spotted something about the image. I moved closer to the light. I stared and then I realised what it was. The strokes were too uniform and the places where the shading was darker showed no sign of any different level of pressure on the paper. So, it was traced. Suddenly it was obvious. Someone had traced it. And I realised what else was bugging me. I knew this shot and, if this had been in colour, I would have recognised it immediately.

I switched on my computer and flicked through my Facebook profile pictures.

Yes, I could see where my face was copied from. It was a group shot from the Christmas before last. There were a bunch of us in town. Eight of us I think. There was me and Ben, my brother Charlie, this girl he liked from college who wasn't interested in him and then Jess with her boyfriend. I couldn't remember his name. Paul, maybe? Phil? I didn't know. He turned up just before Christmas and was gone by the first week of January.

And then there was Andy and some girl he'd met the night before. They went out, maybe three times. Andy had grabbed a waiter and handed him the camera and we'd all grinned into the lens, saying something stupid like 'Mistletoe' or something. 'Sprouts,' I think we actually said.

And there, that was where the photo of my face had come from.

No one had access to this page any more. My Facebook account was private and, even back then, the photos were only visible to friends. Just friends, not friends-of-friends. How many friends did I have? It was hard to remember. I had none left but I guess there had been fifty or so back then.

So, that narrowed it down a little. But not very much.

WEDNESDAY 14 JUNE, 2017

I didn't really pay attention to the time when I phoned Charlie. It had gone twelve o'clock though. I didn't expect he'd care and, sure enough, he didn't.

He sounded as though he was in a room full of people.

'Where are you?' I asked.

'Just in my flat,' he replied.

'Sounds like a party.'

'No, no. Six of us live here you know, sis? By the time you add on visitors, there's always about twelve of us in the front room. Anyway, how are you doing?'

'Not too bad. I need help with something. It's a bit . . . awkward.'

Charlie hesitated. Not because he wasn't willing to help, I know that. He probably hesitated for about the time it took to think, *What the fuck now?*

But he managed to sound cheerful about it.

'I've been getting anonymous letters,' I told him, and I heard him move out of the room and shut the door behind him. I guess he was standing in the hallway.

'Abusive letters?' he asked.

'Uh-huh,' I replied, and the relief of telling somebody brought a lump to my throat. I breathed steadily until it passed.

'How many have there been?'

'Eight, so far.'

'Eight? That's not a small number, Em. What do they say?'

'It's not just what they say. Look, you won't tell Mum and Dad, will you? I really don't want to worry them.'

'Hey, if I told our parents, think of the things you could dob me in for. No.'

'Two of them had a drawing. It was explicit.'

'Of what?'

I chewed my lip for a moment and decided to tell him.

'It's crude, it's stupid, it's just . . . somebody used a photo of me from Facebook and it's a photo where I'm saying something or other and my mouth's open. They've drawn a close up of my face with this . . . penis . . .'

He cut in. 'A dick?'

'Yeah, Charlie, yep. It's like, right in front of my mouth. Like I'm, you know . . .'

'Eurgh, too much, sis . . .'

'Well exactly. So, what I want to know is, could it have been done with software? I mean could a photo be turned into a picture with software? Well actually, I know it can but how difficult is it?'

'It's a piece of cake. You can download an app on your phone. It doesn't even have to cost you anything and, you know, it's fairly idiot proof. Even you could do it.'

'Yeah, well thanks . . .'

'Oh, you know, I mean, anyone could.'

'Hmm . . . that doesn't help me much.'

'You want to find out who's done it, right?'

'Yeah, course I do. Look, I'm assuming it's not a stranger but someone with a personal angle. I'm not going to the police with this but you know, if I could . . .'

'If you could what?'

'I don't know . . . talk to them.'

'I don't think that's the recommended approach for, like, a stalker.'

'Well, they're not stalking me, are they? They're just pissed off because I took Andy to court.'

'So, you want to know who it is?'

'Course I do.'

'Okay. Any clues?'

'No. All I know is my Facebook profile was set so that only my friends could see the photo. It hasn't been shared.'

'Could it have been downloaded?'

'Yeah, but even if it had, only by one of my friends. They couldn't have seen it otherwise.'

'Okay, so who are they?'

'Well, there's nobody left now really and nobody even knows my Facebook account is still there, privacy's so tight. I'm invisible.'

'Yeah, okay, but back then, who were your Facebook friends? Go back through your posts.'

'Once they've de-friended me, don't they vanish?'

'Just go back. Look at the photos. See if you can remember who liked it, who put what, what you responded to. Get a list of people who were your friends.'

I exhaled slowly. 'That's a hell of a lot of work.'

'Well, it seems to me you have a hell of a lot of free time on your hands.'

One thing I could always rely on Charlie for was hitting the nail on the head.

I slept badly and woke just after 5 a.m. There was a net curtain at my window and at first light it glowed dingy grey.

I had every intention to try to go back to sleep but it was easier to get up in the end. I stood at the window and watched the cars below. I already recognised them from the sound of the gravel under their wheels but this time I watched them pulling out.

First were the husband and wife with the matching BMWs. They left a couple of minutes apart, driving slowly and turning slowly so the gravel made a grumbling sound, but none of it moved.

Then Frank, he was out early. He must have gone to buy more than a paper; milk or bread, perhaps, because he came back ten minutes later with a small carrier bag in his hand.

The final car, the Audi, was moved by a woman who looked around sixty. She had close-cropped hair and a tall thin frame, and from where I stood, her golf bag looked twice as wide as she did. Funnily enough I'd never seen this woman closer than this and barely glimpsed the two matching BMWs; I'd been here almost a month and I was a stranger to all of them. She drove out of sight and I accepted that it would be another day in an almost empty house.

Visiting home was dangerous, like being on a diet and then suddenly letting yourself have chocolate. Or being dry and kidding yourself you'll stop at one glass of wine.

My parents had lived in the same house since before I was born and I'd grown up with the feeling that Foxton was in the middle of everything. Not that it was the most important place, but that the rest of the world was positioned around it. Perhaps that's not always the way with kids, but it was certainly the way with me.

Returning to Foxton stirred too many memories.

I had other friends apart from Jess. Claire and Mia, Laura and Jody. At one point, we used to go out as a group, you know, for something to eat, have a laugh, get drunk, go to the cinema. Not in that order, probably. And then, one by one, we started spending our time in other places, with other people, and the only person I always stayed close to was Jess. I'd never expected to fall out with her. It felt impossible, like she was a sister – as if not being friends with her any more would be like us changing our common DNA.

I understood how uncomfortable she'd been about the case and I hoped, after time, she would soften and that we could get back to where we'd been. Marriages came back from worse. I knew it wouldn't be easy; you can't just pretend that the painful memories never happened but I also wasn't ready to believe that she'd just washed her hands of me. I realised that it might have to wait until her relationship with Andy hit its certain end. Of course, I had no idea when that would happen but I suppose it was almost inevitable that when I crept back in to Foxton, I'd creep back round to see her too.

Her Jaguar F-Type was parked on her drive. I was on foot, and in time to see the lights flash and hear the muted double-beep of the central locking. The shadow of Jess disappeared into her house.

75

She'd bought the car a couple of years earlier. I'd laughed when I'd seen it, not that I wasn't kind of impressed by it too. I was driving my second-hand Focus, which was already eight years old by then, and she went off and splurged a whole load of money on some car that looked as though it should have been driven by a middle-aged man having a midlife crisis.

I stopped about fifty yards from her house, not really conscious of the fact that I was just standing in the middle of the pavement or that somebody might see me and tell her I'd been there. Instead, I was thinking of all the other times I'd been in this road, when I'd come here straight after work with my make-up bag and a change of clothes. When we'd call a taxi and it would wait at the end of her driveway until we climbed inside. Full of banter, full of energy, full of our 'bring it on' approach to having a night out. Then hours later, when we were dropped off at home, we'd have trouble navigating the narrow strip of driveway that lay between her car and the grass and, when I wobbled, she'd hiss, 'Don't scratch the paintwork.' And if I wobbled too far the other way and felt my heels sink into the grass, I'd whisper, 'Can't you widen the path?' or 'I've ruined my shoes.' Then we'd take drinks to the sitting room and the banter would carry on. We'd replay patches of our evening and giggle and push a few more drinks at each other until one or other of us would crash out on the sofa and the other would crash out on the bed. We had that kind of closeness where I could crash out on her bed without asking. Where I could get up and make myself breakfast or look through the DVD collection to see what was new. These things don't sound like a big deal but when you realise you've lost them, then they are.

I watched the light in her downstairs window blot out as she closed her curtains. She didn't pause or look across. Perhaps I should have left her alone but I knew then I needed to speak to her.

I never used to be an emotional person. I suppose I still wasn't in some ways, but when I knocked on her door and she didn't answer immediately, my thoughts began to drift again. I was silently asking myself what I would do if she refused to open up at all. Let's face it, I knew she was in there.

I counted to thirty and knocked again. It was just about possible that she'd had time to shut her front door, run upstairs, strip off her clothes and jump in the shower, but I doubted it. I sensed that she was there, staring at the other side of the front door, maybe from her kitchen or from the top of the stairs, chewing her lip and wondering what her next move ought to be. I counted another thirty and knocked again, deciding that I would wait for as long as necessary. This time there were only a few seconds before the door opened and her face appeared in the long narrow crack. She smiled tightly.

'Hi. I was upstairs. Sorry.'

'Don't worry,' I said. But I didn't volunteer anything else and after a few awkward seconds of silence, she asked me if I wanted to come in.

'Sure,' I said and I followed her through to the kitchen but she didn't offer me a drink. Instead she leant against the worktop but faced the window.

'How are you?' she said at last.

'Could be worse. How about you?'

She shrugged, folded her hands across her chest. 'I'm fine, work's fine. It's picking up again after . . . you know.'

'After me?' I asked her and couldn't help the sharpness in my voice or the way I pressed my lips tightly shut afterwards. I had to remind myself to unclench my jaw.

'That's not exactly what I meant, but I'd be lying if I said that it hadn't damaged the company.' She looked at me like I'd done it, not Andy.

I wasn't sure what I could say that wouldn't sound like I was feeling sorry for myself. I could have put my heart on my sleeve and said, 'Jess, I miss you,' but was I really expecting her to say, 'Oh Em, I miss you too,' and for it all to be all right, with a hug?

But I stood there looking at her for a few minutes and I wasn't sure what else I'd come to say. I felt the skin tingle near the top of my cheeks, the way it always does when I get the first sign that I'm going to cry. 'I never thought it would work out like this,' I told her.

'Well,' she replied, 'I don't think any of us could have predicted it turning out quite like it did. But there you are. And the damage is done now, isn't it?'

'Is it? I mean, is it irreparable?'

'Between who? You and me? Or you and Ben? Or you and your family? What did you expect?'

'I'd like us to still be friends, the way we always were.'

'Andy and I are happy together.' Jess unfolded her arms and rubbed her palms down the outer thighs of her jeans. 'Ben's seeing someone else,' she said. 'I thought you should know.'

I was momentarily wordless.

'You didn't know then?' she said. Her voice softened a little. 'He took it really hard when you and he split up.'

I blinked a couple of times, trying to retain my composure. 'It wasn't what I wanted,' I said.

Her eyes narrowed for a second.

'After that day in court, there wasn't going to be any other outcome, Emily.'

Emily. Not Em. She'd only ever called me Em. For as long as I could remember, anyway.

'I don't want any nastiness between us,' she said. 'But I'm not doing this any more. I'm not going to be here for you when you show up unexpectedly.'

'I don't understand. What did I do that was so wrong?'

She looked at me as though I was stupid. Like I was really, really dumb.

'You had it so good,' she said. 'Ben adored you. I adored you. Great job, great home. And then there was Andy. He'd always been a laugh. The joker. It feels to me that everything was fine until I started dating him. Was that what the problem was?'

'Did you ever believe me?'

'I didn't know what to think. I couldn't believe that you would be so destructive; if you'd lied I couldn't understand your motive unless it was to break up Andy and me. So, I went to see Andy, to have it out with him.'

'And?'

'And he's not a rapist. If he'd raped you, if he'd *really* raped you, you'd have had bruises, you'd have . . . someone would have heard you cry out. He's not some big musclebound bloke who would have pinned you down, or an aggressive man who would have made you felt too terrified to speak up. I know him and I know you. I wanted some other answer but when it came to the trial I had to face up to what it really meant to all of us. I had to make a decision.'

'I didn't make it up.'

'Emily, I know that you are honest, but only until you are in a tight spot. Then you'll lie to cover your own back. I've seen it a hundred times.'

I bit my lip and didn't reply. She had a point.

She'd seen me get out of homework, pull a sickie, lie to ditch a previous boyfriend.

'And you've never been the quiet, mousey type. If you hadn't wanted it, the whole house would have heard. So just let Ben get his life back together. He's my friend now and I hope he and Shannon make a go of it. I will tell him you stopped by but please don't turn up here again.'

I didn't drive straight home. I went to Edis Way. To the house I'd owned with Ben.

There was a red Vauxhall Corsa parked on our driveway. I didn't know anyone with a Vauxhall Corsa. I parked along the road and pretended to be studying my phone screen each time a pedestrian passed.

It was almost midnight when our front door opened and a woman stepped from our house. I was too far away to see her clearly but she stood with her car door open and talked to him until he left the doorstep. He continued the conversation, their faces just inches apart.

They didn't kiss.

Wouldn't they have kissed if this had been a new relationship?

She reversed from the driveway and I should have let her go but panic hit me. I had to know who she was, didn't I? I thought I might need to know for later.

I drove towards her, I didn't get too close and I passed our house before Ben had finally closed the front door. For a moment, he stared at me. And for some stupid reason I smiled back at him, as though it was the polite thing to do or something.

I was still following her car ten minutes later. She drove steadily as though she was a new driver and I wondered how old she was. I wondered whether she was a student and found myself remembering how hard I'd had to work to pay my share of the bills and wondering whether this time he'd be happy to pay them all.

What did that say about me?

I couldn't describe the way I felt just then. I didn't think it was jealousy or anger but it was some kind of pain.

At the next junction, she signalled right and I pulled up behind her, ready to make the turn too. It was all I could do to not follow her.

I kept my hands gripped to the wheel and refused to let myself release the handbrake.

She pulled out and I saw her glance over her shoulder at me. Her expression was wary. That time I didn't smile. It was over in a second and I stayed in the same spot until a car pulled up behind mine and sounded its horn. I turned back and I don't remember the journey home to Mill House.

FRIDAY 16 JUNE, 2017

It took me a couple of days to find out who she was.

Her name was Shannon Bridges. She was six years younger than me. She was at primary school when I left secondary, and was eight years younger than Ben.

I know they're just a bunch of numbers that shouldn't mean anything but I found myself looking for an answer in them when I didn't even know the question.

Twenty-seven is an age when things happen. I was twenty-seven when Ben and I married.

She was twenty-four.

I'd reached twenty-four and felt pressure to start to make adult choices. It was pressure I put upon myself but I remember it felt wrong to march towards thirty without hitting at least a couple of milestones. Not children though. Not yet. We both wanted them but Ben was in less of a hurry than me. It was okay. Because I thought I could wait.

THURSDAY 22 JUNE, 2017

I woke up to the sound of a car turning on the gravel. I could tell by the noise it made that it was a vehicle arriving, not leaving, and within seconds I picked out the sound of another, larger vehicle whose engine was idling somewhere at the front of the building.

I looked out of my bedroom window. The car was a Porsche Cayenne, not a vehicle I'd ever seen there before. Whoever had driven it had already parked up and gone, so I moved to the front of the house and, from my kitchen window, saw a medium-sized removal van. It reversed close to the front door. They killed the engine and two men jumped out. Well, jumped was perhaps a little too enthusiastic. The driver was a large man who slid from the cab and landed on his feet in a move that made his belly wobble. The second was younger, taller and about a third of his weight.

They opened the rear doors and I found myself studying the contents of somebody else's home. The first objects I saw were a pair of children's bikes. The larger was pink and white, with tassels on the handlebars and a flower-covered basket on the front. The smaller was a bright green BMX-style bike. They leant against a chest of drawers and behind that I could see the underside of two bed bases.

So there'd be children downstairs. I hadn't thought of that. I supposed it didn't bother me. I'd never had much contact with kids and, although I always knew that one day I'd like to have my own, I also felt that they were rather alien. I wondered what the rest of the residents would think. But to be honest, with their flat directly below mine, no one would hear as much of them as I would.

I paused to listen for any childlike sounds coming from below. There was nothing but, after a couple of minutes, I could make out a woman's voice. I made myself a tea, positioned myself near the window and watched for about half an hour as various items were unloaded. Finally, the woman came out to the van.

I wasn't at the best angle but she looked about my age. She had dark blonde hair that hung down to her shoulders and although she was dressed for the practicalities of moving in old jeans and a hoodie, I could see that she was slim. Elegant, even, in the way that she moved. She took her turn to go back and forth with several smaller boxes and I decided it was time to venture downstairs.

The men were carrying a sideboard, grunting at each other with 'back a bit' and 'mind the corner', 'your end first' and 'left a bit, left a bit'. I'd looked at the flat through the windows. It was bigger than mine. It didn't have the disadvantage of the second staircase cutting through it for one thing, and from the outside I'd worked out that it had an extra window, front and back. The other flat on my floor was larger; it had three bedrooms, where I just had the one.

The woman downstairs had three bedrooms but I suppose that's what you need with a boy and a girl. I glanced through the doorway as she was coming out. She stepped aside to let the movers through with a cupboard, then stooped to straighten the pile of post that they'd knocked across the carpet as they'd gone past. She glanced up at me from that kneeling position and gave me a tentative smile. I kind of waved at her which was a bit odd, considering we were about eight feet apart. I'd really planned to walk on and just have a quick look on the way past but now I'd been caught being nosy, I had to do a bit better.

'I live upstairs,' I said. 'I wondered if you had electric yet. I could put the kettle on if you wanted?'

It was only the offer of a cuppa but she looked ridiculously grateful.

'I have electric,' she said, 'but I'm damned if I know where the kettle is, or a mug, and I don't have milk, never mind teabags. In fact,' her smile broadened, blossomed, 'I'm not even sure my kettle will work. I think it might be the wrong voltage. But I really would kill a cuppa.'

She walked away from me, back into the flat and called to the men, 'Do you want tea or coffee?'

The two men both wanted the same. Coffee, strong, white with two sugars.

'Do you mind if I have a coffee?' she asked. 'Just white, no sugar.'

'No problem. I'm Emily.'

'Joanne.' she replied. 'Joanne Carter.'

We both looked a bit awkward, not sure whether to shake hands or what, I guess, and in the end, she held hers out. I shook it and that job was done. Five minutes later I brought four mugs downstairs and she stopped for a minute to talk to me. The conversation never went beyond the trials of moving and questions about the nearest shop and the nearest take away and what it was like to live in the building.

'You can walk to the pub, but the nearest shops to us are a car ride away.'

She looked disappointed. 'I think maybe I was busy looking at the house and not thinking about the amenities. Ah well, it'll come right,' she said.

That was the first and only time in the conversation where I caught a twang of an accent in her voice.

'Are you Australian?' I asked her.

She smiled. 'No, my husband was. I just picked up the odd hint of it, I guess. I'm amazed you heard that; in Sydney I was constantly told I sounded like a pom.'

'It was faint, but I definitely caught it in there.'

'Oh, you can hear it more with the kids,' she said. 'Molly and Luke. They're my two.'

She smiled as she said their names. 'They're in one of the bedrooms. I've told them to stay there, just until I get everything in the building. They are dying to help me unpack,' she said. 'I think that will probably make it worse. What d'you reckon?'

I thought the question was rhetorical but she looked at me for an answer. 'I don't really know. I don't have much to do with children.'

'Well, I hope they won't bug you too much,' she said. 'They're not

85

always quiet, but they're usually well behaved. Thanks for the drinks. I can wash the mugs up and bring them back up, if you like?'

'I can take them,' I said, 'if you're finished. Otherwise just give them back later.'

It was obviously my cue to go. I shouldn't have minded. On my scale of things, at least recently, this had been a major conversation but the ache of loneliness was ever present and it began to throb before I'd even walked away.

'See you around,' I said.

She was already slightly distracted though. She'd bent down and picked up the pile of post and had flicked through the first couple of items.

'There won't be anything for me,' she said. 'I don't know whether to bin the whole lot, or what.' As she flicked through, I spotted something familiar amongst the rest. I stepped closer and reached out for it before she had the chance to pick it out herself.

'I think that's for me,' I said.

Her gaze followed the envelope as I took it. 'Are you sure?' she asked.

I held it up enough for her to see my name on the front. It had no flat number.

'Oh,' she said, 'I'll check if there's any more for you.'

I was sure there wouldn't be but I waited while she went through the rest of the thirty or so items and by then I was fidgety and breathless and I could feel cold sweat forming across my back.

She studied my expression for a moment but said nothing.

'Thanks,' I said. 'Please, just post it through if there's anything else.'

And I hurried back upstairs.

I returned to my flat and closed the door. For once the postmark was clear: Cambridge, 20-06-17. It had been sent two days ago. I leant with my back to it at first but as I opened the letter, I slid down to a seated position, my flat in front of me and the rest of the world at my back.

It was one page. I'd been treated to a picture again. It was me all right, taken from a photo I vaguely recognised and drawn or computer morphed in a very ugly, caricature-ish way. My jaw was heavy and my lips were over-emphasised so the expression had a cruel twist to it. Technically I suppose it wasn't bad. I stood full length down one side of the page. It looked like I was soliciting under a lamppost or at the kerbside.

The headline was:

YOU ARE NOT WELCOME IN FOXTON

So subtle. Beneath it was a simple list:

Goodbye Ben.
Goodbye Jess.
Goodbye nice little home.
Goodbye successful job.

It really wasn't a threat. It really wasn't anything. Just an intrusion. I turned over the sheet and glanced at the back. There in small neat writing was written:

Don't try to work out who hates you. They all do.

They wish you were dead.

And then a smiley face and the word:

Whore.

I released my breath slowly, refolded it and returned it to its envelope. It was nothing. Meaningless. That's what I told myself. I didn't feel hurt or scared or anything by it, but I stayed where I was for the next hour, the energy sapped from me. The whole point of what I might have done with my day suddenly seemed redundant.

No husband, no friend, no home, no job.

Not quite no home, but not the home I wanted.

Everything the letter had said in those few words was true.

I don't know what it was about that letter that hit me so hard but, suddenly, everything I'd been afraid to feel for the previous months rained down on me. Or maybe it was just that after a certain length of time I couldn't avoid the emotion.

I felt everything then.

Grief and loss.

The pain of it hit me like something physical. Everyone I knew apart from Mum and Charlie had somehow abandoned me or turned their back. Ben and Jess and Andy and even my own dad.

I couldn't imagine walking through my own village or bumping into people who had been my clients without feeling shame. Perhaps Jess was right. I considered that for a moment. Perhaps those ten minutes in the bathroom should have stayed ten minutes in the bathroom.

Perhaps sex with Andy, even non-consensual, could have been brushed under the carpet. Would I be in a better place now if I'd simply kept quiet? It was never going to be easy to put all this behind me now. I didn't think I could have kept it from Jess, she would have needed to know what her boyfriend was capable of. And then Ben would have found out and I had no way of knowing whether the outcome would have been any better than this.

But no, how screwed would I have been if I had tried to ignore what Andy had done? To keep it secret from Ben and go through the pretence of socialising with somebody who thought it was all right to do what he wanted, when he wanted.

I'd made the right choices, it was destiny or fate or some other force that had backed me into this corner. And I had blundered from one obstacle to the next until I'd found myself here; alone in my flat and pretty much alone in the world.

Our minds play tricks on us, releasing chemicals to excite or sedate and sometimes to numb. I had been numb until that moment; I had understood everything that had happened but the full shock of it hadn't hit me until then. I sat on the carpet behind the door and I sobbed and I shook. And heavy breaths wracked my body until I thought I was going to vomit. I heard wailing, a from-the-gut sound, and at first I didn't even realise that it was coming from me. I don't know how long I sat there and, even when I calmed down, I remained motionless.

It felt as though getting up would be the same as saying, *Well that's all right then. That's out of my system.*

No part of me wanted to move. In that moment, I was neither hot nor cold, hungry nor thirsty, nor needing anything. It felt as though it might be best just to lie there forever.

The knock on the door behind me surprised me, but I didn't jump. I pressed my lips tight. For some illogical reason, I wondered if it might be Frank. He'd never knocked before but that was my first reaction. After the second knock, there was woman's voice.

'Are you okay?'

That should've made me smile. I didn't reply and hoped she'd leave again. I listened and couldn't tell whether she was there or not, but I hadn't heard footsteps. It felt as though about two minutes had passed before she knocked a third time.

I just wanted her to go and before I knew it I was swaying and banging my back against the door and shouting, 'LEAVE ME ALONE. JUST FUCK OFF AND LEAVE ME ALONE.'

When I still didn't hear footsteps, I began screaming words.

'FUCK OFF, WILL YOU? LEAVE ME ALONE.'

I didn't even stand up. I crawled across to the sofa and used my mobile to call my mum.

Of course, she knew it was me because my number would have come up on her phone but she still asked, 'Emily? Is that you?' She waited. 'Take your time,' she said. It was always so straightforward with Mum. 'Do you want me to come over?' she asked.

'No,' I managed to say but underneath it was really a yes.

'Tell me what's happening.'

And although she couldn't see me I shook my head in reply. My cheeks were wet with tears and I could feel my face was red and puffy and my lips swollen and ugly. She didn't need to see me like this.

'Who knows where I live, Mum?'

'Oh,' she said. 'Do you mean who have I told? I haven't told anyone. Okay, well your dad knows and your brother. People have asked me in passing how you are doing, where you are. I haven't given anybody an address, but you know that. I'll just say, "She's in a village on the other side of Cambridge." I don't think I've even mentioned Wicken. Why?'

'It doesn't matter.'

'No, why? Come on, Emily.'

'Something came in the post.' I'd started now, hadn't I? 'I had a letter. It was spiteful.'

I heard her draw a breath.

'Go on,' she said.

'It's nothing. It wouldn't matter if it had been forwarded on from you. But it was addressed to me here and that's weird. It's come from somebody who knows me. They know Ben and Jess and about my old job. Would Dad have told anyone?'

'No, you know what your dad's like. He wouldn't remember your address. He'd know where to look it up and he's not going to be looking up your address for anybody we know, is he? We'd check with you first. Perhaps it's appeared somewhere public? You know, like, I don't know, one of those online searches you can do?'

'I'm not sure. I haven't been here long and I use my maiden name for everything now.'

'There's plenty of people who know what your maiden name is, Em. Look, if it's worrying you, contact the police.'

I wheezed out an impression of a laugh. 'Yeah, well I don't really get on very well with contacting the police, do I, Mum?'

'That's not my point. If someone's threatening you . . .?'

'It wasn't a threat, Mum. It was just spitefulness and it's probably a one-off. It really doesn't matter. I just don't want somebody, anybody, apart from family knowing where I live.'

'Do you want me to come and visit you?'

'Really, no, it's fine.'

'Have you thought about work yet?'

'Well, yes and no. I need to look for something. My money will run out otherwise, but a career's not the thing right now. There's a pub in the village. There's a few local businesses, I suppose. Perhaps I could get some office work. And there's a recruitment agency in Soham.'

'Go in there,' Mum said. 'You know, just have a chat. Tell them that you're looking for something, see what's about.'

'*Why did you leave your last employment?*' I mimicked. 'I think I want a job that doesn't require a CV and references. And after that, I'll see.'

Mum didn't reply and to me it sounded as though she was thinking.

'You are going to have to be careful, aren't you?' she said at last. She spoke slowly and she was testing each word before saying it, as if she was worried that wherever she was leading was dangerous territory.

'What do you mean?' I asked her.

'People can be vicious and if someone knows where you live, they might want to stir things up when you find a job. It might be best you don't do something like pub- or shop-work, when anyone off the street can come and find you.'

I said something to brush away what she was suggesting but I could see it was true. Around me, my little world seemed to constrict a tiny bit more.

One option was to move again, but what difference would that really make?

'Can I ask you, Mum, are people treating you any differently?'

'Like who?'

'Anyone. People you deal with at the school or see at the garden centre. Or people in the street. Friends, neighbours. Has all this done you damage?'

'Emily, there are always small-minded people. You matter to me far more than they ever will.'

91

'Mum, I'm so sorry.'

'Don't be,' she said.

'I thought I was doing the right thing,' I told her.

'Well, I'm not sure about that,' she replied.

FRIDAY 23 JUNE, 2017

I was up and out of my flat at half-seven the next morning. I caught Mr and Mrs Watts first. I'd come face to face with Mrs Watts a couple of times since I'd been here. She had one of those smiles that only goes up at the corners and never reaches her eyes.

She looked as though I'd already annoyed her before I even spoke.

'Hi, I'm Emily Jenkins. I live in Flat 2.'

She had her car keys in her hand and looked pointedly towards her vehicle.

'Yes?'

'A couple of bits of my post have gone to the wrong flat,' I said, 'and I was wondering whether anything else had been delivered for me?'

'Would it have said Flat 2 on it?' she asked, her lack of enthusiasm obvious.

'Well, one piece that went astray had no number on it. The other things I've been receiving have been correctly addressed, but if anything arrives with incomplete details, it could go anywhere, couldn't it?'

'I doubt it,' she muttered. 'The postman knows me well enough. I'm sure he would work out if we suddenly had somebody *extra* living with us.'

She said the word *extra* with particular coldness in her voice.

'So, there's been nothing then?' I smiled and thanked her.

She didn't say anything else and drove away without even telling me her name.

I walked back towards the house in case she was looking in her rear-view mirror, then hung around until the next person came out. In this case, the next person was her husband. He didn't smile either but it turned out he was a little bit more amiable.

'We just get the usual,' he said. 'Circulars and bills. I'm sure my wife would have said if we'd had anything in the post that wasn't ours. I certainly haven't seen anything. I'm Dan, by the way. My wife's Sally. I bet she didn't introduce herself, did she?'

I shook my head. 'No, she didn't actually.'

'Well,' he smiled cheerlessly. 'She'd be quite happy if the whole building was unoccupied and we were the only ones in it. I'm sure she'll thaw out eventually; she seems to manage to when it suits her. And I hope you find your post. Are you missing much?'

'Not as far as I know. Just once, an envelope went astray, but it made me wonder if anything else had gone to the wrong flat.'

'Have a word with Gerald,' he said.

'Gerald?'

'The postie. He'll be along in a bit. He's normally around by nine.'

'Okay, thanks. Yeah, I'll do that.'

When Frank came out, he frowned before he smiled. 'Good morning, Emily.'

'Hi,' I began. 'I've been asking around to see if anybody's had any of my post. It seems one item went downstairs to Flat 1.'

He frowned again. 'You look different today.'

'Do I?'

I didn't think I did, and when I looked down at my clothes I was sure I was wearing the same old jeans and shirt as I had the day I met him.

'You look as though you've been crying.' I didn't reply. Thankfully he was tactful and quick to fill the silence. 'There's a woman who's moved in downstairs from you,' he said. 'Have you seen her?'

'Yes, her name's Joanne. She has a couple of kids.'

'Oh,' he said. 'Is that a good thing?'

'Well,' I smiled, 'you are on the opposite side of the building.

I reckon it's more sound-proof between them and you than it is between them and me. I don't mind though.'

'No,' he said, 'me neither. I never had kids but, in theory, I don't object to them. Mostly. Sometimes actually. Hmm . . .' He paused and seemed to be weighing up the question, and I wondered if he was going to come back with a percentage split. But no. 'I like the place without them but I suppose it depends on each kid,' he decided. 'Anyhow, I haven't had your post. So, the one that went astray had the wrong number on it, did it?'

'No number.' I showed him the envelope. 'See and mine's number 2.' I hadn't thought about the flat numbering before but I realised then that number 1 was straight below mine. 'I would have thought that 1 and 2 were the ground-floor flats. What number's yours?' I ask.

'Four,' he said. 'They went up the left-hand side then up the right-hand side. No logic to it. There should be some sort of numbering convention to it. Like, you do all the ground floor first, then the first, or something like that. Or if you go up one side, you might as well come down the other. That would make me Flat 6. I like the number 6. I'd have preferred that.'

The longer Frank talked, the more I realised that, while he was obviously quite astute, his mind wandered continually.

'I've met Mr and Mrs Watts, the couple with the BMWs, the matching cars, you know?'

'Two flats above me?'

'Yeah, that's right. Dan and Sally,' I offer.

'Bloody woman.' I thought for a second that he meant me. He pointed up the driveway towards a patch of aubrietia at the entrance. 'Bit my head off when I planted that, she did. I don't see what the problem is. Wasn't like I was asking her to chip in for them. I just did it out of my own pocket. Just made the entrance look a bit brighter for people when they arrived. But she said the flowers looked common. How could a flower look common?'

'What did you say to her?'

He smiled impishly. 'I told her not to generalise. I said that's like saying all second-hand BMWs look like they belong to pimps. That made her cheeks flush. She hasn't spoken to me since. Stupid woman.'

95

'So that's number 6?'

'That's right.'

'And Flat 5?' I asked. 'That's the empty flat?'

'Mostly unoccupied but not empty. The guy comes and goes. He's a property developer – whatever that means these days. He owns the building. I'd say that you won't see him much but you've already met him.'

It took me a second. 'Edwards? The guy with the Tesla?'

'That's him.'

'He was checking out the ground-floor flat.'

'Checking his assets, you mean?' His tone was sharp but he stayed deadpan. 'And look,' he said. He nodded behind me and I turn to see the tall angular woman from the flat above mine. 'I'm off, but ask Maureen,' he said, 'see if she's had your post.'

'Maureen,' she said and held out a bony hand. I guessed she was in her sixties. She was the lady who golfed, whose set of clubs was always in the boot of her car.

Her voice was firm and her back very straight. I could imagine her being a teacher of some kind. The sort who would have looked across the top of the children's heads and picked out the misbehaving kids at the back of the class.

'Was it you making that noise last night?' she asked.

I felt my cheeks redden.

'I'm sorry if I disturbed you.'

'As long as you're fine now?'

There was a question at the end of the sentence but it felt as though the only correct answer was to say, 'Yes I am, thank you. I'm sorry if I disturbed you.'

'So, you are after some post?' she asked.

'Not exactly. I just wondered if any post had come to you by mistake. One item went downstairs. It was wrongly addressed.'

'Well, unless somebody had planned to go through every flat that was available, I'm sure they'd correct themselves after getting it wrong once. Have you let them know?'

'No, not yet.'

'Well, speak to Gerald,' she said. 'I'm surprised he put it through the wrong door in the first place, but you're new. Both flats were empty for some time so he had no way of knowing, did he? Is that everything?'

I nodded, but that didn't seem good enough. 'It is, thank you,' I added.

It occurred to me then how easy it was to take on the mannerisms of others. She drove away and for the next five minutes I felt the need to stand straight and enunciate properly in case she reappeared.

So, the only cars left were my Focus and the Porsche belonging to the flat downstairs.

Ten minutes later the post van arrived in the driveway and the postie everybody told me was called Gerald stepped out.

'I had a letter,' I said.

'Well done you,' he replied.

'I mean a letter that went to the wrong flat. It had no number, but it had my name on it. So, I was wondering if you can keep an eye open, in case anything else that's meant for me goes to the wrong address?'

'Well,' he said, 'I don't think you'll want it but I do have one here. I noticed it when I was sorting out the letters this morning. If I'd known you better I probably would have caught the first one. But here you go. Advertising bumf, by the look of it.'

He handed me three envelopes. They all had my name on the front but the top two had me down with no flat number. None of the post was spectacular. Another brochure for blinds, one for central heating and the third was an advert for accompanied coach tours. I didn't think I was quite ready for that.

'Thanks,' I told him.

'Now I know who you are, I'll look out for your name and make sure it goes to Flat 2,' he said, 'even though officially, if it says another number, that's where I'm supposed to deliver it. But, you know, mistakes get made. Just let them know where you can, so it doesn't carry on happening.'

'Thanks,' I said again.

As I was going in the front of the house, he was already knocking on Flat 1. I followed him inside. He knocked again and, as I went up the stairs, the door opened. I was halfway up the second flight when I looked down and I saw Joanne signing for a parcel. She looked up at me and managed a small smile.

'Hang on, Emily,' she called out.

I didn't go back down but stopped where I was and, when Gerald the postman left, she came out into the hallway.

She wore a sweatshirt and jogging bottoms. Her hair was tied in two bunches and she was as make-up free as me.

'I just wanted to ask if you were okay?' she said.

'I am now, thank you. I feel a bit embarrassed about it.'

'You don't need to be,' she shook her head. 'It's none of my business, obviously, but I do think the kids would have been distressed if they'd heard you upset like that.'

'Oh, well, I'm sorry.' All I seemed to be doing was apologising.

'I can just explain to them, you know, if it's something that's likely to happen often?'

'No, I'll try and keep it down,' I said. 'I just had some bad news and . . . well . . . I'm sorry.'

'That's fine,' she said. 'Don't worry. We'll keep ourselves to ourselves and we'll try not to bother you either.'

She didn't immediately turn back inside though and I didn't immediately head up the stairs. I didn't want her to close her door. 'Perhaps it would help them settle in, you know, if they met me and knew they had friendly neighbours?'

'Okay,' she smiled. 'Well, we'll see.'

'Okay.'

I returned to my flat and I wondered what 'we'll see' might mean. I didn't think I had been too pushy. I mean, I hadn't really been after anything. But perhaps, if I was their mum, I'd have been a little hesitant at my children meeting the mad, screaming neighbour.

At least that made me smile.

I turned on the kettle and decided it was time to make some kind of plan for the rest of my day. I didn't know what; anything to fill my time would have done.

SATURDAY 24 JUNE, 2017

The first I saw of her children was on Saturday morning. Molly was seven and two years older than her brother. She had long, straight, dark brown hair falling to just below her shoulders. Not really long, but the perfect length to wear in braids or a ponytail.

Luke's hair was short but the same shade as his sister's and the same brown-coloured eyes. Molly's face was heart shaped and Luke had long dark lashes that fanned out across his cheeks. Of course, I couldn't see that from my window. I heard their voices first and went across and looked down on them playing on the grass.

They had a ball, football-sized but made of sponge. They kicked it back and forth a couple of times but then Luke carried on dribbling it around the edge of grassy area. Molly asked two or three times for him to pass it to her. He ignored her and she stood with her arms folded. I waited for her to wail and call for her mum but she didn't. She just stood and watched him until he'd finished. Then she grabbed it and I heard her shout out, 'It's my turn now, Luke.'

The gap between me and Charlie was too big for any of this. I would play a game to amuse him but if I played a game to amuse myself he wasn't interested. I always liked the age gap between us. There was no competition. I liked the way he looked up to me, but I suppose a sibling nearer my own age would have been interesting.

I watched Luke and Molly for a while before I decided to go outside and join them.

'I'm Emily,' I told them. I stood on the edge of the path with my hands in my pockets, trying to make sure that I didn't seem too forward, like I was encroaching too much on their game. 'I live upstairs from you.'

Luke ignored me. Molly smiled and sort of waved, raising her hand to just above her waist, spreading her fingers like a star.

'Hello.'

Then Luke looked up. 'We don't know you,' he said.

He was right of course. 'That's okay,' I said brightly. 'I'll go and find your mum.'

I was about to knock on her door when I realised that it was on the latch. I pushed it gently so it opened by a few inches and called quietly, 'Joanne?'

She was kneeling on the floor, unpacking books from a heavy removal box. 'Oh, hi.' There was no enthusiasm in her tone.

'I just said hello to your kids and then I thought, well, they probably ought to meet me properly, with you there, I mean.'

She clambered to her feet and wiped her hands on the front of her jeans. 'I've told them all about stranger danger,' she said. 'I know you live next door, but that's what you are, isn't it?'

I felt my face redden. I'd done the wrong thing already.

'I'm sorry,' I said lightly, 'I'm not used to kids.'

She didn't relax. 'I'll come out with you.'

If I thought we'd made a friendly start yesterday, it felt as though it had vanished today. She seemed partly preoccupied and partly annoyed. Once we were outside she called the children over. 'Molly, Luke, this is Emily. She lives upstairs.'

'I know, Mum,' Molly told her.

'Yes, but you know how important it is that you meet people properly. People shouldn't come up to you and talk to you, should they?'

Both children nodded solemnly. 'Well, now you've met Emily, you know she lives upstairs. You don't know her properly yet, but she's a neighbour so it's fine to say "hi" when we see her. Then, if Mummy gets to know her a bit better, then you can too. But what do I always say?'

Luke replied fastest, 'You are the only one we know in this country.'

'Exactly. So, let's get to know Emily a bit better and then she won't count as a stranger, okay?'

Molly smiled when she nodded and glanced at me shyly. I thought that perhaps she liked me a little and I smiled back. I was about to speak to Joanne but she'd already turned away, heading for the house. I hadn't been given permission to play with the children. I hadn't been invited to socialise with Joanne either.

I went back to my flat and watched them play some more from my kitchen window.

TUESDAY 27 JUNE, 2017

It was Tuesday before I saw any of them again face to face. I came home with some shopping and it was about half past four. Molly was sitting on the second step of the flight that led up to my flat.

She was wearing school uniform and she was holding up a copy of *Gangsta Granny*, looking at it as if she wanted to be seen to be reading. She looked over the top of the page.

'This is my new book,' she said.

'Is it good?' I asked her.

She shrugged. 'I've only just started it.'

'Oh. I haven't read it.'

'No, I think you're too old,' she said and I smiled.

'How was school?'

'It was my first day. It was okay. There's lots of kids in the class. It's bigger than my old school because we lived in the country.'

'Well, this is the country,' I said.

'Yes,' she said, 'but there's more kids in my class than my old class. And there's only three weeks until the summer holidays. Mum shouldn't have made us go at all.'

'Are you all right sitting out here?' I asked her.

'Uh-huh,' she said. 'It's quiet because my brother's watching the television and he talks all the time.'

'Oh.'

'And Mum's a bit stressed.'

'Is she?'

She nodded. 'Yeah. She's unpacking. She was unpacking yesterday and when she goes through the boxes, it makes her unhappy.'

'Oh.' I said. 'Moving house can be a big thing. Pretty tiring.'

'Yeah, I suppose. She's unpacking my room though.'

'Are you going to help her?'

'Maybe. At the moment, though, she's doing books and photos albums and even ornaments. I don't like ornaments. I worry that I'm going to knock them over. I don't want to make Mum sad.'

'I'm sure you don't,' I said and, without thinking about it, I sat on the step next to her.

'She wouldn't want to make you sad either, would she?'

Molly shook her head. 'My brother died. And my dad. Mum's always sad since then.'

'Oh.'

I didn't know what to say then. I didn't want to ignore the comment but I didn't want to stir anything up either. I couldn't just run back to my flat after hearing a revelation like that.

'Is that why you moved house?'

'Uh-huh,' she nodded. 'We lived in Australia because that's where my dad was from but Mum said she needed to come home. But she's never lived in this house before so I don't see why she thinks it's home at all.'

'She means back in her own country.'

'Yeah, I know. But I had friends there.'

'Well, you are going to meet new ones, aren't you?'

'Yeah, I met two today. I like meeting new people,' she said.

Just then the flat door opened and Joanne appeared in the hallway. I wondered for a second whether she would be annoyed with me for sitting and talking to Molly like that. 'Molly, it's time for tea. Come on in.' She ushered Molly inside. 'She talks, a lot,' she said as a parting shot to me.

'I don't mind,' I replied.

'Thanks. It's been a big day for her today, first day at school.'

'Yeah, I can imagine. I don't mind chatting to her, anytime.'

Joanne smiled, and her expression was warmer than it had been the day before. She nodded again before going inside.

SUNDAY 2 JULY, 2017

They kept themselves to themselves for the rest of that week and seemed to be away for most of the weekend, back during the evenings but out during the day.

On Sunday morning, I saw Joanne and the kids all wearing wellingtons, packing up the car and driving off somewhere.

It was teatime when they returned home and I could hear the distant sound of water running as they bathed before bed.

The weekend had been quiet throughout the building. I'd spoken to Frank briefly. He'd spent a few hours picking weeds out of the lawn, trimming the edge of the grass. He did it because he liked to, he said. 'There's supposed to be a man that mows the lawn, but I've always done it by the time he gets around.'

I saw Mrs Carson come and go with her golf clubs and Dan and Sally Watts driving in and out in their separate BMWs. It felt as though I lived in a building full of isolated people but from my viewpoint I seemed to be the only one who minded.

Mum phoned me. I was in the middle of something so I didn't pick up and I planned to ring her later, when I was sitting down and unwinding for the rest of the evening.

But on Friday I didn't get around to it and on Saturday I didn't either.

Hearing the children downstairs getting ready for bed, hearing them squabbling and Luke losing his temper and having a cry, was eventually broken by Mum phoning back.

'The weekend was good,' I told her.

'I was wondering if you'd had any more thoughts about a job?' she asked, straight to the point.

'I haven't decided.'

'You'll need to sort something before the money runs out.'

She was right, of course. We'd made a good profit on that house when Ben had bought me out but, by the time I'd paid the legal fees, it wasn't an amount that would last me forever.

'Why are you bringing that up now?'

'I've just seen a couple of jobs advertised,' she told me. She'd obviously been looking on my behalf then.

'Where?'

'In Cambridge.'

I hadn't been into town for a long time.

'Would you email me?' I asked her. I wasn't sure. Cambridge was twenty miles away but seemed a whole lot further. I'd started to feel secure in my little country home. Perhaps I should just let the real world drift off without me. But she was right: having enough money to live on was going to become an imperative.

I finished the call and then went downstairs. I knocked on Joanne's door.

Her hair was pinned up in a ponytail. Her sleeves were rolled up and she held a tea towel.

'I was wondering,' I said. I was jumping in, just going with my gut instinct before I even had a chance to think it through. 'I was wondering if you ever needed a child-minder. I mean, I don't know if you are planning to work or anything. But . . . err . . . I'm at home and I would actually be able to do a few hours each day and I would only charge a reasonable hourly rate. Whatever it is for one child, you could have both for the same price. I don't know what child-minders charge.'

'Oh, I see. Well, I hadn't really thought . . . I'm not planning on working at the moment,' she said. 'I've just been concentrating on moving in and getting the kids settled. Are you registered then?' she asked.

I was tempted to bluff something but I'd already begun to shake my head and I didn't even know what I would need to do to be officially recognised as a child-minder.

'I just like kids,' I said.

'I thought you didn't know much about them?'

'I'm not an expert but I'm right here. I thought perhaps, if you needed to get a job . . .'

'Okay,' she said. I could feel her brushing me away, but at the last minute, she paused. 'I'm sorry if I was abrupt with you, the other day. You know, about you talking to the kids. They've been through a lot and I worry about them and . . .'

She dropped the tea towel on the bookshelf near the door, then folded her arms but not in a defensive way. More as though she was hugging herself.

'It wasn't that I'd planned to come here,' she said. 'Everything just got turned on its head and once that happens you start to look for the next thing that's going to blind-side you. I'm careful with the kids, that's all.'

'I understand.'

'Thank you.'

Again, she was about to go but just before the door shut, I managed to say, 'Would you like coffee sometime?'

The door was only open by a couple of inches by then.

'Sure,' she said. When she smiled her whole face lit up.

'When?' I fired back and then stopped short; I realised that I was pushing it too much. But how long had it been since I'd had a cup of coffee with someone? And it wasn't such a terrible thing to ask.

The door fully opened again. She seemed to have finished weighing me up.

'Tomorrow morning?' she asked. 'I do the school run first thing and I'm back by quarter past nine. If you want to, that is?'

I nodded and had to stop my smile from spreading too wide. 'Half past? My flat? Or yours? Or we could go to the coffee shop on the Fen?'

'I'll come up to yours, if that's okay?' she said. 'But I can't stop too long. I still have a lot to unpack.'

106

MONDAY 3 JULY, 2017

The part of my brain that dealt with hearing woke up before the rest of me the next morning. I lay still, as disconnected from my body as if I were still asleep, but listening to the sounds from below. I didn't know the time. I didn't look either but I guessed it must have been somewhere around seven.

From time to time their voices were raised, but not in anger. Calling at each other from different rooms and sometimes with a sense of urgency.

I heard Molly clearest. Every couple of minutes it was 'Mum, Mum'.

I could picture her face, the way that she was so small that whenever she spoke to me she looked up and tilted her head back. Her eyebrows sat like two perfect little arches.

Downstairs fell silent.

I wouldn't have guessed she was a Molly. I thought maybe a Poppy or a Sophie. Yes, I imagined I might have picked a name like Sophie if my baby had looked like her.

I still had time to have children. Thirty's not old, not these days. But how do we ever know what's in front of us? If I could have had some glimpse of the future and seen that it was all sorted out, that I'd meet somebody and those things would happen, then I might have felt less anxious.

But emotionally I knew I wasn't in the right place to start again and I didn't have any idea if or when that might be.

There. I heard them again. A door must have been opened because the voices were suddenly clearer.

'My PE kit, Mum. I need my PE kit.'

And Luke was babbling on about his lunch, how he didn't want sandwiches again, how he wanted to take a slice of pizza to school. Joanne said 'No' and then Molly chipped in with 'Pizza's bread and cheese. That's like a cheese sandwich, isn't it?' and I couldn't work out whose side she was on – Luke's or her mum's.

My bed was warm. I had no real desire to move and, when I heard the front door close and then the car doors open and shut, I drifted off to sleep for another half an hour.

Then, when I woke, I showered and dressed and hurriedly cleared space in the front room. I wanted it to look as though my flat was in some semblance of order.

I opened the windows to let the fresh air in and I boiled the kettle, ready. By half past nine, I was sitting near the kitchen window and watching for her car to come back. I felt strangely anxious. Like that feeling when you are meeting somebody and you are wondering whether they are going to stand you up. Of course she wouldn't; she lived downstairs. I didn't know what my problem was except that my days seemed endless and increasingly silent. And just having a cup of coffee had turned into a really big deal for me.

It wasn't just a long time since I'd had social contact, but the first time I'd met someone of my own age who didn't know exactly what sort of mess I was in.

The kettle finished boiling and a few minutes later I boiled it again. And a few minutes after that, I stood in the doorway between the kitchen and the sitting room replaying our conversation in my mind. Had it really been a firm arrangement for her to come around here? Or just one of those 'must meet up for coffee'-type comments? As I looked around the room with the stack of still packed boxes and the disorganised heaps of paperwork on the table I wondered why she'd want to visit anyway. Why would anyone?

Maybe it would be better if she didn't come today. Give me a chance to do something with the place. Make it half presentable so that when the casual suggestion of coffee was finally firmed up, she'd have somewhere comfortable to sit and not realise how chaotic I really was.

If I'd stood there then and told myself to do a better job of tidying up I probably would have found something else to do or found it too daunting. Instead, without thinking, I began to pick through the things on the coffee table. Most of it was post that had arrived since I'd been there. Most of that was previous tenants' mail or junk mail. Three in the bin, one for me, three in the bin, one for me.

Official paperwork like bank statements were starting to filter through now. I had a folder for them but sitting and filing them away felt like too much effort. I scooped everything off the table top, plonked it in my lap and then fished out only the ones that I really needed to keep.

If I'd stayed by the kitchen window, I guess she never would have turned up because nothing happens when you watch for it. But after about twenty minutes of paper sorting there was a knock at the door and I answered it, holding close to my chest the pile of junk mail I'd sorted out.

Joanne tilted her head to one side and smiled as she saw me. 'Is it still okay?' she said.

By then her failure to show up had left me feeling stung, but I pushed that to one side and smiled.

'Of course.'

She had a small square box clutched in both hands.

'I have cake,' she smiled. 'I'd have been here sooner but I had some paperwork to fill out at the school. I should have let you know, I suppose, but I don't have your number.'

'Really, don't worry.'

In the box was a Victoria sandwich bought from the Co-op.

The nearest Co-op was a few miles up the road in Soham.

'Isn't there a school in Wicken?' I asked and felt stupid for not knowing the answer when I lived in this village.

She shook her head, 'There would have been once, I suppose. It doesn't make any difference at this age. I'd be going to the school to pick them up anyway. But when they are older, well, I'll still be going to pick them up anyway. I couldn't let them cycle along that road.'

'It must be hard on you, doing it all on your own, I mean.'

I asked her what she wanted to drink and she opted for tea. I left her in the armchair next to the newly cleared coffee table and went backwards and forwards to the kitchen, talking to her while the kettle boiled.

'You're right about Molly's accent,' I said, 'and Luke's is very subtle.'

'I never picked it up much. I was there for near enough ten years though. I know there's the odd word that's crept in. Luke has one or two very Australian phrases too. You probably haven't heard them yet. It was more obvious when he played with his friends. Over there, I mean. He used to sound like a local boy sometimes.'

'Are they good company?' I thought my voice sounded a little too wistful so I chatted on, trying to sound more casual. 'I mean they seem like good fun. They're nice kids.'

'Thanks,' she said. 'There are plenty of days when they drive me mad. I'm not naturally maternal.' I thought she might have been about to say more but she pressed her lips firmly shut and changed the subject. 'How about you then?'

'Me?' I asked. 'No, I don't have children.' Then I realised that I'd misunderstood her question. She just meant in general, what about me. This wasn't like a conversation with Jess; we'd known each other's thoughts and half-sentences. But, I reminded myself, that level of harmony would take time. 'I broke up with my husband and I moved here to start over.' I nodded a little as I said the words, perhaps hoping she'd nod too and not ask any more. 'It was difficult but, of course, nothing like a bereavement.'

She smiled tightly. 'No, I guess not.'

She stared into her cup and a heavy silence dragged out between us.

'I'll sort out the cake,' I muttered and returned to the kitchen to find a knife and a couple of plates.

There used to be evenings when I'd sit on the computer and play patience or some other mind-numbing computer game. Most of us do it at some point, don't we? Kid ourselves that we're going to have half an hour zoning out and then three hours later find that we've wasted most of the evening.

My conversation with Charlie came back to me and I convinced myself that I'd just spend a few minutes on Facebook, but as I went through my old photos and saw the faces that had once been tagged and the friendships that had now disappeared, I started looking up the profiles. These were my former friends and I suddenly wanted to see if their lives had changed, or how they'd changed. It had only been a few months but it was like a snapshot that I could compare to the last time I'd seen them. And yes, they'd moved on.

Jess had finally updated her relationship status and in her profile picture she was side by side with Andy. Jody had a new boyfriend too and Mia had changed jobs. A couple of the others had visibly put on weight. That's Christmas, Valentine's and Easter for you.

It was inevitable then that I found myself typing in Ben's name. His security settings were tighter than most so his newsfeed seemed to contain only things that other people had posted on his wall, with big gaps in between.

I told myself that he wasn't posting anything right now but I didn't believe it. I was convinced there had to be other posts filling the gaps. I clicked on his list of friends and there didn't seem to be any security there. He currently had 108. The few I had left were the ones I didn't really know. Friends of friends where we'd ended up making a connection because of some event that we'd been at together. They'd probably forgotten that I was on their friends' list and that's why they hadn't bothered deleting me yet.

But Ben's friends were all there. I scrolled down. Usually when a relationship breaks up people's loyalty keeps them with the half of the couple they'd originally started with. Not in this case. Ben's friends' list was made up of my friends plus his friends, all amalgamated into one big happy group.

Half a dozen names from the bottom I saw her.

Shannon Bridges.

Her security settings were non-existent and when I clicked on her newsfeed I could see every happy event that she wanted to share with the world. From a 'girls' night out' to 'I've met a cute guy'.

I scanned back as far as I could. She was a sharer of relentlessly happy photos, interspersed with life-affirming memes and cartoons of cats and rabbits. I have nothing against cats and rabbits but, at that precise moment, neither appealed to me.

I looked at her 'likes', pages she'd signed up to, her choice of films and music, where she'd worked, where she'd been educated. She had a degree in tourism. But she worked in the medical records department at the hospital. If I'd looked at her page in a completely detached way, there would have been nothing that rankled me. But basic human nature made me critical of every entry.

Some were too dumbed down. Some were too low-brow. Others seemed pretentious. I thought of the snide comments I could post against various photos and shared videos and I realised that my hand was gripping the mouse too tightly, my shoulders were tense, my jaw rigid and I felt like I hated her. I tried to remind myself that she hadn't done anything. Not really. She'd met a man who was getting divorced. Unless, of course, it had been going on before.

The thought was ridiculous but once it had entered my head I found myself scrolling back, trying to pin down where we'd been at the various times she'd marked her location.

I tried to remember, wondering if Ben and I had spent too little time together, whether he could have been seeing her when I thought there was only me.

I spotted it in a folder of photos grouped together under 'Weekend in Cambridge'. I'd think if you want a romantic weekend you'd go more than ten miles away and, if you don't want to see the sights, why leave the house at all?

And there it was, among the pictures of punting and close-ups of food. A picture of the two of them. A selfie, like the ones everyone used to take in the photo booths with your faces squished together, your cheeks right up against each other. And next to it the same picture but this one had been modified, turned, like Charlie had said, by some computer programme, into what looked like a pencil drawing. It was only when you saw the two together you realised nobody had drawn it, only the computer.

I sank back in my chair, my finger tapping gently on the top of the mouse. What did this Shannon know about me? Why did she hate me so much? What right did she actually have to torment me when she had the life that should be mine?

I picked up my mobile, found Ben's number and pressed call, only to immediately cancel it. This was no good over the phone. You can't see people's faces on the phone, can you? And I needed to know. I needed to know whether he knew or whether he'd feel betrayed or want to stick by her, whether he felt any sympathy for me.

I grabbed my coat, my phone and my bag and hurried from the flat.

I knocked on my front door feeling like a stranger and when Ben opened it, the familiar smells of cooking and the plug-in air freshener we always used hit me straightaway. In the first moment, his expression was open and relaxed, as though, if he was expecting anything, it was something good. But his features became stiff when he saw it was me, his mouth tight. His eyelids flickered in a double blink.

'Em,' he said. 'What's up?'

Words filled my head, the angry ones fighting with the reasonable. I could hear the sound of the television somewhere behind him, no other noise, but I knew he wasn't alone. Houses feel different when they're empty and that wasn't an empty house behind him.

'I've been getting letters. Anonymous letters, hate mail, if you like.'

'Why? Who would . . .?' he began to ask and his question drifted away. 'What sort of hate mail?'

'I don't have it here,' I said. 'But trust me, it's unpleasant.'

'What do you think I can do?'

'I need it to stop.'

His expression changed slightly as he realised what I was saying. 'It's not me,' he said. 'Look, Em, I feel for you. I don't want anything to do with you but I don't want to see you messed around either. Enough's enough now.'

'I want to speak to her,' I said.

He half glanced over his shoulder, 'Why?'

'She's got it in for me.'

'Em?' He held his hands out, palms upwards. 'She's not behind them.'

'When did you start seeing her?'

'What does that have to do with anything?'

'Come on, I need to know. Was it when we were still together?'

He dropped his voice to an urgent whisper. 'Of course not. What would make you think that?'

'I don't know. Perhaps I don't. But I want to speak to her.'

He kept his voice low and I knew he was trying to calm me. 'Her name's Shannon . . .'

'I know what her name is.'

'I don't think you are in the right frame of mind.' So much for trying to calm me.

I snapped back in response, 'Is there a right frame of mind to confront somebody who's been sending you abuse?'

'Shannon wouldn't do that. She doesn't even know you.'

'I want to hear her say it.'

'Well, you're not speaking to her.'

'I am. I am going to speak to her, if not now then I'll make sure I find her. I'll find her and I'll talk to her face to face. Shannon,' I barked over his shoulder, 'I need to talk to you.'

I heard a voice from inside the house. I didn't hear what she said but Ben told her, 'It's all right, don't worry.'

I looked down the hallway. I might have been paid off but it was still my house. This was still the man I'd spent years of my life loving.

'Shannon.' I yelled it louder this time. 'If you don't have the guts to face me, just know you have to leave me alone. Stop sending me those letters.'

'She hasn't. Em, please.'

'Stop her writing to me. I'm out of your life, isn't that enough?' I'd asked him a question but there was no answer he could have given that would have satisfied me; my despondency was all consuming.

Ben reached forward. He tried to grab hold of me but I stepped back then changed my mind and pushed myself forward, trying to fight my way past him into the house. And she appeared a few feet away in the entrance to the kitchen.

'I haven't sent you anything.' Her face was white. She looked frightened. 'I wouldn't do something like that. I'm sorry it's happening but you need to go now.'

I couldn't reach her because Ben was holding on to me. He was much stronger than I was. He always had been. I wanted to keep shouting at her but the better part of me realised that there was no point.

I saw her face and, despite wanting someone to blame, I knew it wasn't her.

They were just two people with a cosy life and that life had nothing to do with mine.

Ben's tone dropped and he spoke quietly, close to my ear, 'You can't keep making scenes, Em. You can't make things up to get attention. I'm with Shannon now and you need to get used to that.'

'I'm not lying. Is that what you think? That I'm lying?'

'Em.'

'I'm not a liar, Ben. Is that what you think of me?'

He didn't reply and Shannon looked sorry for me.

'It won't last,' I told her. 'You've known him five minutes. We had a life together. That's my home you're in.'

'Emily.' He had rarely called me that. 'I don't want you to come back,' he said and guided me towards the door. 'But I need you to hear this from me. Shannon and I are having a baby. It's what I want. *She's* what I want. Please don't come back.'

It felt as though my dad came from nowhere to bustle me away. He clamped his left hand around my left bicep and his right arm behind my back and he propelled me out through the door, holding me tighter than he needed to.

Mentally I didn't feel any stronger than I did when I was five or six and he used to whisk me out of the room if I was having a tantrum. I remember that clearly, the feeling of floating, flying almost, and how his anger filled my entire vision. That's not fair, really. Mostly, my dad was a placid man.

But whenever he had lost his temper it had happened quickly; the colour would rise in his face and he seemed to puff up somehow. Or perhaps it was me who shrank.

I've always felt like that. Never wanted to annoy him. He was pretty reserved I guess. He liked routine and knowing who does what and what goes where and I wasn't exactly following that pattern, not any more. I don't think he said anything until we were in the car apart from apologising to Ben and muttering my name at me. Well, if he did, the words have completely slipped from my memory.

But at that point, I didn't even know what I was saying. I'd relinquished control and what was spewing out of me was this unchecked torrent of anguish and accusations and insults I didn't mean. All those words were somehow releasing pain in me, or that's how I felt, and they were my words but not from my conscious brain. They were spilling out from somewhere deep down and it wasn't the words themselves that mattered but the anguish of their delivery.

I should have jumped straight to the point and just screamed 'Help, help, help' because all I wanted was for someone to save me. Maybe Dad would have done that if I'd just asked him.

He pushed me roughly into the passenger seat, shouted, 'STAY,' slammed the door and marched round to his side of the car. He started the engine immediately and drove towards his house and then pulled up a hundred yards from home. He turned off the engine and swivelled in his seat.

'What the hell are you playing at?'

I shook my head but I was shivering so much by then that I don't know if it was even noticeable.

'*What* are you playing at Emily?'

'I don't know,' I sobbed back. 'I've been getting letters, hate mail. Obscene letters.'

I rummaged in my bag as though I expected to find one in there even though I knew I'd left them at home, but he grabbed my hands and pushed them down into my lap.

'What did you expect, Emily? You can't seek attention and then complain it's not the type you wanted.'

It took a few seconds for me to grasp the meaning of his words.

I looked at his face and his lips were a hard, straight line and the expression in his eyes was the same as it had been as he left court; filled with disgust.

'You can't blame Ben and Shannon. What do you expect Ben to do, Emily? He has to pick up his life and get on with it. He's met Shannon and she's a nice girl. It's all too quick, I get that, but it's his life and you're not part of it any more.'

'I still love him.'

Dad snorts. 'Yeah? Well, show it then. He doesn't hate you, you know. He just wants to move on. But after what you've put him through, I know why he doesn't want you round the house.'

'I really didn't do anything wrong.'

And finally, there was a glimmer of softness in his voice.

'I believe you didn't mean to,' he said, 'but if you had any sense you would have seen that there was going to be fallout that reached way beyond you and him and even beyond our family. You need to get some help. Counselling, proper help. We can try and find someone for you, if you'll go.'

'No. I don't need to go to see somebody. I think I'm doing fine.'

'Well that's not how it looks to us. I'm happy to check it all out. I'll find somebody who's right for you.'

'No.'

'They won't judge you.'

'Dad.'

'Your mother doesn't quite have it straight in her head yet, but she will and you need to put it straight in yours. You can't play people, you can't tell stories for your own benefit and not expect repercussions.'

There was no answer to that and, even if I'd had one, I wouldn't have been able to say it. My throat had closed up. It was all I could do to stop myself from howling again.

'I want you to go home. I'm taking you home,' he said. He didn't mean to their house, to Mum. He started the engine. 'Give me your postcode.'

'I want to see Mum.'

He shook his head.

'I picked up Ben's call before she reached the phone. She doesn't know what's going on and you think just because she's always there for you that this hasn't taken a toll on her? Thank God for your brother. Being there for him is the only thing that's keeping her sane in my opinion.'

His finger was poised over the satnav and he waited until I told him my address before he headed on to the main road. I glanced at him and then over my shoulder.

'What about my car?'

'I'll get it dropped off tomorrow,' he said. 'You're not fit to drive right now.'

I guess that was a perk of running a workshop: a pickup truck and a garage hand who would drop my vehicle back so my dad didn't have to.

'We'll keep this between us,' he said. 'I know Ben will be discreet.'

And that was it. The rest of the journey in silence.

Isn't it funny how when you're a kid, your parents are your whole world? You think they have the wisdom of the whole bloody universe. And when you're an adult they still have the power to shrink your universe back down to child-size.

I had enough tissues in my pocket to dry my face and I held my emotions in for the thirty minutes it took for us to get back to my flat. He pulled up at the door and kept the engine running, clearly a sign that he didn't want to see me in. But then I didn't want him to.

'Think about counselling, will you?' he said.

I shook my head wordlessly, managed a rebellious slamming of the passenger side door and hurried in the building, not stopping to watch his taillights disappear. I didn't even make it to the bottom of the stairs before I began to sob again.

I didn't hear the sound in the hallway. The first I knew was an arm reaching round me, across my shoulders, and a hand on my hands as they lay in my lap. I knew it was Joanne without needing to open my eyes or look up at her.

'Don't cry,' she whispered in my ear. 'Emily, it will be okay, don't cry.'

She nudged me off the second stair and coaxed me into her front room. She scooped a box of tissues off the side table, sat me on the settee and then pulled a few from the box and pressed them into my hands.

'I'll make you a drink,' she said, but then rather than going to the kitchen, she sank on the sofa beside me and wrapped her arms around me fully and held me tight, my forehead pressed into her shoulder.

My heavy breaths gradually subsided but she didn't let go then, and we stayed like that for two or three minutes longer until I was the one that pulled back first.

'Sorry,' I said.

'Hey, we've all been there,' she said. 'We think we're resilient but when it comes down to it, sometimes it's just too much, isn't it?'

I nod.

'I'll make tea. Or coffee. Whichever you'd prefer?'

'A glass of water, thanks.' Then I realised that I sounded a little too martyred. 'Coffee, thanks, no sugar.'

She came back with two mugs and sat beside me on the sofa, our bodies angled slightly towards each other so our knees almost touched.

'I didn't mean to disturb you,' I said.

'Oh, it doesn't matter. It can be hard to know what to do in the evenings once the kids are asleep. The last thing I want to do is wake them up and there's only so many books I want to read.'

The bookshelf was across the room from us. It wasn't large and contained a mix of biography, classics, cookery books and plenty for the children.

'I haven't read anything for ages,' I told her, 'apart from the news-paper, of course.'

I didn't think the bitter edge to my voice was at all audible but there was no reason for her to pick up on it anyway.

I held the mug in my hands and I could tell by the heat in my palms that it wasn't too hot to drink but it was kind of comforting just sitting there like that and, if I'm honest, I wasn't in a hurry to move. But she didn't seem to be in a hurry to make me either.

'Isn't there always a lot of shenanigans at the end of a relationship?'

I nod, then shrug. She was kind of on course, I supposed, but it didn't feel right to lie to her, even by omission.

'I have broken up with my husband,' I said, 'but it's not that. Or not entirely. It's way more complicated.'

She leant with her elbows on her knees and her coffee held just a couple of inches above the table. Her hair had dropped forward over her ears, her fringe over her forehead but I could still see her brow furrowed and her curious expression.

'Look, I don't want to be nosy, but it seems to me neither of us are in a good place and I could certainly do with somebody to chat to sometimes. I don't mind if you don't?'

'I thought we were off to a bad start. You know, with me chatting to the kids and everything.'

She closed her eyes as she shook her head.

'No. No, I'm cautious that's all. You know, when something hits you out of nowhere, it leaves you that way. My life is nothing like the one I had last year and it certainly hasn't come about through any-thing I've planned.'

'Yeah, well,' was my answer, 'I know that feeling.'

Joanne didn't push me for any information, but after a while and in the warmth of her company I felt like I needed to tell her something.

'My husband and I are going through a divorce. I can't explain the details but it's caused this massive family rift.'

I hesitated, chewed on my lip for a few seconds. I wasn't lying, I wasn't telling the truth either though and things like that tend to come back and bite you, unless you are really careful.

She didn't push me though.

'Families are always the toughest,' she said. 'Their disapproval hurts the most, doesn't it?'

If Molly hadn't told me about her dad and her brother, I guess right now I'd be asking Joanne about her past. But knowing the small amount I did know made me feel like I was prying. The conversation had stalled and she seemed lost in her own thoughts.

'Molly told me,' I ventured, 'that you lost your husband and your son.'

Joanne looked startled. 'Did she?' She shook her head. 'Well, I'm surprised, but it is Molly's story too, isn't it?'

I didn't ask her what had happened but I didn't know what to say either and there were a few seconds when neither of us spoke.

Perhaps she told me because she thought I was waiting for an explanation. 'We had a little boat that we used to keep moored a couple of hours away and Grant had promised to take Connor fishing. We used to go up there when we were first married, just to hang out, but when Molly and Luke came along there wasn't the space so it was just the two of them.' She took a breath and I could see that she was struggling to speak and I wished I could think of any words that might help.

In the end, I remained silent.

'I didn't think twice when I didn't hear from them,' she continued. 'Then the police arrived. Told me there'd been an accident with the boat and just like that, the boys were gone.' I could see the pain in her expression. 'And that's three years ago now.'

Her gaze had been focused a long way off but now her eyes found me again.

'Whatever it is that's hurting you,' she said, 'it doesn't always get better but it gets different. I don't cry anymore. Well, not so much, and yet there was a time when I thought I'd never be able to stop.

Now I cry so little that people must think I've left it all behind. I haven't. Some days when I think about them I feel so detached that it's almost like I imagined them and then other days it's so real that I can't believe they're gone.'

I made good eye contact with her and I mumbled that I was sorry. What else can you say in the face of something like that? It made my tears feel trivial.

'How did you carry on?'

'Molly and Luke,' she said. 'Of course, when you have children like that, what choice do you have? They were two and four when it happened and that's the saddest thing. They don't remember much about their dad or their brother. But then, that's the best thing too. They escaped some of the hurt, didn't they? Imagine if it was now, how much the loss would be.'

We talked for longer and although I was tired I felt it would be wrong to just run back to my flat after hearing that somebody had suffered like that. I must have drifted off to sleep because, when I woke in the morning, sunlight was hitting my face. She'd spread a duvet over me, put a pillow under my head and left a glass of water on the coffee table.

I guess none of those things were much of a big deal really. Plenty of people had crashed out at my house and I'd crashed out at plenty of theirs. But right then, it felt like the biggest thing.

I could hear the children moving around in their bedrooms but I stayed still for as long as possible, shutting my eyes against the warm sun and pulling the duvet up around my face. Although my flat was only one floor away, it felt as though I was in a safe bubble there.

FRIDAY 7 JULY, 2017

That was the start. We weren't immediately in each other's pockets and for the next few days I had that same feeling that you get when you first start going out with somebody. I didn't want to pester Joanne but I kept going over our conversations in my head, wondering when it would be too soon to call on her flat on some pretext, and finding myself coincidentally out in the garden when she brought the children home from school just so I could smile and say 'Hi'.

It was another three or four days before I saw anything more substantial of her. She stopped on the way out for the morning school run.

'I was wondering,' she said, looking a little apologetic, 'is there any chance of your mobile number? I could have done with you yesterday. I had to take Luke to the doctor's and I was worried I wasn't going to get back in time to pick Molly up from school. If something like that happens again, would it be all right if you went to pick one of them up?'

I grinned. 'Of course. Yes, that's fine. I'll let you have my number in a bit. I'll write it down for you.'

She smiled warmly and carried on to her car. She didn't seem to notice that I was disproportionately pleased by that little moment. Then after she'd gone I began to worry that she might find out about the court case. Would she want me near her kids then? I batted the thought around my head for the rest of the morning. I wasn't a criminal. I didn't have a conviction. There was nothing to say that I wasn't responsible with children. But then, on the other hand, I had been outed as a supposed liar.

I wrote my mobile number on a sheet of paper in any case and slid it under her door.

It was a couple of hours later when I was in the Co-op in Soham getting groceries that my phone pinged with a text message. I stopped mid-aisle.

Hey, Emily. Now you've got my number too. ☺ *See you later. J x*

I had plenty of contacts in my phone but this was pretty much the only one that mattered right then. Her and Mum, I guess. At the end of the aisle I took out my phone and read the message again, and sent her back a smiley face.

I put the groceries in the car and was about to pull away when I had a sudden thought and texted her again.

I'm at the shop. Is there anything you'd like me to get?

My finger hovered over the send button and quickly added an 'x' on the end, then pressed. There was nothing she needed but she replied quickly, adding another smile.

I didn't see her when I arrived home but my evening was peppered with little batches of texts going backwards and forwards between us and I guess that's when our friendship started properly.

SATURDAY 8 JULY, 2017

By Saturday, Joanne had asked me if I wanted to join her for a walk around Wicken Fen. I hadn't been before. It wasn't something that I'd fancied doing on my own. In fact, I'm not much of a walker. I probably wouldn't have bothered at all but the idea of spending time with her and the children made it seem far more appealing.

I didn't own wellingtons or even walking boots so I wore trainers. Molly looked at them with amusement.

'They're going to get muddy,' she said. 'I'm not allowed to wear my trainers when I go anywhere muddy.'

'Well, it's the best I have,' I said. 'It will be all right. I don't mind a bit of mud.'

And, actually, it wasn't too bad. The footpaths were mostly well laid out with boardwalks over some of the boggiest patches, at least initially. Molly wanted to see the Konik ponies. That's all she talked about. 'Where are the ponies? How far to the ponies?'

When we finally spotted them, they were in the distance. A herd gathered round a small clump of trees. Molly didn't look impressed.

'They look like little dots,' she said. 'Can we get closer?'

Then the ground started getting boggier.

'This is no good for my trainers,' I said to her.

She smiled. 'Ponies are better than trainers,' she said and suddenly slipped her hand into mine. The trainers really weren't any big deal. We made it to within a few hundred yards of the ponies.

'I wonder what their names are,' she said.

'Maybe they don't have names,' I replied. 'They are wild, aren't they? We don't give names to other wild animals.'

'Do you know,' she said, 'there's rabbits that come in our garden at night and I've named some of them? I call the biggest one Bertie because I think Bertie's a kind of round sounding name. I was at school with a boy called Bertie. He was fat.'

She chatted on like this, jumping from subject to subject the whole way around, and just ahead of us Joanne was walking with Luke and they were hand in hand too and abruptly, in the middle of this wild and desolate place, I had a sudden feeling of home, of belonging and, briefly, everything felt perfect.

And then Molly said to me, 'Has Mum told you about her boy-friend?' and I felt my smile become pinched.

'No.'

'She likes him. They're like, on the phone all the time.' She made the chatting mouth gesture with one hand. 'Yabber, yabber, yabber, yabber. He's been working away but he's going to come back soon. Are you going to meet him or have you met him already? Oh no, you didn't know. Oh well. I bet you'll like him. My mum says he's very special. Eurgh.'

She screwed up her nose and simultaneously poked out her tongue.

'And I bet they'll get married and move into a big house and we'll have to pack up our toys all over again. I wouldn't like that,' she shrugged and flapped her hands against her thighs.

'Well, I wouldn't like it either.'

'Boys are horrible,' she grinned then ran off after her mother, leaving my hand empty.

What is life really, but a series of goodbyes? I just wasn't ready for another one and I felt indignant, like I had some right to complain because Joanne hadn't told me. I knew that I'd only just met her but I suppose I'd pinned too much illogical hope on our friendship.

I kept walking behind them, Joanne following a path and the other two zigzagging around her like summer flies. After about a hundred yards she turned to wait for me. Then, when I'd covered about half the ground between us she started walking towards me.

'What's wrong?'

I looked at her, confused at first, then I suppose slightly dumb-founded. I didn't know what expression I had slapped across my face but it was obviously intense enough for her to recognise distress from fifty yards.

I shook my head a little as if to say 'nothing', but I didn't trust my voice. She hurried towards me, glancing back at the children and calling for them not to run off and then when she reached me she grabbed me and hugged me close. I held my breath. I don't know what I'd expected but it wasn't this.

'Has one of the kids upset you?' she said. 'I'm sorry, I didn't real-ise. I was so busy with them . . .'

'It's fine,' I muttered.

She pulled away and looked into my face. 'You look like you want to cry.'

I drew a breath and it sounded like a sniff. 'I've been crying too much. I'm like this sobbing mess at the moment,' I muttered.

'It doesn't matter,' she said. 'If you're in that place where you need to cry, then don't stop it.'

She linked her arm with mine and we began walking, following the children as they walked along a footpath of ankle-deep grass. She left it for a full minute at least, then I felt her squeeze my arm. 'So, what was it then?'

I kept looking ahead. 'It's stupid. It's nothing.'

'Okay, well if it's nothing . . .'

'Yeah, I know, share it. I feel stupid . . .' I began, and even though I knew I was starting one of those conversations that might, with hindsight, prove to be a bad idea, I'd made my decision and I carried on. 'Molly told me you have a boyfriend.'

I paused. I could see Joanne's concern shifting towards curiosity.

'And?' she asked.

'And I know it's none of my business.' I hoped that reassured her. 'I do. I really do know that it's none of my business. But at the same time, when she said that you were going to buy a house and move away . . .' I couldn't find the words to finish the sentence, or at least ones that didn't sound obsessive or as though I was crossing some unforgivable line. 'I know we've only just met but, if I'm honest Joanne, our friendship already means a lot to me and I just felt sad that you might move away.'

We kept walking and although she didn't reply for a few seconds, her hold on my arm didn't loosen. She took her time choosing her words but when she spoke she sounded resolute. 'Look,' she said, 'it's like this. I don't know what's happened to you but, for me, I've moved back to England after a long time away. I don't have friends here, not really. I'm starting over, just like you.'

'We only met a couple of weeks ago.'

'So what? People go on a two-week holiday and make friendships that last a lifetime. Grant and I decided we were going to get married after our third date. When it feels right, then why question it?'

'I suppose . . .'

'And I should've told you about my boyfriend. I knew him years ago. He was my playground crush and I was his, apparently. We connected over Facebook and, I swear, neither of us was looking for anything. Certainly not me, not after what had happened. But after a few weeks the tone of our messages began to change. There was a bit of flirting, I suppose, and it seemed so separate from everything that was going on there that it didn't feel wrong or a threat to my life, the way meeting anyone else would have done. Does that make sense?'

I bit my lip and nodded.

'He flew out to see me once, and I flew back here for a week and I don't know whether it feels like we've been together for a long time or only just met. Because on the one hand, we've spent about twenty days together and, on the other, I've known him for most of my life.'

'And you're marrying him?'

Her expression broke into a broad and spontaneous grin.

'Did Molly tell you that? Oh gosh, no, we're not that far ahead. I think that's a seven-year-old getting romantic for you. See, the thing is about Molly and Luke, their memories of their dad are fading pretty quick and Molly, with her ideas of princes and castles and everything else that you dream of when you are that age . . . well, I think she's jumping the gun a bit. I'm not planning on moving out of that flat for a while. We have the money to buy a house but I'm not ready for that either. Just taking things slowly with the kids and, I'm sorry if this is a stupid thing to say, Emily, but I feel like this is the first time in years really when I've had a proper friend. And although I didn't have any reason not to tell you about him, I probably wouldn't have done anyway because you're having a hard time and I wouldn't have wanted to ram my happiness in your face.'

'Ram away. It gives me hope to know it's possible.'

'I guess.' She sounded doubtful and, as it had already happened to her, I guessed that she was doubting whether it could also happen to me. Although I was pleased for her, if I'm honest there was a little part of me that hoped it wouldn't work out.

By mid-afternoon I was still with Joanne and we were back at the downstairs flat. Molly and Luke occupied themselves, Luke with Lego and Molly with a book.

'I didn't know kids still did those things. I mean, read and play quietly.'

'I keep them away from video games,' she said. 'We have a PlayStation but it's just for a couple of hours on Sundays. I hate the noise of the thing,' she said, 'and the relentless colours and flashing of the screen. Stresses me out. Imagine what it does to their brains.'

I watched Luke with his Lego. He was picking through his box, hunting out all the green pieces. I offered to help him. He shook his head. 'It's okay,' he said, 'I know what I'm looking for.'

'The green ones?' I asked him.

'Yep,' he says, 'but the ones, twos and fours, not the big ones. You can look for mini-figure heads if you want.'

I didn't know what he meant so he showed me a little cylindrical piece with the features painted on. Obvious really, I suppose, but it just reminded me how little I knew about children.

Even so, I figured, if they were mine, I might like to see them playing together on the PlayStation, joining in with each other instead of Molly being on one chair and Luke being over on the other side of the room. But still, they weren't my kids, were they?

130

Joanne passed me a glass of wine. I thanked her but I didn't drink it.

'You don't like red?' she asked.

'Only white. Red doesn't agree with me,' I said and pulled a disappointed face, so it seemed as though I was missing out rather than being a killjoy. I didn't like red anyway. It always tasted of vinegar to me. I knew I'd probably drink again at some point but then I was nowhere near ready; I was still at the point when even the sweetest drinks tasted sour.

'I think we're going to have a takeaway. Do you want to join us?'

I didn't want to overstay my welcome. My gaze drifted towards the ceiling though and I knew my flat was dark and unwelcoming right then and this room, with its pools of light and human warmth, was where I wanted to stay, while I could.

'Yes, that would be lovely.'

'Chinese?'

'Sure. Do you want me go?'

'No, no. They'll deliver. Anything over fifteen pounds apparently. Hardly seems worth their time coming all the way out here for fifteen quid but there you go.'

'Do you want me to chip in?'

'No, don't be silly.'

'Well, as long as I can get the next one,' I told her. She looked pleased and I was sure that today wouldn't be a one-off after all.

'Do you fancy watching a film?' I asked her.

She shook her head. 'I would, but you know, I'm having trouble receiving anything in here, even the internet.' She seemed resigned. 'Well, they can't fix it until next week anyway. But still, you can't expect everything from day one, can you? I have running water, electric and a working washing machine. Let's face it, a washing machine and microwave are the two main things you need with kids.'

I looked her straight in the eye. 'I wouldn't know,' I said.

She lowered her glass. 'Did you want children?'

She'd said *did* not *do*.

Then she raised her hand, with a stop gesture. 'Sorry. I shouldn't have asked that.'

'No, no. It's fine. I thought that one day we would. Me and Ben, I mean. But it never worked out, never seemed like the right time.'

Shannon's face flashed up in my mind. I blinked and waited for it to pass. I lied, 'It's not something I really think about now.' I felt lost for words and for a second she looked the same.

Then she said quietly, 'I tell you what, it's better not to have them than to have one and lose it.'

MONDAY 10 JULY, 2017

I was on the driveway on Monday morning and planning to take a walk when the post van arrived.

Gerald, the postman, wound down his window. 'This is lucky,' he said. 'There's only one letter for this building today and it's for you.' He started talking then about which days were busier than others. All the while, my letter was in his hand and I could see what it was. I kept smiling, replying as little as possible, hoping he'd hand it over and go away. Finally, he did and I stood there until his van had gone out of sight.

It was only then that I looked down at it, at the now familiar envelope.

I turned and walked slowly back to the house as I ran my finger along the inside. It was a single sheet of paper again. It wasn't a conscious decision to stop walking but I did and stood a few feet in front of the entrance, my head bowed, staring down at the contents.

No picture this time. Just the words.

You are going to pay.

You are going to pay.

The second line was a repeat of the first and the third line was a repeat of the second but this time the word 'are' was underlined.

You *are* going to pay.

Three lines the same, then:

When you are lying in your bed and you can't sleep and you're staring up at the ceiling, remember you are nothing. You deserve what's happened to you. Everyone hates you.

I didn't think I felt scared but my hands were shaking and my bottom teeth were biting into my top lip.

I wanted to throw it away. To bin it, to burn it, but I knew I had to keep it.

When I looked up I realised that Joanne was in her flat and staring at me through the window.

She looked as unsure of what to do as I felt but I wasn't surprised when I opened the front door to find her in the hallway.

'Do you need a coffee?' she said.

I nodded silently and followed her back inside.

'Do you want to talk about it?'

I shook my head, 'It was just a letter . . .'

'You look upset.'

I studied the envelope, tempted, just for a moment, to share its contents with her. I didn't even begin to know Joanne's struggles but I knew she didn't need mine too. I wanted to be the friend that she could count upon, not the other way around. 'It's just paperwork.'

'Hey, Frank.' It was a couple of hours later when I called down to him from my sitting-room window.

He was kneeling at the edge of the car park, weeding the grass. He looked up at me and I made the tea sign with two hands.

'Ah, milk no sugar, thanks,' he shouted up, and a few minutes later I took two mugs of tea and joined him.

'Who's supposed to do the gardening then?' I asked.

'There's a guy who comes around once a fortnight with a sit-on

134

mower. That's all that happens so I try and do bits and pieces with the rest. I'm a bit long in the tooth for it all but I figure a few hours here and here helps keep me fit.'

Frank was quite lightly built and when I saw him it was the word sprightly that always came to mind. 'You could ask the landlord?' he said.

'The letting agent?' I query.

'No, no, the actual landlord. He was back yesterday, briefly. You know, your man with the Tesla.'

'He's not *my* man.' I laughed.

'He usually keeps himself to himself. The building's under the name of a holding company, Peterson Properties. Anyone would think his name was Peter Peterson or something but we all know he's Matthew Edwards,' he said. 'And I have no doubt that Flat 4 knows even more about him, but he was friendlier to you than he was with the rest of us when we first moved in.'

I brushed aside the comment. I planned to steer clear of Matt Edwards but I couldn't help feeling a little pleased by it.

'He came yesterday afternoon when you were busy with your friend, Flat 1,' he added as if it was her name.

'Joanne,' I reminded him, 'and Molly and Luke, the children.'

'Yeah, well, he went inside Flat 5. He was moving around a lot. I heard him walking up and down above my flat, over my ceiling. A couple of hours he was here, pacing around, restless. Then he was off again. God knows when we'll see him next. October or something I expect, in time for Halloween.'

I laughed. 'You're mean.'

'He shouldn't keep the flat if he doesn't want to use it.'

'So, what's your interest in him?'

'Nothing. I just like to know who's in the building, who I'm living with. He's a bit of a mystery, but then, so are you.'

'Am I?'

'You're a very attractive young woman with no job and no visitors. How does that add up?'

As soon as he said it, I wanted the conversation to move on. I could feel from my expression that it looked as though I was floundering and, for one horrible moment, it looked as though Frank was going to hug me. But he didn't.

'It took me a while to settle in,' he said. 'Now I wouldn't want to live anywhere else.'

I certainly wasn't in that camp. The idea of moving anywhere else would have been a mountain but I didn't belong here either. But as soon as that entered my head, I found my thoughts drifting to the flat downstairs, to Joanne and the children, and I realised that as long as they were here, then I'd be happy here too.

TUESDAY 11 JULY, 2017

I woke early for me, just after six. Through the window I could see the sky was clear but there wasn't enough light to see anything more than a hint of blue. I lay there for a long time, listening to the traffic in the distance. I heard the matching BMWs go, one after another, five minutes apart.

I must admit, I envied them a little with their routine and their careers of being busy for forty hours a week, no matter what those forty hours contained.

I didn't think I'd fallen asleep but the next time I noticed the sky it had brightened to the colour of forget-me-nots. The gravel outside churned slowly and, though I couldn't hear the engine, I knew there must be another car down there somewhere. After a few minutes, I thought I could pick out the burble of voices. I couldn't tell whether they were from somewhere else in the building and speaking normally, or outside somewhere and conversing in very low tones.

My bed was comfortable. I was lying in the position that left me perfectly relaxed and precisely the right temperature, but still the faint sound of voices was enough to make me go to the window. From that angle there was nothing to see so I went to the sitting room and looked down on the view of the parking area.

And there it was, the black Tesla.

Without any further thought, I pulled on yesterday's clothes, sprayed myself with too much deodorant and pulled a sweatshirt over the top. I brushed my hair through just a couple of times, enough to make sure that it wasn't sticking out at any unpredictable angles. Then I went out on to the landing outside my flat.

It took a few seconds for me to home in on the talking but as soon as I did, I worked out that it wasn't coming from his flat, the one across the landing, but somewhere downstairs. I moved towards the sound and stopped at the bottom of the stairs. It was hardly any louder. I opened the outside door by a few inches, thinking perhaps he was standing out there, maybe on his phone. It was then I realised that his voice was coming from the other side of the wall, from inside Joanne's flat.

I found myself outside her front door, with my hand poised, ready to knock, and it was only then that I suddenly queried my own actions. Did I really want to know what they were doing? And if I knocked on the door, what would I say? *What's going on?*

I'd met him once and, yes, something about him had piqued my curiosity. And maybe, just maybe, alongside spotting his flirty nature, I'd sensed something darker. Or perhaps that had all been in my head. And I couldn't claim to be perceptive because it was only at that moment that it occurred to me that he was the one, this boyfriend that Molly had mentioned, whom Joanne had admitted to. An unidentified wave of something flushed through me and I felt heat rise at the sides of my neck and onto my cheeks. I wasn't ready to come face to face with him again.

I went back up the stairs, stripped off and stood in the shower, the jets of water flooding my ears until I wasn't thinking about the world outside.

Then I began cleaning the flat. It needed doing but I stopped short of running water or turning on the vacuum cleaner. Although my intention was to keep myself occupied, I couldn't help but listen for any other sounds downstairs. At half past eight I heard Joanne's front door close. I moved across to the side window and waited to watch her load the children into the car. I glanced at my watch. It was time for the school run.

The Tesla remained where it was. I wondered whether I'd hear him leave her flat and go into his own but I heard nothing at all.

I took window spray and a cloth from under the sink and went back to clean the glass, probably doing a more thorough job than was necessary. She was back by twenty past nine, driving quickly into her parking spot, slamming the door and hurrying towards the house.

She didn't look up at me and, the last I saw of her, she was taking off her coat as she walked.

I stood stock still. Her door opened and closed. The murmur of voices resumed and a few minutes later I heard her laugh playfully. His voice became louder. I couldn't hear the words but I could tell from the rhythm and the pitch that he was teasing her. I sat on the floor and carried on listening. Another ten minutes and they fell silent.

In her own way, Joanne was beautiful. I say her own way, because she wasn't conventionally beautiful, not like a perfume model or a movie star. She had the eyes, though, these beautiful blue, almond-shaped eyes, the kind that draw you in. She had a strong jawline but the rest of her features were delicate. Her skin was smooth and soft, and I imagined she'd never sat out in the Australian sun.

I closed my eyes for a minute and tried not to imagine what they were doing down there. But as my ears retuned, I could hear the tell-tale rhythm of the bedroom.

Inexplicably, I felt a lump in my throat and the words *it's not fair* fell in to my head.

She knocked on my door at mid-morning. About five minutes after I had heard the Tesla pull out of the car park.

'Come in,' I said, and let the door swing wide, walking away towards the kitchen. 'I'll put the kettle on.'

She'd begun chatting to me already when I came back through, filling the silence with lots of nothingness about the school run, about shopping and unpacking from her move.

The 'just had sex' mellowness hung around her and her face and neck were slightly blotchy, as though the friction of his skin against hers had left her tingling. She smiled as though everything was normal. I decided to say nothing, to wait to see whether she told me. I'd drunk half my tea before she did.

'Matt was here this morning.'

'That's his name?'

'Didn't I tell you?'

'No, you didn't. So, he's back?'

'Yes, he has a few things to do now but he'll be here later.'

'I think I heard his car,' I said.

She smiled. 'He caught me by surprise. I wasn't expecting him till the weekend. Obviously, I'm glad he's here but I hoped we could spend a bit of time together today.'

'I'd like that.' I wondered if she meant it, though, or was trying to make me feel better.

'And I wanted to talk to you. If you didn't mind, that is?'

'Of course not.'

'The thing is, I don't have anyone else I can open up to and I know we've only just met, but I feel like you understand me.'

The tension was already drifting out of me and now I felt a surge of relief. She did value our friendship.

'My husband wasn't my first boyfriend, but pretty close to it and this is the first time I've been with anyone since. If I'm honest it scares me and I can't shake off this feeling of guilt, like I'm betraying Grant somehow.'

I nodded slowly. 'I can see that. I think if I meet somebody one day, however long it takes, I'll still feel guilt and I'm not bereaved like you.'

I tried to say the right words, the ones that encouraged her, the ones that were right for a friend to say.

It would never take Joanne long to find someone else and at least Matt lived in the same building. If it worked out between them, I'd still be close to her and, if it didn't, then I could be the friend who would see her through it.

I leant a little closer to her and risked placing my hand on hers.

'If this feels right with him, you need to go for it.'

'I didn't mean it to happen. It's just because I knew him already. I trusted him enough to start chatting and, well, he had this long-term girlfriend and she went off with someone else and he was pretty devastated. So, we were just catching up, talking about the things that have happened between school and now, and it turned out we had some things in common. Good experiences and bad. That's what falling in love is, isn't it? Fifty per cent admiration, 50 per cent sympathy.'

'Is it?' There was a little laugh in my voice but out of bewilderment. I'd never heard that before.

'This guy, a friend of my husband's, told me that. I thought it was a very unromantic way to explain love. But when you think about it, when you meet somebody there has to be a connection, there has to be somebody that you look up to in some way and there must be something about you they have a reason to look up to. But at the same time, it's that vulnerability, isn't it? And he'd lost his girlfriend and I'd lost my husband.'

'You don't need to justify it. And you don't need to rush it either, do you? Think about it,' I said, 'you're here, he's here, he works away. You get the perfect arrangement. You get time together and then you get space in between and you can take it as slowly as you like. Nobody is having to hurry into anything, are they?'

She seemed to brighten then. 'You're right, of course,' she said. 'What do you fancy doing today?'

'Lunch somewhere? I tell you what, though, I need to sort out my hair and make-up.'

'You look fine. I'm not exactly dolled up either.'

I shake my head. 'No, you can get away with natural. Hang on a minute. Did you want to bring your laptop up and jump on my wi-fi, while I'm fixing my face?'

'No,' she said, 'I can't be bothered to go downstairs. It's just a couple of orders I can chase up. They can wait.'

I grabbed my laptop from the table and passed it to her. 'Just use mine. I'll be out in a minute.'

And I headed to the bathroom feeling excited, glad to have something to do but more excited that I'd found a friend.

I brushed my hair through a few times. I didn't bother straightening it and I applied as little make-up as I thought I could get away with. The idea of spending the day together cheered me, but I knew we had to be back when the children came out of school so I hurried.

When I returned to the room she spun the computer towards me. 'Look,' she said. She had the Cambridge tourist website up on the screen.

'What are you thinking?'

She grinned. 'I haven't been to Cambridge, not properly, since I was a kid. Would you be up for doing some of those tourist things, like going on a punt?'

'Well, the funny thing is,' I said, 'I know I live here but I always make sure I still do it once a year. You can forget what's right under your nose. The colleges were designed to face the river. Have you ever been on one?'

'Maybe, but like I said I haven't been there since I was small so I wouldn't remember.'

'Okay, let's do it. We'll get one of those chauffeured ones, they tell you the history of the colleges and there's no risk of falling in the way there is if you are doing it yourself.'

She handed the laptop back to me and she was on her feet immediately.

'That's a plan then,' she said. 'We'll do the river tour, then grab some lunch and be back in time for the kids. There's probably time for a shop or two. Are you up for shopping?'

I shrugged.

She tapped me on the arm. 'Course you are. I'll drive,' she said and before I knew it we were heading to Cambridge. Acres of open fields rolled past us, giving way to small industrial units and groups of houses that dotted the roadside. When we finally turned onto the A14, it was as though we'd left a world that only trickled and re-joined the gush of real life. A few minutes after that, I saw Cambridge sprawled across the horizon. It was small, as cities go, but in that flat and often bleak part of the world, it was a metropolis.

We queued to get into town and we queued for the car park. We even queued for the ladies' toilets. In my old life, this thronging of people seemed normal but now the first half an hour came as a shock to me. I found myself people watching with a sense of fascination.

We walked through the Grand Arcade where high-end shops lined our route and hit us with an array of items we didn't need. If I was excited, then Joanne was more so, especially when we reached the market. We'd only need to skirt round the edge of it but she pulled at my elbow and she darted us down one of the rows and back up the next.

'I never went out much when I was over there,' she said. I assumed 'over there' meant Australia.

'My husband wasn't the going-out type. Quite traditionalist really. He liked me being at home with the kids. I didn't mind, but this is awesome.'

She stopped to buy a scented candle and held it up to my nose. 'What do you think?'

'Yes,' I said vaguely. I found the smell overpowering but I didn't really think she wanted my opinion. She was already paying for it. Her enthusiasm was infectious, though, and a few stalls on I stopped to buy a scarf. It was a decorative scarf rather than a warm one, made of a fabric that was like an imitation chiffon. I guessed it read 100 per cent acrylic or viscose or one of those synthetic things on the label. I looped it round my neck a few times.

It was covered with an image of blurred pink and blue flowers and as I walked I could see it just at the bottom of my vision, looking cheerful.

Joanne stopped again at the fruit stall at the end of the row and bought two cartons of freshly squeezed orange juice. She didn't ask me whether I liked it and, in truth, I wasn't a fan but it didn't seem to matter just then.

Ten minutes later we were on the punt. It was pretty full. We were with a group of Chinese tourists and we squeezed side by side on to one of the seats. The tour guide gave us a travelling rug and I spread it across our laps. The weather wasn't hot considering it was July and cosiness was good.

We didn't say anything to each other, we just listened as the guide talked us through the architecture and the history. We stared where he pointed but my thoughts were really on Joanne and how much this moment meant to me.

We forgot about shopping in the end. We sat near the river at a table by the window of one of the restaurants on the quayside. I liked being here as a tourist. I was seeing the same sights but without the blinkered eye of a local. Joanne's attention darted from one thing to the next. On the punt, she'd asked questions about different buildings, about Cambridge's history, about local events, and I dragged up the answers that were buried somewhere in my head. Things I didn't know I'd known, and I occasionally wondered if I'd just made them up.

We didn't eat anything complicated. She chose a goat's cheese salad then followed it with panna cotta. They were my first choices too and each time she ordered I smiled and ordered the same.

I still wore my wedding ring. Nobody had commented on that except my mum. She just seemed curious. She didn't tell me it was time to take it off or anything like that.

My thoughts settled on this as I noticed that Joanne's left hand was unadorned.

'I'm sorry if this is a personal question, but when did you decide to take off your wedding ring?'

She laid down her cutlery and spread her hands in front of her. On her right hand, she had three rings, one on her thumb and one on each of her smaller fingers. She wiggled the ring finger.

'This was my engagement ring,' she said. It was ruby, set with three diamonds either side. Quite traditional, I thought. 'I put the others away, the wedding ring and my eternity ring. I suppose I took them off when I started to feel less than married. After he died I still felt married for a long time. People would ask me. They do when you fill in forms, don't they? I didn't want to put "widowed", I just wanted to put "married" but legally, you know, it is what it is, right?'

I nodded.

'And then you go through those stages of grief, however many there are.'

'Seven, I think,' I said.

'Right. Well, one of them is anger.' She hesitated and chewed on her lip, looking at me as though she was not sure whether to continue but, after a few seconds, she did.

'Our marriage wasn't perfect. I don't suppose any are. But when your husband dies, that's how it's framed. And of course, his friends and family loved him. I don't suppose they knew he hit me some-times. Not often, but near the end he did. He'd been drinking. He'd had a problem in the past and it seemed to be behind us. Well, behind him anyway, and then it started again. He'd been drinking the night they died. I lost our oldest child because of him.' Her voice wavered slightly. 'My Connor. Once the shock slipped away and the anger arrived, I didn't even want to write "widowed" anymore.' She was fighting not to cry and I was sorry that I had asked. 'I got rid of my wedding ring. Well, from my hand anyway. I had to move away unless I was going to live a lie or tell his family what he was really like and hurt them even more.'

All her previous lightness of mood had vanished and I realised that she must have been constantly living with all of this close to the surface and, if I didn't count Matt, she had been facing it all on her own.

I had carried on wearing my rings but I could now see that was wrong. I slid them off and dropped them into my pocket and later, when I reached home, I put them out of sight.

We walked more slowly back to the car, not ignoring the city but just letting its beauty slide past us.

I changed the subject to Molly and Luke and she brightened a little. 'Can I buy them something?' I asked.

'Sure,' she nodded.

We were passing the doors of Heffers bookshop and I slipped inside. I bought *Tintin in Tibet* for Luke and *101 Dalmatians* for Molly.

'They were two of my favourites,' I explained, 'when I was a kid.'

'Thank you. And thank you for today,' she said, slipping her arm through mine. She rested her head on my shoulder for a second as we walked.

'You'll like Matt,' she told me. 'At least I hope you will. He's fun.'

And I forced myself to smile.

We were home by half past two and from the first glimpse of the car park I saw the Tesla. Joanne's face brightened as she saw it too.

'He'll be in his flat. I'll introduce you this afternoon, if you like?'

'Sure.' I pinched the inside of my lip with my teeth and thought quickly. 'I tell you what,' I said, 'why don't I pick the kids up from school? Then you and Matt can have some time together, not long, but you know, I'll take the kids to the park if you want.'

Her smile widened.

'Seriously?' She didn't wait for me to reply. 'I'll phone the school. I'll let them know. You just need to identify yourself to the teacher, maybe take your driving licence or something with your name on it, so they know you are who you say you are. Then they'll let the kids know. Ask Molly, she'll show you where the park is. We go there sometimes.'

'I'll have them back by four.'

'Oh, that's brilliant. Half past is fine,' she said.

'No problem.'

I slipped my driver's licence into my bag, glad that I'd already updated it with my new name and address. The children's presents were on the back seat. I'd give them to the children before they came home. Everything felt perfect.

Picking up the children was incredibly easy. Molly's teacher came out and I went to speak to her. She said, 'Oh, you must be Emily?' She checked Molly's expression, making sure the little girl recognised me. It was as straightforward as that. The same with Luke's teacher.

'How was your day?' I asked them both. I took their lunch boxes and book bags from them. They didn't say much but before we'd left the gates Molly slipped her hand in mine. She held Luke's with her other hand and the three of us headed off in a little walking wave.

We reached the car and I opened the door and dumped their lunch boxes and book bags on the front seat.

'Now,' I said, 'I'm going to be taking you for something to eat and I could take you to the park too. Do you want to go to the park here or on the play equipment in the pub?'

'Are we going to a pub?' Molly's eyes widened like I'd said Disneyland or something. Luke pointed in the direction of his friends still streaming out of the school gates.

'My friends are going to the park,' he said.

Molly cut in, 'There's more to play on at the pub,' and within a couple of seconds the two of them were brewing into some kind of primary-school stand-off.

'Okay, okay. I'll tell you what, Luke, next time I pick you up we'll go to the park. This time we'll go to the pub because if we get there now, we can have ice creams.'

Luke scowled and stared at the floor and said nothing.

'And,' I said, 'I bought you a present each when I was in town today.'

I'd barely finished the sentence when his frown disappeared and he looked at me.

'What is it?'

'Come on,' I said, 'jump in the car and I'll show you.'

Luke opened the door and was straight in. Molly stood, looking inside then up at me.

'We need car seats,' she said.

'Oh. Your mum didn't say anything.'

Molly sighed deeply in the dramatic way that only an under ten knows how to do.

'She *always* forgets,' she said. 'They are built into her car and she forgets when it's anyone else's. She thinks everybody has car seats. Well, they don't, do they? Not everybody has children do they? You don't.'

'Not yet, no. Let's not worry about that. We need to work out how we can get you home. Can you sit on your coats or something?'

Molly shook her head emphatically. 'No, that's not right.' She looked around towards the trickle of parents still entering the car park. 'Some of the mums have spare seats. That's what you need to do.'

I shook my head. 'You're smart for eight, you are.'

'I'm seven,' she said.

'Well then, you're even smarter.'

'Did you think I was eight?'

'I have to keep reminding myself you're seven.'

She seemed satisfied with that and she and Luke sat in the car to wait while I explained to a load of strange women my predicament and my incompetence.

I only had to ask three or four parents before I'd borrowed two spare booster seats, and nothing eventful happened between then and our food.

The pub was on the route from school to home. I'd passed it a number of times and noticed the play area and the banners advertising their family meals. The menu offered about a dozen variations on burger and chips and another dozen versions of pasta and sauce. I chose a table with a view of the play equipment and watched Molly and Luke tackle the climbing frame while we waited for the food.

I sent Joanne a text, *Don't worry, still waiting to eat,* then went outside and joined them until the meal was served.

We drove back and I didn't pay attention to how long we'd been until I saw Joanne's face at the window. I could see anxiety in her expression even before I could pick out her features. It was all in the tilt of her face and its paleness.

I hurried the children out of the car.

'I think your mum's going to be cross with me,' I said.

Only Luke spoke. 'Probably,' he said.

'I'm so sorry,' I began as soon as I was within earshot.

She shook her head. 'It doesn't matter,' she muttered and turned away from me.

I was still carrying the children's book bags and lunch boxes so it seemed only natural to follow her into the flat.

'I texted you.'

'I know, and it's fine,' she said. 'I could have rung you, but I need to keep my anxiety in check.' She didn't need to mention Connor because the parallel was clear; he'd gone out and never come back.

I wasn't sure whether to apologise again. I decided to stay quiet.

Up to that point my eyes had only been on the back of her head but in my peripheral vision I caught a movement. I turned sharply and there he was. Matthew Edwards.

I smiled awkwardly. He was straight up from his chair and across the carpet to greet me. I held out my hand and he shook it. His hands were thin.

'This is a bit formal,' he grinned. His eyes were hazel and his hair was dark, almost black. I wondered whether he dyed it.

I was a lot shorter than him; the top of my head was somewhere level with the top of his breast pocket so he had eight or nine inches on me. I reckoned that made him about six-two. His flirtatious expression had gone. Instead he was studying me with a well-practised and earnest air. Andy had looked at Jess that way when he was first chasing her. Both men were used to trading on their looks.

Entitled.

Arrogant.

I wondered whether Matt would take what he wanted, when he wanted it.

I felt a pang of regret for losing Jess but I didn't dwell on it, and instead turned my attention to Joanne. 'Can I make the drinks?'

The children took no notice of the adults; they were quiet again, like before, Molly with her book and Luke with his Lego. Luke had liked the Tintin book I'd bought him but now it was on the floor, being used it as a base for a scene involving mini-figures.

Matt sat next to Joanne on the sofa with his hand on her lap. They barely seemed to notice the children either. They were close but not cloyingly loved up, the way they might have been, and when Matt spoke to me he seemed to take a genuine interest.

'How are you finding the flat?' he said. I watched his fingers wrap themselves over hers.

'It's good. It's a nice flat.'

Those first questions were quite stilted and then I asked him, 'Do you remember how it was before it was split up?'

He grinned and his expression broke into something natural and enlivened and warm.

'Of course I do. It's been divided up like this for about fifteen years and before that it was one big house. It came into my dad's family in the late 1880s. I don't really know much about it before that. But I know we owned it throughout the whole of the twentieth century. It was commandeered, or whatever you call it, for soldiers to convalesce at the end of the First World War. It wouldn't have ever come to my dad's branch of the family except the first two in line for it died in action, the third of influenza.'

I wondered if it had become one of those big houses that had fallen into disrepair, too expensive for the upkeep. 'Why the change to flats?' I asked.

He shrugged, 'Who needs a house that size, seriously? It made sense, good business sense that is. The family had other property too and, although I lived in it when I was kid, it wasn't really what my mum felt was a proper home. She was fed up rattling around this place. Your room is my old bedroom. I always loved the second stair-case. I could sneak out that way, spend time in the garden. Nobody noticed.' He leant closer and lowered his voice and I guessed this was for the benefit of the children. 'When I was a teenager I'd leave the outside door open, get girls to come upstairs. That bedroom's seen its fair share of action, I can tell you. Ha. Don't pull that face. It's not the same bed, I'm sure.'

My gaze drifted across to Joanne.

'He had a reputation at school. That's why I wouldn't go anywhere near him. One girl after another.'

Their eye contact was flirtatious with no hint of any friction.

'I think it's probably time I left.'

But neither of them was paying any attention to me.

'Are you going to leave the back door open for me then?' he asked Joanne.

She tilted her face closer to his, 'It's your building. I can't stop you.'

'That wouldn't be ethical.'

'I didn't know we were together for ethics, Matt.'

He shot a glance in my direction and I knew he wanted to hurry me along but illogically that made me stay longer; I didn't want to show him that I was running away on demand. I wanted to show him that when I left it would be on my terms. I could tell Joanne felt awkward then but she smiled anyway. It hadn't been my intention to put her in the middle of anything but my expression had become chilly. I tried to hide it and hoped she didn't notice. The conversation limped on.

When Matt had been talking about the house, I had almost warmed to him. A couple of minutes earlier, his smile had seemed genuine. Now it seemed false. And yes, they were leaning towards each other but I was sure the body language was wrong. And when I thought about it, it had been wrong from the first second I saw them together.

I couldn't explain it to Joanne; I suddenly felt on the outside.

'When do you go back to work?' I asked him.

'I work for myself, so my time's my own. I was planning to go to the office tomorrow.' He kept one arm around Joanne but leant back in the chair, spreading his other arm then folding it behind his head, which he tilted back a little. He was watching me now through half-closed eyes. 'But I could make it the next day, if you prefer? Perhaps we could all do something together?'

So, it was cat-and-mouse now. He was trying to make me uncomfortable. Trying to make me back away.

I kept control. 'I'm busy actually,' I told him.

Joanne glanced at Matt then back to me. She had finally picked up on the undercurrent but I could tell that she didn't know where it had come from. 'I need to get the kids to bed.'

'Right.' I stood. This was a good moment for me to leave.

He stood too, perhaps to follow Joanne, perhaps to leave. I had no idea which but I made up my mind that I had to be in my flat before he left hers. I gave Joanne a hug. 'I'll catch you soon,' I whispered in her ear.

Her goodbye to me was brief and I slipped away.

I heard their low voices as I climbed the stairs and the last thing that reached me was the sound of his laughter in the hallway below. I wondered what he could be laughing about if it wasn't about me.

WEDNESDAY 12 JULY, 2017

It was half past nine the next morning when I saw her again. There was a tap at my front door. She didn't use the knocker; it was just the sound of knuckles on paint.

I opened up and she pushed past me into the front room. There was tension in her expression but I couldn't tell whether she was upset or angry or something else.

'What's happened?'

'I don't know. I just had a feeling, a feeling that . . .' She tried to stand still but she was too restless. 'Something was going on last night, wasn't it? There was a subtext I wasn't catching.'

'What do you mean?'

'You know what I mean. Something between you and Matt, like you had a private joke or some secret conversation I wasn't part of.'

'No, no. No, you're wrong about that.' I held up my hands in an 'I surrender' gesture.

I stepped towards her but she seemed panicked.

'I know he's a flirt. He always has been, but you're my friend . . .'

'Hey, Joanne . . .' She let me step closer, 'I wouldn't do anything to hurt you and I know we don't know each other very well, but I'm not after your boyfriend.' Her concern couldn't have been more misguided. My thoughts flashed back to Jess again and how I wished I could have warned her about Andy before it was too late for her to listen.

For a few seconds, there was no reaction from Joanne. She seemed to be reading my face and I kept very still, meeting her gaze. Finally, she gave a sigh and it was mixed with a small laugh. 'I didn't think you were.' She shook her head as though confirming to herself how ridiculous she'd been. 'It's just, I'm a widow with two kids. And, at the end of the day, I have way more baggage than you. I don't think for a second you'd want to do anything, but you couldn't help it if he fell for you, could you?'

'Hey. Where's that come from?'

'He didn't take his eyes off you when he was talking to you.'

'Well, I think you're wrong there. Besides, we were talking about the house. He obviously loves the place and he must have wanted you living here.'

'That's true,' she conceded. 'I have money, enough to buy some- where outright, but I wanted to settle back in England first and he's let me stay here rent free for now. I don't want to rush into it. I was happy to pay, but he insisted.'

'Well then.'

I said *well then* as if I was trying to convince her that he was a decent guy when instincts told me the opposite. 'I do think though, you shouldn't rush in too quickly. How much do you really know about him?'

'It's mostly what I remember from years back but it feels special.' Her expression softened. 'It feels like I've always known him.'

'A lot will have happened between school and now.' I felt like my own mother dishing out the kind of cautionary advice that I never would have listened to. 'He looks older than you anyhow.'

'Yeah, he wasn't in my year. He was a few years above. As I was in the bottom of the school he was at the top. It was like, you know when you're in year four and everybody fancies the year sixes. It was like that.'

'And he had a thing for you?'

'So he said. I don't remember at the time to be honest.'

'So, what's this relationship with him based on exactly?' I shouldn't have said it but I did anyway.

She grinned then. 'Sex, for one.'

153

'But that's . . .'

'That's not enough, I know. I feel connected, sane when I'm with him, as though I don't need to have doubts about the future. And that would be so great for me and for the children,' she said. 'I want this to be love.'

'But you're not sure?'

She took my hand and squeezed it gently as she spoke. 'I'm falling for him, Em, but I'm scared. I told you that, right?' Her skin was pale. 'It's a big jump after what's happened in the last couple of years. And he's a good bloke. He knows I can take care of myself but he's looking after me too. Like with the flat. Despite what he says, I know they converted this to flats because they had to and I know money's sometimes short for him. He's just a really sweet guy, even if he is a bit of a flirt. And I'm sorry. I wasn't accusing you of anything. It's just, like, you have a whole lot more going for you than I have. You're really pretty.'

I wasn't dumb, though. We all know where we are on the looks scale, don't we? If I was a six, Joanne was at least an eight. But maybe she was worn down to the point where she'd become unaware of her own attractiveness.

'Don't rush into anything,' I told her. 'He might be all right for a fling but I don't think he's the long-term kind.' I carried on thinking about Matt. And, more specifically, the uncomfortable feeling I'd had when I'd seen them together. 'You said he's short of money? But he's in property?'

'That's right. He works for himself.'

'Doing what?'

'He buys buildings, does them up, rents them out and then sells them on. Those kind of things.'

'But you said that money's short . . .'

'They're big investments, they tie up his capital. Asset rich, cash poor, that's the saying, isn't it? He doesn't have problems.'

'But you're the other way around, aren't you?' I was thinking out loud when I said this and I saw her expression harden instantly.

'He's not after my money. Besides, you should be happy for me.'

The last thing I needed was to throw suspicion back onto myself.

'I am. I really am. I wasn't trying to cast any doubt. I don't know him well enough for that. Just an instincts thing, that's all. I'm just worried about you.'

She didn't seem convinced so I tried again.

'Two minutes ago, you were worried that I liked him, or he liked me. This is no different; I'm concerned that he's going to mess you around, or that you'll end up hurt. Maybe neither is the case but my concern's still real.'

'Honestly?' she frowned, 'If I was single and not so messed up by everything I'd be jumping at him. Having a boyfriend is a huge adjustment for me and the children.'

'He barely seems to notice them . . .' I let the words trail into nothing.

'He's giving them space.' Her expression softened. 'I'm sorry, Emily; I've been stupid. In fact, I think that's my first pang of jealousy since college.'

'Well then, I'm flattered.' I said it as though I was joking but, in truth, I did feel pleased.

'And I'm embarrassed. God,' she exhaled, 'I'm an idiot.'

'Forget about it. Tell me about Molly and Luke.'

The change of subject seemed to please her. 'They asked about you at breakfast. Wondered when we'd be seeing you again. I thought maybe you would like to pick them up again one day? With the booster seats this time.'

'I'd love that.'

We talked for a while longer before she went back to her flat and I felt happy to spend the rest of the day alone.

Matt had left early in the morning and, in the afternoon, I watched him come back. I heard them downstairs. I lay on my bed and listened. I picked up just enough sounds to work out which room they were in when they were chatting, when they were using the kettle and even when they were in the bedroom.

Each time I thought of Matt, I thought of Andy. And I considered the possibility that I was inventing a connection between. But there had been plenty of times when I'd had small doubts about Andy,

155

when I'd ignored a niggle of doubt or overruled myself when I'd occasionally felt uncomfortable in his company. If I regretted anything it was dismissing my own intuition; that's what had ruined my life and left Jess vulnerable to him.

How stupid would I have been to let the same thing happen twice?

Matt was using Joanne. I was absolutely sure of it. My instincts were screaming it at me and, as I lay on my bed, I stared at my ceiling trying to clear my mind of everything except what I actually knew about him.

He was three years older than her, or thereabouts. He owned the building and from my contract I knew the company name. He grew up round here; he lived in this house. His birthday was in June. And he had a small scar on one side of his neck.

And he was too old not to have a past.

That, I realised, was what I needed to find to prove to Joanne that he wasn't right for her.

I grabbed pen and paper and began to write. I made a list of what I knew, of what I needed to find out. It was a random way to spend my time but then, what else was I doing with it? Even if I couldn't convince her to break it off with him immediately, I could prepare her. Make sure that she knew I was there supporting her and looking out for her and the children.

I remained convinced that I thought more of the children than he did.

I'd bought them a ball each. Molly's decorated with a Disney princess and Luke's with Spiderman. They weren't expensive: they were the sort you buy at the petrol station, a couple of pounds each. I figured Joanne wouldn't mind as long as I wasn't spending much each time. Molly and Luke weren't old enough to understand the value of money but they would like the things that were bright and fun and for them.

By late afternoon it was warm and dry, and by the time they came back from school Matt was nowhere to be seen. And I wanted to be certain that every shred of this morning's awkwardness had gone so I took the balls down to the garden and I played with the children while Joanne made their dinner.

She invited me to eat with them and everything was right again.

I checked for him on social media. That's always my starting point when I'm looking for anybody that I know. He'd set up a Twitter account, gone as far as adding a photo. He followed the BBC news site and never tweeted anything beyond his first 'hello world', and his profile description was simply 'lives near Cambridge'.

Facebook wasn't much better. He was there all right but he'd locked down everything apart from his name and his profile picture. I jotted down details as I went, though. Next, I googled him, just his name and Wicken. I figured that, bearing in mind the size of Wicken, there wouldn't be any other Matthew Edwards in the village. He appeared on a phone directory listing. No number, but it told me that I could check for him on the electoral register, that I could find out whether he had any county-court judgments against him. There was a fee, of course. I added it to my list and moved on. Maybe I wouldn't have spent so long on it if I hadn't had so many free hours every day, if I'd had a job and a life and all those things that create enough noise to fill up other people's days.

I used up most of the day looking for him, seeking out the financial details for his property company, finding out that year on year they were barely breaking even. I'd found an option that said, 'Credit report available'. I could view it for £20. I hadn't started out with any intention of spending money on this, but then I figured £20 wasn't much. And within a few minutes I had a report that promised to include the risk score, credit limit, charges against property, shareholders and all those other bits of information that are meaningless unless you are really interested.

I wasn't a financial expert but I didn't need to be to see that he'd borrowed heavily against the properties. It wasn't just this house, there were five more. Addresses that included two houses broken up into multiple-occupancy student occupation in Cambridge, a small workshop unit on a trading estate halfway between Cambridge and Wicken, and two small terraced properties in the village itself. I checked out all the addresses. They were all occupied but then, when I looked at the loans secured against the buildings, I could see that he'd borrowed and borrowed again.

Letting Joanne live in that flat rent free was close to being the difference between turning a profit and only breaking even. It astonished me that banks still lend like that; letting the faith that people were managing their money and thinking they could repay override the facts that proved they really couldn't.

But as far as Matt Edwards was concerned, it was irrelevant.

Loads of people had stretched themselves too far. It didn't prove intention of anything else.

I looked across at the CCJs. There were two minor non-payments, one of parking charges, the other I guess was a dispute over some sort of delivery fees owed to a company called Baxter Removals. On the scale of things both were inconsequential and had obviously done nothing to affect his ability to borrow increasingly large sums of money. But then it wasn't money I was worried about, was it?

I shut my eyes to block out the computer screen and tried to relive the moment when I had first felt that creeping sensation that seeing him with her was wrong. There are many kinds of 'all wrong' in this world.

Hadn't I known since I first met Ben that Andy had been 'all wrong'?

We've all done it; we've pushed our instincts to one side and convinced ourselves that those gut reactions were baseless and then, later, berated ourselves for not listening. Well, I was listening now and something was wrong. And not just his blatant flirting that first time he'd met me.

I told myself again: anyone Matt's age has history, and I needed more than dry financial records.

FRIDAY 14 JULY, 2017

'Tell me about your emotional state,' Dr Lahiri studied me over the top of his half-moon glasses. He had been our family doctor for the past ten years and whenever I booked an appointment I asked for him rather than one of the others at the practice.

'I think I'm doing really well,' I told him.

'I see,' he replied but he may as well have said, *I know you're not.* 'You've been through a lot of emotional difficulties in the last few months. A divorce is always traumatic.'

'It's not finalised yet,' I pointed out, as if that made any difference.

'Does that frustrate you? Or are you dreading the day that it is?'

'I don't think of Ben every day, like I used to. He seems to have moved on. He has a girlfriend. They're having a baby.'

His expression gave nothing away. I guessed he knew this already; after all, there was only one doctors' practice in the village and I could imagine Shannon coming in here with her ever-swelling bump.

'And how are you moving on? Can you?'

Dr Lahiri had always looked old to me, like he'd been pulled out of retirement and had dragged his tweed jacket with him. I imagined he was old-fashioned even when he was young.

I swear he looked right through me. That and the fact that I knew it was all confidential meant there was no point in lying.

'I'm trying to move on. My parents struggled with what happened,

Dad especially. I lost my job over it. I had to move out of the village really.'

'Don't tell me that bit,' he said. 'You'll have to register somewhere else if you make it an official move.'

'I don't know if it's permanent or not. Part of me wants to move back but the bigger part of me . . .' I sighed. 'I don't know . . .' And it was true. I didn't.

'I met someone though.'

'A man?'

'No, a woman who lives downstairs. She has two children. I think she's going to be a good friend. Perhaps she is already and I like her a lot.'

I hesitated, like I needed to say more, to give him the true picture.

'Are you remembering to take your prescription?'

I nodded. 'Mostly at least.' And just like that I threw out the truth. 'There have been some days I've missed.'

'Well, you shouldn't. You need the support of keeping your mood even. You won't always make good choices if you're fighting with depression or anxiety.'

He knew it was both.

'I sense there's something you want to say about this friendship?'

That was funny. I hadn't known there was. I looked at the clock. My appointment had already taken too long. What was the allocated time? Six minutes or something. I didn't know what it was, but knew it was short.

'I don't think I should be taking up your time.'

He shook his head. 'Some patients need more and they deserve to have it. You haven't been to see me for months now. I am totally within my rights to spend that much longer with you.'

'I wondered whether I was wrong to have pressed charges against Andy Tyler. Wouldn't it have been easier if I'd just come to see you and increased the dose of the anti-depressants and not let myself worry about it?'

'How am I supposed to answer that? I think I said to you at the time that it was down to you to find the right solution.'

'You think I was wrong.'

160

The corner of his mouth pushed downwards. He didn't reply.

'You do, don't you?' I persisted.

He put down his pen and pressed his palms flat on the desk. 'What I feel,' he said, 'is that you are a young woman who gave herself a lot to deal with. The investigation and the court case, they would have taken their toll on the strongest person and you've always been . . .' he paused for a little too long, 'you're not the most thick-skinned, are you?'

Well, I couldn't disagree with that.

'You were going to tell me something about your new friend?'

'Was I?'

Out of nowhere I had a thought and I jumped for it rather than letting him make me drag up the wrong thing about Joanne. My sidestep, I thought, was rather neat.

'I met somebody,' I told him. 'A man, I see him occasionally in the village. And I'm scared of getting to know him any better and I wondered if there was any way I could check on him, you know, discreetly, like employers do when they want to get one of those background checks, to see if anyone's been convicted of any offences. Can I do that for a boyfriend?'

He looked at me for a long minute before he answered.

'I don't know. You'd have to find out from the police but I would assume that you are not a fan of theirs. Google it, why not? That's what everybody does these days. My advice, I'll be honest with you, Emily, would be to leave it alone for a while. I would imagine your family have been finding it very tough.'

'This has nothing to do with them.' I looked past him and out of the window. I could just see the road through the narrow slats in the venetian blind.

'I can refer you if you need more support. It isn't something you have to handle by yourself.'

It.

You'd think a doctor could say depression or whichever other word he wanted to use for my frame of mind.

'I'm trying to start again and that means a new relationship at some point, doesn't it?'

'It does.'

'And I need to be careful.'

'Which is why you must move slowly. Don't rush into anything with this man. I'd like you to come back and see me in, say, two weeks. Will you do that?'

I nod but I'm sure I won't. 'Do you believe me, doctor?'

'About what?'

'About everything that happened.'

He leant back in his chair as though he needed to view me at a bit more of a distance in order to take stock properly. 'I'm sure, from your perspective, you think you've been accurate and you've certainly presented all the symptoms of somebody who's been traumatised. But dealing with something like that in public, the court case I mean, I suspect that was enough to cause the trauma and I didn't see you before that, did I? Just in these months since.'

'Do you think I'm lying?'

'No. I believe you've told me the truth, as far as you're aware of it. But I'm not in a position to say anything more specific than that. And that's not a slur on your character.'

'Of course it is.' I said it calmly, but afterwards I wished I'd shouted at him.

'That's not the way I intended it. Just make sure, for both your sakes, that you take it slowly with this new man.'

I rose to go. The genial Dr Lahiri clearly thought he needed to protect this fictitious new man in my life and he even needed to hedge his bets with me for his own benefit. I wondered who else he was a doctor to. To Ben? To Jess? To Andy, even?

The bitterness of hearing his doubt finally caught up with me. He tried to carry on talking but I snatched up my jacket and my bag and I was out of the door as fast as I could move.

'Do you have children, Matt?'

I could guess what the answer was going to be before I'd asked the question. He'd tried talking to Molly and Luke but the conversation had been brief and awkward. Especially so with Molly who replied with exaggerated shrugs and obvious disinterest. He fared a little better with Luke and managed to be convincing as he admired Luke's latest Lego model. Even so, I couldn't imagine he'd ever had much contact with children.

'No, I don't,' he replied. But it wasn't the words that told me what I wanted to know. I'd surprised him by suggesting it and his expression showed that the idea of it was ridiculous.

He was heading for his mid-thirties, and perhaps there were some dads out there who were overly preened and well-kept and who could afford flash cars and designer clothes along with the cost of having children, but I'd never met any like that.

I have heard people say you can judge a person by their shoes. I'd always gone for hands. I was sure his were manicured. He wore a signet on the little finger of his right hand and an expensive looking watch on his left wrist. It was one of those understated ones with the leather strap and a muted face and with hands so thin that they were barely visible. I could just tell it was expensive. The same as his clothes. They were smart and neat and they didn't shriek anything at all. They just showed him off, right down to the cuffs and those well cared for hands. His fingers were long and thin. Not in a freaky way. They were a man's hands; strong and broad across the backs.

My gaze drifted away and up to his face and I found him looking at me, his eyes bright, slightly amused even. And all this time Joanne was there too. I started to try to cover it up by clumsily changing the subject but she didn't seem to mind. Perhaps she hadn't noticed. Her previous moment of insecurity had been completely forgotten and she seemed comfortable in a way that I never had been.

Women hanging around Ben almost always made me feel uneasy. But as if to prove that none of it bothered her, she left the room with the children, helping them to find their pyjamas and brush their teeth. Matt leant to one side in his chair. He rested his elbow on the arm and pushed his fingers through his hair.

'Joanne tells me you're single.'

I nodded. 'Recently,' I said.

He nodded slowly as if that made complete sense.

'Did he deserve it?'

'Deserve what?'

'Dumping. I assume you dumped him?'

My cheeks flushed. 'It wasn't quite like that.'

I didn't mean to do it but I fixed him with a steady gaze and a small smile. I wasn't going to be intimidated by him.

'Well,' he said, 'I suspect your ex wasn't all that smart.'

It was me who broke eye contact first. I'd read before that it's the strongest one who does that, the one who's ultimately going to get the upper hand in the relationship, but whenever I'd needed to look away, I'd felt I was the weaker one.

I'll be honest, I didn't feel uncomfortable being alone with him in the room like that and, yes, there was something mildly flirtatious passing between us but, for me, it was contrived. I wanted to see how he'd respond. And what challenge would there be in bagging a man who was obviously such a player? I was sure he'd never been that discerning, not until he met Joanne.

I left for the bathroom as soon as she returned to the room and when I came back I sat in a different chair, turning my body forty-five degrees away from him, so that she was in my line of sight instead. I spent the rest of the evening not exactly ignoring him but making sure that she was the centre of attention, that she was the important part of the conversation. And, every once in a while, in the periphery of my vision I felt his gaze drift across to me and I knew he was curious. I knew what sort of bloke Matt was.

I returned to my flat well before bedtime. Of course, I had no idea whether he'd stay the night or leave after they'd had enough time alone. And, if he did leave, whether he'd just cross to the other side of the building or take off somewhere in that car of his. For the next hour, my mind drifted through the various possibilities, creating scenarios, weighing up the outcome. Inventing, I suppose, if you wanted to look at it that way. But these were things I'd always been good at. And when I sensed a change in mood downstairs and heard that the murmuring of voices reaching me through the floor had taken on a more formal rhythm then I slipped outside to my car.

I drove out onto the road, into the nearest side street, then turned around. From where I sat I could see the entrance to the house and the road as it disappeared in both directions. Perhaps he'd just go to his flat. Perhaps he wouldn't. I kept one eye on the digital clock on the dashboard, and the colon blinking in between the hours and minutes. I thought I'd give it twenty minutes but then allowed another twenty after that. It was almost an hour before the Tesla pulled out onto the street. By then I was cold and tired but there was no way I wasn't going to follow him.

He turned in the opposite direction, away from the side road where I was parked, and headed in the direction of the A10. I kept my lights off for the first mile. I hung back. There was little point chasing his car – I couldn't catch up with him if I tried. But he was in no hurry. He stayed at thirty in the thirty-mile-an-hour zone and only accelerated to a maximum of fifty once he was out of the village.

I kept the dots of his taillights in sight and only attempted to catch up as we approached the junction with the A10, where he would have the choice of driving straight over, going left to Cambridge or right to Ely. He took the left and I expected him to accelerate away into the distance once he'd hit this larger road. He did accelerate but not beyond sixty.

The traffic here was busier and I kept a couple of cars between him and me. By the time we made it to the lit streets on the outskirts of Cambridge it was easier to make out the shape of his car from the others up ahead. We'd come in at the Science Park, the traditional site for the innovative and high-tech businesses in town, although the way Cambridge was expanding, anything could be anywhere. But he didn't stop there and carried on towards the centre, past the tree-lined avenue where schools had tied yellow ribbons around the hornbeams and horse chestnuts, hoping to save them from the expansion of the busway.

He drove around the junction at Mitcham's Corner, treating the bends like a chicane and suddenly darting through the lights as though he'd realised I was there and had made the decision to leave me behind. But when I came out the other side on to Victoria Avenue, he was there again, back under the thirty-miles-an-hour limit. I kept tabs on him until, finally, he found a parking spot in King's Parade and made his way on foot down Bene't Street. I stayed in the car. I kept my distance but kept him in sight too and spotted him going into the Eagle pub. I drove back out and parked a hundred yards along from his Tesla. At first, I only planned to wait a few minutes, just enough to determine whether this was a flying visit or something longer.

But as time passed I convinced myself that I needed to stay for the duration; just following him to a public place told me nothing, so I waited. When he finally returned, it was almost an hour after pub closing time and I was on the point of wondering whether he was coming back at all.

He reappeared in a group of six, two other men and three women. They all looked about his age. They stood for a minute on the corner across the road from his car. He was the only one who wasn't dressed for a night out. The woman close to him wore a mink-coloured dress. It had a satiny finish and spaghetti straps. The hemline stopped halfway up her thigh and she wore those shoes that looked like high-heeled gladiator sandals. Ugly, in my opinion.

What she was wearing could have been mistaken for lingerie, but then that was just my opinion too. She was tactile and didn't seemed to be able to speak to Matt without wrapping her hands around his bicep or touching her cheek on his shoulder. I tried snapping a photo with my phone but they were too far away and the image was pix-elated. I really expected the other two couples to head off in one direction and for her to accompany Matt to his car.

They were like that for about ten minutes and the cool night-time air was nipping at the women's legs. They were all underdressed although perhaps not quite as provocatively as the blonde girl standing with Matt. In the end, she began to tug on his arm. He shook hands briefly with the two men and kissed cheeks with the women before following her back down Bene't Street.

This time my approach was different.

I locked my car and began to follow. The streets were all but deserted now and there was nobody between me and them. I kept close to the shops on the left-hand side, hurrying across the patches of pavement that were lit by the shop windows. They made it to the corner ahead of me and turned out of sight. I broke into a run, not pounding the pavement but moving as quickly as I could and still managing to stay silent, thankful for the soft soles of my pumps.

When they came back into sight, his jacket was round her shoulders and this time it was he who was hurrying her along. His jacket came low enough to hide her dress and I could imagine what she would look like naked and just draped in his cast-off clothes. I dismissed the idea of trying for another photo. They were still too far ahead. I don't know what I expected to see but I kept pace with them, watching their body language. They looked so much more than just friends but there was nothing I'd seen that could prove anything to me.

Finally, they found the arched entrance to a small private club on the opposite side of the marketplace. I'd heard about it but never been inside. I knew that guests were welcome so I could follow them in there but, in jeans and an old T-shirt, flat pumps and no make-up, I'd stand out a mile. I stopped there and then, took a photo of the doorway and texted it to myself so I'd know for sure what time it had been. I made my way back to the car and sat and watched his Tesla until first light. By then I was queasy with tiredness and the cold had overtaken me. I turned on the engine and drove back home.

The dashboard clock said 6:24 when I pulled back in the driveway. I saw Frank immediately. He was in the flowerbed closest to the ground-floor windows, kneeling with a trug beside him and a trowel in his hand. He looked up and raised the other hand in greeting. I wasn't really in the mood to talk but I had to walk past him between parking the car and going indoors.

'You're up early.'

'Well, at least I had a night's sleep,' he said. He raised one eyebrow and his comment was clearly supposed to be an opening so that I could explain. I didn't.

'Weeding's therapeutic,' he told me and waved the trowel at the heap of plant debris that was filling the trug. 'I spend a lot of time out here, thinking, and it works because I'm not trying to think, I'm trying to weed. And before I know it, my thoughts are somewhere else.'

I smile politely. My thoughts are actually on nowhere but my bed.

'It would be good for you,' he said.

'I'm sorry?'

'Good for you, to come out here, do some weeding with me, tend to the garden.'

'Ah, gardening's not really my thing.'

'Nope. A means to an end,' he said firmly. 'You obviously know what it's like to watch the sun come up but come out here a few minutes after that and it's a magical experience.'

I nodded and took a step backwards, not wanting to be rude but thinking I'd been there long enough to get away with making an excuse. But before I could go, he'd clambered to his feet.

'It's not my business,' he said, 'but you seem troubled.'

The ability to deny it and shrug it off didn't come to me. Instead I felt my forehead pucker. 'Troubled, how?'

There was a hard edge to my voice and I wished it wasn't there. He had small grey eyes and they registered surprise.

'In a sad way, of course,' he told me. 'I can see what it looks like when people are weighed down. You're weighed down and you're miserable with the burden of it. I know you split up with your husband and I know that's tough but come out here.' He waved his trowel at the garden behind him. 'It would do you good.'

'No, I'm fine, thank you.'

'Just a suggestion.' He raised both his hands skyward and the tip of the trowel waggled at the clouds.

'If I'm not happy, it's not going to be fixed by a bit of gardening, Frank. I appreciate the thought, but no.'

He started to speak again, maybe to convince me, I don't know. I raised my finger and pointed. Not at him but up at the sky, in that same place that I thought he was just gesturing towards. 'I'm not in the mood right now, I'm really not. You are being friendly. But it's not what I need. I don't want help. I'm tired, I don't feel well and I just want to go to bed.'

He had looked so sure about his suggestion that half of me expected him to carry on defending it. Instead he nodded and turned away, almost shrinking back towards his gardening and I caught the word 'sorry' as I too turned away.

I was unlocking my door when I heard Joanne's front door open. She called upstairs to me but I pretended not to notice. I closed the door behind me and tried crashing fully clothed onto my bed. But Molly and Luke were awake now and the sounds of the children downstairs didn't comfort me as they usually did. I wanted the kind of peace that comes when you are pretending the rest of the world doesn't exist. In the end, I did the next best thing. I ran a bath. I made it as hot as I could stand then sank into it, sliding down until my ears were submerged and I was soundproofed from the rest of the building.

I lay there and slept, waking much later when the water was tepid, the children had gone to school and the house was genuinely silent.

FRIDAY 25 AUGUST, 2017

It took me a few weeks to work out the pattern but it turned out to be always the same. The children went to a holiday activity club on Mondays, Wednesdays and Thursdays, and Matt and Joanne would spend time together in the daytime and that invariably involved sex. I could hear them sometimes and other times just silence, broken by the flushing of the toilet or the running of the shower.

I saw them go out together too. Sometimes in the car or, more often, heading out for romantic walks, no doubt holding hands as they strolled through the village. I hadn't thought either of them was the holding-hands type but they proved me wrong.

He was spending more time with the children, too. I noticed that straightaway. In the first couple of weeks I dwelt on the worry that the children might be his real target. I watched him every time Joanne looked away; I didn't want there to be a single second when one of us didn't have them safely in view. I'd read about men singling out mothers with children but Matt's behaviour towards them was masked by awkwardness. He tried hard to make conversation in front of Joanne but their replies were always heavy with disinterest. He made no attempt to befriend them the rest of the time. I suspected that they intimidated him and I found it amusing to watch him struggle.

There were several evenings when I offered to babysit and Molly and Luke stayed with me, hanging out in my flat, watching DVDs I had bought until it was time for their bedtime and I took them back downstairs and settled them down for the night.

I started going out more too during the daytime. Finding the next DVDs we'd watch, or the next games we'd play, became a bit of a hobby of mine. I tended to buy the films online, but for games I'd go into Newmarket. I went into the toy shop and browsed the shelves, finding the ones that were both fun and educational. Molly was really good at English and Luke liked art. I suppose Molly did too really because she never wrote anything without drawing a picture along-side it. They both drew me one day. In Luke's picture, I had long legs, the sort you might make out of string, with beads for feet. Molly drew me in a party dress.

'You'd look pretty in a party dress,' she told me.

And all the time I watched Matt and made notes of his comings and goings and learnt that there was a pattern to his life. He rarely used his flat. He either stayed with Joanne or disappeared back to Cambridge.

I didn't press too hard but Joanne told me that he had work there and would stay over at a little apartment he had in town. That night I'd seen him in Cambridge had been a Thursday. On Thursdays, Fridays and Saturdays he'd leave earlier than on the other nights. I'd followed on several occasions and the pattern was the same, parking on King's Parade and ending up at 12A, the private members' club.

I hadn't seen her again, though, the lingerie woman.

But I'd never managed to wait long enough to see him return to his vehicle either. There was, I knew, no point in following the same pattern again. I had to push it further. I couldn't get the idea out of my head that he was going to hurt Joanne somehow but it was more than that.

Just the sight of him now riled me. I felt his presence, even when he was downstairs with her. I felt his presence intruding into my life. Joanne and I had very briefly had a friendship where he didn't feature and, I suppose, while having a boyfriend was so far off my agenda, it had never occurred to me that it would be on hers.

After all, what did she need? She had the children and a good home and, from what I could work out, plenty of money in the bank.

And the two of us could have been enough company for one another. Perhaps it came down to the one thing she needed that I didn't.

Sex.

I remembered what it was like to enjoy it. But she didn't have to pick him, did she? I knew from the first time I saw him that he liked women for what they could give him, not what he could give them. And I knew from the first time that I saw him and Joanne that it was wrong. He was the fracture in the picture.

Once I started thinking about it, my frustration at his existence made my decisions easy.

I bought a better camera, one that I could adjust so that it would take photos in half-light without the need for a flash. I chose a dress from the clothes that I'd kept. One that I would have actually picked for an interview, not for a night out. I just had to get into the place and blend; besides which, I'd long since walked away from anything that could be even mildly construed as slutty. The shoes I'd picked had been from an interview too, plain with a heel. I straightened my hair and kept my make-up low-key. The overall effect made me feel like somebody's aunt or a single woman, as I was, but labelled *spinster*. It didn't matter.

I made it in to 12A at eight, earlier than he'd ever considered arriving. The place claimed that the bar was themed like a speakeasy. To me it felt like a gentlemen's club, the kind where the chairs are heavily upholstered and the lighting is muted and one private conversation is possible six feet away from the next.

I chose a seat with my back to the door. I figured it would give me several minutes before he spotted me or perhaps he wouldn't see me at all. I ordered drinks, just an endless supply of mineral water, and opened out a copy of *The Times* across my lap. I read a little but made sure I checked the room frequently. No one challenged me and perhaps I imagined it but I could feel the curious glances of the bar staff as they tended to the nearby tables. At 10.45, I glanced at my watch. It was still a little too early and I thought I had time to visit the ladies' before he was likely to arrive. I stood and it was that moment I felt a hand grip my arm just above my elbow, the tips of the fingers digging in to the fleshy bit of my inner arm.

'Outside,' Matt whispered.

Behind him the lingerie woman stood at the bar. She was pretending to notice nothing and stared into her martini glass. I reached down and grabbed my bag. 'I haven't paid,' I mutter.

He ignored me and pulled me towards the exit. I didn't fight him, I didn't ask for anyone's help, but as the two of us went outside I could feel a ball of fear beginning to form in the pit of my stomach. When he finally stopped, my back was pressed against the cold wall that had once been the cinema and his hand was still firm on my arm.

'Why are you here?'

'Why do you want to know?' I replied.

He ran his tongue along his top lip. There was nothing sexual about it but my chest tightened and my lungs felt as though they were locked in hard.

'Why are you here?' he repeated.

'I'm waiting for a friend.'

'Is that so?'

I gathered myself a little. 'I'm waiting for a friend. And I have every right to be here, you know.'

He smiled at that.

'You don't have any friends. Only Joanne. She told me.'

That stung but I managed not to show it.

'What do you want from me, Emily?'

'I don't want Joanne being hurt.'

'And you think I would?'

'You are here with someone else.'

'I'm here,' he said, 'and Joanne knows as much as she needs to.'

His free hand reached up and touched my free arm. 'You're quivering. You're like a rabbit, aren't you? A frightened little rabbit.'

'She's a good person.'

'Joanne? Yes, she is.'

'I want you to leave her alone.'

'But I like her. We like each other. Haven't you worked that out?'

'She can't see what you're like.'

He shook his head. 'She's the best thing that's happened to me. I'm not going to have it ruined. Not by you.'

I think he smiled but I wasn't sure. He'd been leaning into me but now he pushed away and took a step back, studying me with his head cocked to one side, as if I was some sort of exhibit. 'What's your story, Emily?' He tapped his temple. 'There's something going on in that little head of yours. Emily . . . What is your last name?'

I didn't reply. I shook my head a little.

'You know what? I'm actually your landlord. It's not so hard for me to find out about you. It wouldn't be so hard for me to make you move. I think you should give me and Joanne a bit of space, time for us to develop whatever it is that it is going to become.' He released his hold and stepped away from me, 'You are not spoiling it. I won't let you.'

I didn't move until he'd gone back inside. And then I began to shiver properly. Not just out of cold but an uncontrolled shaking that reminded me how feeble I was.

The streets were mostly deserted by then. Stragglers, talking in pairs, ignoring me, smoking cigarettes or hurrying on to wherever they were going. One taxi with its engine idling parked across the square, and the untended market stalls that could hide any number of eyes watched me.

I was not comfortable, even though Cambridge was my patch. In the daytime it was genial, it was order and discovery, art and creation. But at night it was none of those. It stepped away from itself and loitered in its own shadow. That's what I saw just then. And suddenly I realised; that was who I was. Someone who loitered in their own shadow.

I hurried back to the relative safety of my car but this time I didn't go home. I brought it on to the marketplace and found the one spot where I could park and be lined up to a narrow gap between the market stalls, where I could see where we had just been standing, the same spot he would have to pass through when he left. And that was where I waited, still cold, still shivering but feeling a little safer. And it didn't take long, twenty minutes at most and then I saw him and her out on the pavement, his jacket around her shoulders like it was that other time, his arm in the small of her back.

I started the engine and eased the car forward. I edged out onto the pavement and pulled out towards Sidney Street, in the direction I thought they must have gone. I'd travelled no more than ten or fifteen yards when a movement flickered in the corner of my eye. I turned just in time to see a bicycle frame being swung at my windscreen. The windscreen frame took most of the impact so the noise was worse than the damage. The bike bounced away onto the ground and then his face was there at the glass. He was screaming at me.

'Fuck off and stop following me.'

He continued shouting until the police arrived.

They asked me what happened and I told them 'nothing'. He apologised and was smug and easy with his words. She had her arm around him as if he was the one that needed the comfort. I wondered what had brought the police so quickly, whether they'd seen something on CCTV and would charge him anyway. They asked me again what happened and I couldn't bring myself to say a word. I had seen too many police officers in my life and I wasn't going back there again. So, they left and I went home with scratched paint, a broken wing mirror and the knowledge that he was violent.

SATURDAY 26 AUGUST, 2017

It was about ten the next morning when Joanne knocked. I wasn't dressed and I'd slept badly, finally drifting off into proper, deep sleep at about six in the morning. When I opened the door, I was still mellow enough from sleep to seem at ease but I could sense a slight formality on her part.

'I'm taking the children into town. Not Cambridge, just Ely. They need some clothes and I promised Luke some more Lego for his birthday.'

'Oh. When is it?' I don't know why it hadn't occurred to me to find out when their birthdays were. 'I haven't missed it, have I? Or Molly's?'

'No, no,' she said, 'Luke's is early next week and Molly's is in September.'

'The oldest in the year then?'

'That's right,' she smiled. 'So, do you want to come with us?'

'I'm not ready to go out yet.'

'We can leave it for a little while. Have lunch if you like, at that pub by the river? Or perhaps the tearoom?'

'Have they fed the ducks yet?'

'I don't think we're supposed to.'

'No, no, I think it's all right if you have proper duck food. I have proper duck food. Well, at least, I haven't, but I'll get some.'

'Okay . . .' Her voice took on a tentative tone and I realised I'd probably come on a bit strong.

'Well, I don't have to come. I don't mind, it would be nice, but . . . I could stay here?'

'No, no,' she said, 'come with us. We can walk down along the towpath.'

And somehow, I knew that the unspoken end to that sentence was 'and we can talk.'

'Have you spoken to Matt today?' I asked.

'Briefly,' and her gaze drifted off a little. Normally her eye contact was good but at that moment she wanted to look anywhere else but at me.

'I don't want to cause trouble,' I began.

She pressed her lips together and shook her head.

'We'll go to Ely. Will you be ready in twenty minutes?'

I told her I could be but then spent the first ten minutes too restless to concentrate on deciding what to wear, then the next ten minutes scrabbling around trying to choose between a jumper and a jacket, a T-shirt and a blouse. None of it mattered. I just wished I could jump ahead and have whatever it was that that conversation was going to be.

I had always thought of Ely as the hill with the cathedral on top. But of course, it was more than that and the south side nestled up to the river with its boatyard, marina and the whole community that lived upon it. The river headed one way to Cambridge and the other out towards the sea and although there were plenty of pleasure boats, I could never quite shake off the feeling that it had once been a trade highway and that the fields and farms beyond had earned their right to exist in a landscape that was fertile and bleak in equal measure.

Joanne and I ate scones, both with jam but not with cream. Luke chose a brownie and Molly a chocolate cake, which she half ate and then pushed round the plate until the blob of white cream from the centre floundered in a trail of chocolate crumbs.

We left the tearoom and began to walk, keeping them ahead of us on the towpath. I thought it was so that we could always see where they were, but maybe so they couldn't hear us either.

'So,' she said, 'you've been following Matt.'

It wasn't even a question, just a blank statement of fact.

'I had a bad feeling. I can't explain it. Intuition perhaps.'

'He says you are jealous. He thinks you want to break us up. Is that right?' She looked more curious than angry.

My first reaction was to say no and then repeat the denial. 'Of course, I was pleased when I found out that you had a boyfriend, so it's not that. It's just him. There's something off about him.'

'So you do want us to break up?'

I hesitated. Either answer here was the wrong one. 'Look, I don't want you hurt and I followed him this one night. I wanted to know why he doesn't stay here. He has a flat in our building and he goes back to Cambridge every time.'

'Surely that's his business?'

'Yes, but why? You and he are together. Why wouldn't he want to be here? Why have a flat standing empty?'

'That doesn't make him a . . . whatever you think he is. What do you think he is, anyway?'

'A womaniser, for one.' I bit my lip then. Everyone shoots the messenger, don't they?

'Matt?' she gave a small laugh. 'Flirting, yes. Womanising, no.'

'I've been watching him. There's this woman . . .'

Her expression darkened. 'Hang on . . . you've *been* watching him. More than just last night? Is that what you mean?'

'I'd been watching him with you and I felt uncomfortable and this one night I followed him to Cambridge. Not last night, a different night. And I saw him with this woman.'

'I see.'

'He's met her more than once.'

Joanne's voice dropped. She sounded cold now.

'How many times are you talking about, Emily?'

I dodged a tiny bit. 'He was with her last night.'

'Have you been stalking him?'

'Stalking? No. You and I, we've both been through a lot.'

'Have you, Emily? As far as I can see you're going through a divorce like millions of other people.'

'Yes, I am. And there is more, but that's enough isn't it? And you've lost your husband. And if I'm honest, yes, I was a bit jealous. You're the first friend I've made since I've been here and I love the time I spend with you. And I suppose I felt threatened and I suppose maybe a bit envious because it's not going to happen for me.'

'Of course . . .' she began.

'No really, it won't. So, I'm sorry. I'm sorry I've been out of line. But he's out of line too.'

'Because of this woman?'

'Partly.'

'Tall, slim, shoulder-length blonde hair. Long legs, short skirt?'

I nodded dumbly.

'That's his sister.'

'No, no, it can't be.'

'It really is. She's younger. She goes out, gets pissed. He takes her home. He says she's a nice girl, just partying a bit too hard. He's determined to help her.'

I stared down at the monotony of the surface of the footpath, using it as a blank canvas to help me remember, and I reluctantly realised that I could see the likeness. I shook my head. 'It can't be. It's wrong.'

'And what did you see? They weren't snogging, were they?'

'No, but he had his arm around her. She was wearing his jacket.'

'And?'

'It's more than that, Joanne. He caught me. He came up to me. He threatened to have me thrown out of the flat.'

'Well, he wants you to leave, that's for sure.' She made sure the children waited for us then turned to me. 'Matt snapped. I don't think it's a sign of anything more than the way a normal person behaves when somebody's pushing them and is a bit too much in their face. Do you know what I'm saying?'

I nodded but didn't reply. It was all I could do not to burst into tears. I think she saw that and I felt her hand wrap around mine.

'I love it that you care, I really do.' She ducked down slightly and tilted her head to make sure that I could do nothing but look at her. 'You don't lose a mate over a bloke.' It was hard to think of anything

179

more apt that Joanne could have said. Relief swept over me. 'Give him some space, Emily, and he'll give you some space. I'll talk to him. You won't be thrown out of your flat. But please stop following him. He makes me happy, but you do too.'

Frank was gardening again when we arrived home. He didn't look up and we went straight indoors, but I made two mugs of tea and took them out to the garden. I placed them alongside him.

'I bought you a present,' I said and handed him a brown paper bag.

He took it and studied the outside of the bag rather than look at me.

'It's to say sorry,' I added. 'I was out of order.'

The weak sunlight was falling straight on his face. It made his skin look thin and the wrinkles stand out. These signs of frailty made me feel even worse about snapping at him.

'You didn't need to buy me anything.'

'Well, I saw it and thought of you.'

He reached into the bag.

'It's for gardening apparently. It came from the antiques' barn at Ely.'

He took it out, holding it by the wooden handle. It was shaped like a fork but with just two prongs and, on the underside, there was a semi-circular curve of metal. His eyes widened for a second and little creases formed in the corners when he smiled.

'It's a daisy grubber. Look.' He pressed the prongs into the ground and tipped it backwards. The roll of metal underneath provided the leverage to remove the weed.

'Oh.' I felt disappointed. 'I actually like daisies.'

'It will work on other things too. Shall I leave you the daisies?' he said. 'You didn't have to, you know. It was kind, but not necessary.'

'Well, I didn't want to get into that situation where we were crossing on the stairs and avoiding speaking to each other, even long after we could remember what it was that we'd fallen out over.'

'That wouldn't happen, I live on the ground floor.' He winked. 'I didn't think we had fallen out. It was just a few words.'

'Okay. But you were right. I don't want to sit weeding, mind you. But a cup of tea together would be okay, wouldn't it?'

He lay the tool down, picked up his mug and climbed to his feet.

'I need to walk around for a few minutes. My knees are in danger of locking down there. Can we walk?'

'Sure.'

And we made a slow lap of the garden.

'How long have you lived here?' I asked.

'Bought this flat about eleven years after I divorced, not long after they were first converted. I was sixty-five when I moved in.'

'Wow. I didn't think you were that old.'

'*That* old,' he echoed, placing an emphasis on the word I never had.

I laughed. 'I mean you're wearing well. I thought you rented, like me.'

'No, no. All the flats were up for sale once, when they were first converted. But three of them never sold, that's the two on the first floor and the one your friend lives in. The rest of us have stuck it out since the beginning. Says something good about the place I suppose.'

We'd walked past the car park and we were now on the back lawn where the leylandii blocked the view of the fields. 'These trees were about eighteen inches high. Well, that's a bit of an exaggeration. But not as high as my waist when I moved in. They'd planted them over the top of old flower beds and, for the first couple of years, other plants would appear. Nothing elaborate but lupins on this side and on your side, where there's less sun, hellebore and foxglove. All long gone now, of course. Although from time to time I'll slip in some bulbs or a shrub or two.'

'So, Matt's family owned this place?'

'Matt, is it?'

'Peterson Properties.'

'Yes, I know who you mean. Peterson was his mother's maiden name. I've lived in Wicken for a long time and I used to see his family back when he was a kid. Young Matthew liked pushing the boundaries. Snotty little brat. Your room was his old room, you know? And he used to sneak out at night through that back staircase. Probably going off to climb in girls' windows or steal cigarettes. His family have never lived here since I have. I wondered why they kept that flat on although he moved into it for a while.'

Frank stopped, took a couple of swigs of tea and seemed amused at whatever he was thinking. I wondered whether he was about to say something but he moved on again without comment.

'Did I say something funny?' I asked.

'No,' he said, 'I thought something funny.'

'Go on.'

'It's rude to gossip, isn't it?'

'Absolutely,' I said.

'Well, all right then. You know Mr and Mrs BMW, in the top flat?'

'Mr and Mrs Watts?'

'There was a bit of upstairs downstairs going on there, I can tell you.'

'Between who?'

'Your Mr Edwards and Mrs Watts.'

'You're kidding. She has to be, what, fifteen years older?'

'Well, well, young lady, I'm not sure if that's sexist or ageist or both. You wouldn't have made the comment if it had been the other way around, would you?'

He was right, of course, but I still failed to see what either would have seen in the other. 'Are you sure?'

'Absolutely. It's the only bit of drama I've had here in over a decade. They had a scrap on the landing, the men that is. Both went down the stairs. Mr Watts fractured his wrist. Matthew Edwards completely lost it. Ran outside, grabbed my long-handled hoe and swung it through the guy's windscreen. It was going to go to court and everything, but Edwards paid it. Settled quietly and agreed to clear off.'

'I'm not surprised. I mean he broke the guy's wrist.'

'He was lucky not to get a criminal record that time.'

'That time?'

'Well, any time. As far as I can work out, I don't think he's a bad person, but he does seem to have lived his life by overstepping the line and then stepping back again.'

'My friend's going out with him. Joanne.'

'Yeah, I know. I see what goes on. She might be just what he needs. It might be what they both need. And if not, well there's no point warning her off. People in love never listen, do they?'

TUESDAY 5 SEPTEMBER, 2017

I saw very little of Joanne for the next few days. I guess that was a good thing. It gave time for the awkwardness to subside. Even though she'd told me that things were okay between me and her, I still worried. But after two or three days that panicky feeling lessened. I watched them leave for school in the mornings, come back in the afternoons, and I listened for Matt, coming and going. Those arrivals and departures punctuated my days.

Everyone else carried on as normal. BMW man and his wife left separately and arrived separately, and I'd come to the conclusion that the matching cars had been bought in a fit of terrible irony. Even Maureen, the golf woman, seemed to time her rounds so precisely that she was always gone for three hours and never more than three and a half.

I tried watching television but it scared me how I could watch one programme and was already unable to recollect the programme that had just gone before. And I hated the adverts. The endless morning cycle of happy children and glorious domestic bliss and then the afternoon grind of life insurance and mobility aids. It felt like being fed expectations for what a proper life was supposed to look like, only broken by the lunchtime news and the horrible realisation of how fucked up the world had become.

I gave up on TV and tried turning to books instead. I'd read a chapter then pause, listen to the aching silence in the house, then read on again, trying to find that wonderful moment when the contents of the pages managed to shut out the rest of the world.

On the Monday afternoon, over a week after our chat in the garden, Frank knocked. I cracked the door open a couple of inches and assured him I was fine. And it was Tuesday evening before my contact with anyone was more than just watching the children out of the window. I knew it was Joanne. She always knocked twice and firmly. Similar to Frank but without his footsteps rattling on the stairs.

'Are you okay?' she called when I didn't answer the first time. Then she knocked again and I wondered whether she would give up or be resolute and stick it out for longer. But I answered.

'Are you okay?' she repeated.

'Yeah, I'm fine thanks. I just had stuff to do.'

She glanced past me, perhaps expecting to see new wallpaper or paint, or perhaps a sewing machine and yards of fabric.

'I was a bit under the weather,' I lied. 'I just decided to rest up and the last thing you want is me giving it to the children.'

'Absolutely. They pick up enough germs from school.'

I don't know whether I stepped back to let her in or whether she stepped forward and I let her past, but we both ended up sitting on the sofa and I offered her a drink.

She shook her head, 'No, I won't stop long. I just wanted to suggest something, a kind of way forward.'

I frowned.

Her hands were clasped in her lap and she released and re-threaded her fingers. She took a deep breath and the words tumbled out. 'I know you think I haven't known Matt for long and in one way I haven't, except of course I knew him from school, but, yes, you are right. It is a new relationship. But so is my friendship with you and rightly or wrongly I'm one of those people who doesn't take long to form close bonds and I miss all the friends I've left behind. As much as I love them, I'm starting again here, aren't I?'

I nodded, not sure where this was going.

'So, if I ask you for something, just to give Matt another chance, would you do that for me?'

It was her hopefulness that got to me.

'I don't hate him or anything,' I assured her. 'I was just worried about you.'

'Then please give him a chance. And I'm going to ask him the same. I'm making dinner on Thursday and I want it to be for you and for Matt, so I'd like you to both join me.'

I hesitated. She was right, of course. I didn't know him, but she was right in another way too: bonds and impressions can be formed very quickly and can be hard to undo. I loved her and I just didn't like Matt.

'And the children will be there,' she added as if that was what it would take to seal the deal.

I laughed. 'I was going to say yes anyway, but it's always nice to spend time with Molly and Luke. Can I make dessert?'

'Oh no,' she said, 'It's all taken care of. But a bottle of wine would go down well. Matt loves Malbec. And if you wanted to bring sweets or something like that for the children, I think they'd appreciate it. And thank you so much for Luke's birthday present. You should have knocked.'

'I didn't want to disturb you all.'

'Oh, don't be ridiculous. He'll write you a thank you note.'

'He doesn't need to. I'm only upstairs.'

'I know. Well. I would have brought him up to thank you himself but I've put him to bed. It's all that sugar, you know. I took him and some friends for some tea at the bowling alley and by the time they'd eaten a twelve-person birthday cake between the four of them it was "go wild for half an hour and crash". Luke's asleep already.'

'Did he like it?' I meant the present, not the cake, but as was often the case with Joanne, she followed my train of thought.

'He loves it. You can't go wrong with Lego. And he loves *Star Wars* too so he thinks the little Lego Ewoks are great. He called you a *ledge*.'

'Ledge?'

'Legend. You know?'

'Oh, I see. That's good then?'

'Yeah, it's up there with *epic*. Anyway, I appreciate it too. Thank you.'

THURSDAY 7 SEPTEMBER, 2017

I bought the wine but I didn't want to go too far, buying more things for the children. Not this time. So, I chose a big box of Maltesers and left it at that but I arrived with a board game as well, one we'd enjoyed playing several times before, just in case there was the right moment for it.

Molly grabbed my hand and tugged me through to the front room. I put the things on the table and sat between her and Luke as they told me about school. Joanne passed me a glass of white wine.

'You're honoured. I ask them what happens at school and they just say, "I don't remember."'

Matt was there already. I wasn't ignoring him but I already felt awkward. I took a few seconds to check out the room and noticed how signs of him were seeping in: a car magazine on the table, a candle he'd bought her on the mantelpiece and items of his clothing on the ironing pile. I turned back to him and we managed to make eye contact and nod briefly. It was another five minutes before Joanne left the room and I could distract the children with the game. I sat forward in my chair and spoke to him directly.

'I'm really sorry. We got off to a terrible start.'

He looked at me evenly.

'I'm here because Joanne wants this,' he said.

'Me too,' I replied, and that was where the conversation ended until dinner when we both tried harder because we had an audience.

Joanne didn't seem to notice that I never touched my wine. A couple of times I wandered into the kitchen and quietly tipped some of it down the sink and then thanked her when she topped up the glass again. There were signs of him in the kitchen, too, with his spare keys on a hook by the window and later, in the bathroom, I saw his toothbrush and Aventus aftershave. And the massage oil when I looked inside the bathroom cabinet.

Neither of them seemed to drink much. We moved on to a second bottle, though, and the volume and pitch of our conversation gradually rose. The topics became more adult and I really wanted to take the kids off to play the game on the coffee table, but I knew that would have been seen as anti-social so I stuck it out.

'You don't work do you, Emily?' said Matt, with a smile and interest that looked genuine.

'Not at the moment,' I told him.

'That's funny. Letting agents don't normally take the unemployed.'

I didn't bite. 'I decided to take some time out. I'm not exactly unemployed. I will get a job but this is a paid break.'

'Ah,' he said.

Joanne nudged him. 'Since when are you employed?'

'I earn money,' he said, 'that's the same thing.'

'You collect rents.'

'I'm an architect.'

'You're a property developer.'

'I trained as an architect.'

'Okay, but you don't practise do you?'

The conversation between them was mostly playful but I could sense there was an edge to it too. Joanne was touching a nerve. Matt was trying hard not to react.

I tried to change the subject.

'What about you, Joanne?'

'Professional mum.'

'No, I meant before that. Before you had kids.'

'I was a project manager, actually. That's how I met my husband.'

'What sort of projects?'

'Software implementation. Though you wouldn't believe it.'

She waved in the direction of the table and I guess she was implying that all that domesticity didn't fit with the idea of somebody who'd worked in the IT industry.

'My role wasn't that technical actually. It was about making sure that people had the training they needed and the practical side of implementation. So, maybe seeing if their computer or printer needed an upgrade, data migration, that kind of thing. How many project manager roles are really glorified admin? Mine was.'

Matt shook his head and looked at me. 'She's underplaying it. She made a good career out of it. I remember seeing her Facebook posts. They were "Promotion, new project, promotion, new project." And then "Oh my God, I'm pregnant." I didn't think you'd be one of these women who knocked your career on the head just because you had a baby.'

'That's because I wasn't. I didn't stop working until I'd had Luke. When he arrived, trying to juggle kids with a career really did become too much. Besides . . .' Her voice trailed away. 'Perhaps I would have gone back to work, but things didn't work out the way I planned.'

There was a long silence, broken by nothing but the sound of cutlery on dishes. Molly spoke next and her little voice is firm. 'Mummy means because Daddy and Connor died.'

Then she looked at me. 'Connor was my brother.'

It wouldn't have been right to baulk at the subject.

'I know,' I said. 'Your mummy told me. What was he like?'

'Bigger than me. And funny I think. I can remember he made me laugh.'

She smiled at the memory but this slipped into a frown. 'It was a long time ago and Luke doesn't remember much at all.'

'I do.'

They were the first words Luke had spoken since he'd been at the table.

'He took my Han Solo action figure and sold it to his friend.'

'Luke,' Joanne chipped in, 'That's not what happened.'

'I can remember.'

'He didn't mean to do it,' Molly said and the two children glared at one another from opposite sides of the table.

I caught Joanne's eye.

'Is it a good time to play a game with them?' I whispered.

'Please do. Come on, Matt. Let's make the coffees.'

Luke was too tired to play properly and it wasn't as fun as the time we had played it upstairs, when it was just the three of us.

'It's your bedtime, Luke.' I checked myself and added, 'Probably.'

Joanne was bringing the coffees. I glanced across at her, checking that I hadn't said too much.

'No, she's right. You two get your pyjamas on and, if you're lucky, Emily will read you a story. Do you mind?'

'No, of course not.'

And I did read to them. Luke first, and only a few pages. He was lying under his Darth Vader duvet. The bed was low and I sat on the floor with an elbow on the mattress. After a couple of pages, I could hear my own voice begin to croak with tiredness so I told him he could carry on looking at the pictures and I went to the next room to see Molly. At first, I thought she was asleep but she was just pretending. Her eyes were closed and her lashes made dark crescents on her face but they flickered as soon as I sat on the edge of her mattress.

'Which book are you reading?' I asked.

'I don't want you to read to me. Would you make one up?'

'Oh, no. I can't do that.'

'Why?'

'Because I'm not very good. I wouldn't know where to start.'

'Oh. My dad used to make up stories for me. Perhaps men are better at it because Mum's not so good either.'

'Maybe,' I agreed.

'Mum's not so good at cooking either. Dad used to make this spaghetti. I think it was the best spaghetti ever. It wasn't straight though, it was wavy.'

'I expect it was fusilli lunghi.'

She shrugged. 'He called it Rapunzeletti-spaghetti and it was extra-long and you could never suck it all in in one go. It would go on and on and on. Mum's tastes the same but it isn't as much fun.' She rolled over onto her side and I stroked her cheek. 'Do you like Matt?' she suddenly asked.

'Well,' and there I was, caught between the truth and diplomacy. 'Your mum likes him, doesn't she?'

'But I don't think he likes children much,' she said. 'He's a bit boring and when I tell him anything I don't think he listens.' In the half-light, I could see that she was screwing her nose in distaste. 'He bought Luke a book for his birthday.'

'That's not so bad.'

'It was a science book,' she whispered.

I had to fight to stop myself from smiling.

'Ah. Well, sometimes, when people are not used to having children they don't know how to behave.'

'That's what Mum says.'

'Does that make sense?'

'I guess,' she said.

She sighed deeply and her eyes closed again.

'Are you okay?' I asked her.

She gave the tiniest nod. 'I'm going to sleep now.'

FRIDAY 8 SEPTEMBER, 2017

I didn't remember much about the rest of the evening.

I still don't.

The next I knew, I was waking up on Joanne's sofa. Before I opened my eyes, I was trying to work out where I was and I felt the disorientation of realising that I wasn't in my own bed. My head was at an awkward angle, one shoulder twisted under me. I moved my arm very gradually and opened my eyes.

At first, I saw nothing but a rectangle of light peeping around closed curtains. Then, as my eyes adjusted, I traced the outline of the table and chairs by the window and the coffee table closest to me. It was too dark to see my watch but from the way the light still looked grey and insipid, I guessed it was around half past five.

I wanted to slip back to my flat but as I pushed myself upright, my head began to thump and I could feel pressure pulsing behind my eyes. I groaned and even that hurt. I managed to make it into a sitting position. I had to, it was the only way to restore the circulation in my aching shoulder and help the stiffness in my neck, but it was hard to get any further. I knew as the daylight became more intense, so would the pain in my eyes.

It was long time since I'd had a headache like this, alcohol induced or otherwise. I stayed put for a while and then when it felt safe, made my way to the kitchen where I hung over the sink and ran the water until it warmed slightly, because I knew that drinking it cold would hurt too much. I was still like that when I heard Molly's voice.

'My mum's sick.' She was right behind me.

I gripped the edge of the sink and turned towards her.

'What's wrong with her?'

'Her head hurts and she said she's going to throw up.'

I nodded but it made the pounding worse. 'Where's Matt?'

She shrugged. 'He doesn't live here, you know.'

Then I realised that last night had been a Thursday; I had no recollection of him leaving but if it had been like other weeks he would have gone to Cambridge.

Molly's expression was disapproving. 'Did you both drink alcohol?' she asked.

'No, no we didn't.'

'I saw the wine,' she said.

'We didn't drink much and this isn't a hangover. It's something else, maybe something we ate.'

'Uh-huh.'

Just the few words I'd spoken hurt too much but I asked Molly to take me through to see her mum. It was the first time I'd been in Joanne's bedroom. I hadn't even glanced at it in passing. The door had always been shut.

I don't know what I expected. Certainly not pinks and frills, but the room was more romantic than I imagined, with a wooden sleigh bed and covers and curtains that were heavily embroidered. It reminded me of a fairy-tale. Not the Disney kind. More like Brothers Grimm. And Joanne was lying there in the centre of the bed, half propped between two great cushions.

She had a bowl on her lap and her skin shone, heavy with sweat. I leant against the door frame.

'I didn't think I'd drunk this much,' she breathed, panting heavily.

I was struggling to stand still and I wondered how long before I would be as close to throwing up as she clearly was.

'How are you feeling? You look like you're struggling too. I don't think you drank as much as me though, did you?'

'No. No, I didn't. Do you want water?' I asked.

She was barely able to shake her head. Then she pressed her hand across her eyes and groaned.

194

'I don't understand. Could it be something we ate?'

'We all ate the same,' I pointed out, 'apart from the coffee of course. That was just the two of us, wasn't it?'

'Shit. You don't get food poisoning from coffee.' She began to move towards the edge of the bed.

'No, stay there.'

'No, the children need to go to school.'

'No, just stay there. I can do it,' I told her.

'Okay. In the kitchen, on the top shelf of the cupboard beside the sink, there's painkillers. Migraine tablets, paracetamol, co-codamol. Just help yourself if you want a couple . . .' She paused mid-sentence and didn't speak again for several seconds. 'Can you . . .?'

I nodded.

I took two myself and the act of swallowing them made me nauseous but I hurried back to her with painkillers and a glass of water.

'They'll sort it out. We just need to wait,' she said. 'How are you feeling?'

'It hurts,' I tell her, 'but I'm not feeling sick yet.' Then I spotted Molly standing in her doorway, looking wide eyed and unsure. I smile at her.

'Maybe your mum and I did drink a little too much.'

'Shall I get ready for school then?' she asked.

'Can you wake Luke up?'

'Uh-huh,' she nodded.

'I'll drive you both. And don't worry, your mum will be fine when you get home.'

By the time they were ready to go, the edge of it had gone. The painkillers were beginning to work but I drove the car gingerly, relieved that I hadn't really drunk any alcohol the night before and feeling sorry for Joanne, suffering a hangover on top of whatever this was. I waited in the playground and watched them line up, I made sure they had everything they needed and waved to each of them in turn as their line disappeared inside their classrooms.

By the time I returned, the pain had become muted and the threat of feeling sick had materialised into nothing more than slight queasiness. Gerald the postman was on the drive. He wound down his window as I was driving in and he was coming out.

'You had a package,' he said. 'I knocked downstairs. It needed signing for, so it's in at number 1.' He beamed at me with his best good-morning smile. 'She looks rough and you don't look much better yourself.'

I nodded slowly. 'Must be a bug,' I told him and he replied with something cheerful and several decibels too loud.

As soon as I walked through the main entrance, I saw Joanne's front door was open wide. To my knowledge this had only ever happened when she was inside and the children were playing in the garden. For a split second, I felt an irrational burst of fear, but as soon as I reached the doorway I saw her curled on the sofa, hot-water bottle plastered across her stomach. Despite that, she looked better.

'How are you?' she asked.

'Better now, thanks. You look like you've perked up too.'

'Thank God. A parcel arrived for you. I had to answer the door to sign for it. I couldn't face standing up again so I left the flat wide open.'

There was a small bookcase just inside the door and on top of it was a parcel. It was a small package, maybe fifteen centimetres square, with a slight bulge in the centre.

'It had to be signed for,' she explained.

'I know, I saw Gerald. I'm not expecting anything.'

'Oh, I order things all the time. I forget I've done it and then a parcel will arrive and it will be a book or a DVD that slipped my mind.'

'Well, this doesn't look like either.' I picked it up and sat next to her on the sofa. She had closed her eyes again.

There was no clue on the outside, apart from the fact that it had come from somewhere in the UK and, although I wasn't expecting anything, I wasn't paying particular attention as I tugged the packaging apart. I was too preoccupied telling Joanne about Molly and Luke going into school.

I opened it at one end so that I was looking down on a little gaping pouch. I saw something rounded and a flash of bright pink. It was then I frowned. I still hadn't a clue. I reached inside, so I felt it before I saw it. It was smooth and firm, and I guessed what it was. Joanne started at my gasp. I pulled the vibrator out of the packaging in disbelief. I looked at Joanne in bewilderment. She looked at it and then looked at me and grinned.

'Woah. That's too much information.'

'It's not mine.'

Joanne said, 'It's okay. You are single, it's just personal, that's all. I don't judge.'

'No. It's really not mine.'

Rather than drop it back into the envelope, I pushed the envelope onto the coffee table and dumped the vibrator on top. I wiped my hands on my jeans as though they were contaminated. 'Someone sent me that.'

Joanne's smile's faded. 'How do you mean? Do you mean you didn't order it?'

'Of course I didn't order it.'

'Well . . .'

'Well nothing. Why would I?'

'You are on your own. And even if you weren't . . .'

'Seriously.'

The fact that she clearly thought I was just embarrassed at what I'd bought rattled me more.

'You have to believe me.' I could hear panic in my tone. 'I'm not lying. I have nothing to do with that.' My cheeks were burning.

'Hey.' She reached her hand towards me and placed it on top of mine. 'Okay, I just thought you were embarrassed.'

'I'm not embarrassed. If I wanted to order a fucking vibrator I'd order one. You don't know what's going on.'

'Okay. Tell me then.'

'Someone's been sending me hate mail. And I thought it had stopped. There's been nothing and now this.'

Joanne reached for the envelope, tipping the vibrator onto the table. She felt inside for anything else. 'There's no note in it. How can it be a threat if there's nothing in it?'

'There's nothing there?'

She dropped the envelope on to her lap and grabbed my hand. 'Oh God, Emily. You're shaking.'

'Why can't they just leave me alone?'

'Who?'

'I don't know who. I just wanted to get away and start here and not have to be . . .' I caught my breath. 'I don't want anything about my old life to follow me here.'

Joanne wrapped her arms around me then. 'Just bin it. Bin it and forget about it. Everything's going to be all right.'

I left the delivery in my underwear drawer. It was back in its envelope and I had no intention of doing anything with it apart from throwing it away. But I couldn't quite bring myself to do that. I was sure there would be a way of tracing the sender or at the least the post office it had originated from, but right now I had other things that were pressing. My headache was still there but I could cope and Joanne had managed to stay out of bed too. I was glad she was well enough to be left by herself because the urge to drive to Cambridge was pressing hard on me.

First things first, though, I used the internet to search for Matt Edwards and his company, Peterson Properties. I tried other companies that claimed to give more detailed financial reports but spent another £50 to discover nothing new.

The company's official address was a building in Station Road. I made a note of it and took that with me. As a city, Cambridge is small but driving from one part to another can seem to take a disproportionate length of time.

I started with the registered address and, when I arrived, found nothing but an accountancy firm. I was stone-walled by the receptionist who informed me that a registered address meant nothing more than that.

I drove from there to the centre of town and parked up in a multi-storey. I left the car for the rest of the day, even though the parking charges would be astronomical. The Central Library was in the middle of the shopping centre and it was there that I began my search through the newspaper archives. I was imagining fiche readers and photocopiers, as it had been when I'd studied for my A levels. But there was nothing like that now. The newspapers had been digitised.

Peterson Properties brought up no results. I was luckier when

I typed Matt's name. He came up three times: for a drink driving offence when he was twenty-four and a fine for anti-social behaviour a year after that. His final appearance was at the age of twenty-nine when he'd pleaded not guilty to an assault on a girlfriend. Her name was Melissa McKenzie and there was a side-profile of him as he hurried into court, his head bowed. He'd been a sharp dresser then too. He claimed they had both been drunk, that there had been 'mutual shoving'. He claimed it was self-defence when he'd pushed her to the ground and she'd hit her head on a railing, leaving her with bruises to the side of her face.

I don't know why, but I expected that he would have dodged the conviction. I retrieved the paper from the following day and found that he hadn't. He'd received a suspended sentence and had been forced to pay her compensation. I jotted down her name and the details of where she worked and her age. It wasn't much but it was something.

Melissa McKenzie was easy to find. I traced her to an address just out of town in Camborne but I found her Facebook profile too, where she proudly announced that she worked as a dental hygienist and, not only that, named the practice too. It was a half-mile walk from the library and I arrived at ten past one to find it closed. According to the sign on the door, lunch ran from twelve-thirty to one-thirty. It didn't strike me as very customer friendly to refuse appointments over lunchtime. But then again, perhaps the dentist didn't want to see people when they still had remnants of Cornish pasty stuck in their teeth.

I hung around, hoping that she had left the building and that I could catch her as she returned.

At twenty-five past, a black Mini Cooper pulled into the car park. The driver was attractive and looked the right age; good odds then that this was Melissa. Her make-up was heavy, too orange for my taste with too much mascara, but hey, it was none of my business. I walked over so I was there as she opened the driver's door. Even though we were outside, I wanted to be able to speak quietly, to keep the conversation private.

She looked up at me with a question on her lips.

'Melissa?'

'Yes?'

'I'm sorry to bother you. I need your help.'

'We're not quite open yet.'

'No. It's about Matt Edwards.'

Instantly, her expression became closed. 'What about him?'

'He's going out with a friend of mine . . .'

'Lucky her.'

'The thing is, I'm worried for her.'

'And?'

'I read about his conviction in the paper. I just wanted to know, was that a one-off? Or is that what he's like?'

She stepped out of her car and locked the door without replying. She walked past me and began to unlock the door of the dental surgery. Finally, she spoke, 'I don't want to go back over it.'

'I'm sorry. I just need to ask. I have this bad feeling about him.'

'He's edgy. That's all I'll say. He's not a bad guy, but he's not a good one either. You know, people that walk along that line, he's one of them. That's all I'll say.'

'My friend has kids.'

She stopped then, one hand on the door handle. 'I doubt it will last then. He's not the family type.'

'Well, should I be worried about them?'

She raised her free hand in a *how should I know?* gesture. 'What do you want? I'm not going to start flinging accusations around. Things turned sour between me and him. Don't try to read anything else into that. If I'd ever thought he was genuinely dodgy then I wouldn't have stayed with him for six months, would I?'

'People do.'

She shook her head. 'I don't. That was the one and only time he went too far and I made him pay, didn't I?'

But she stopped halfway through the door, then she turned back to me with a small smile on her lips. 'Of course, if your friend has money, it might last.'

I made it halfway across the car park before I turned and hurried back.

'Where can I find his sister?

'Gemma?'

'Uh-huh.'

It was the first time I'd heard a name.

'Why?' she asked, and continued to speak without giving me time to reply. 'I don't know you and I'm not handing out someone's private details.'

Melissa's expression told me she was already regretting saying as much as she had.

'I want to talk to her, that's all.'

She shook her head. 'You're pushing for a lot of information. What's your angle?'

'I don't have one.' It wasn't meant to be my final word but in reply she snapped a photo of me with her phone, muttered 'Just in case' and turned away.

Gemma Edwards. The name was enough. I spent another £10 on online searches and found her address; a flat, overlooking the market square and within yards of the 12A club. I recognised the block from the outside. Flats above shops, some with tiny balconies that appeared too shallow for more than a flowerpot or two. It took me several minutes to find the entrance and when I did, I was faced with an intercom.

I didn't want to ring up and have to say who I was before I'd had the chance to see her face. I looked around. I could see no sign of a camera so I guessed she would be working from my voice alone, so I buzzed anyway.

The intercom crackled and then she answered.

'Yes?'

'I have a delivery. I need you to sign,' I told her.

'Hang on. I'll just find a cardigan.' Her accent had more of a London edge than Matt's. She sounded chirpy and young. And I waited nearly thirty seconds before the frosted glass door opened and there she was, the same girl that I'd seen with him.

She looked at me and then down at my hands and saw that I was holding nothing. Then she looked back at my face. Recognition slowly dawned. 'What do you want?' The tailend of her smile remained.

What did I want?

I'd half-convinced myself that there was no sister or that she would be somebody else and that the woman I'd seen him with was still an illicit lover. I wanted to ask her what Matt wanted with Joanne, whether he wanted her money or something else. Like she was going to answer any of those things. So, I just stood there while she called out his name and when I heard his footsteps pounding down the stairs, I turned and I ran.

There were two extra cars in the car park when I returned home. One was a police car and the other belonged to Mum and Dad. I parked up but kept the engine running for a couple of minutes, still undecided whether to go in or drive away. But what the fuck was the point?

I looked up at the house; my lights weren't on, but Frank's were. He stood at his window and raised his hand at me, more of an acknowledgement than a wave. Joanne's lights were on too and I knew she'd heard my car because the door opened as I stepped in to the hallway. I could tell she was worried.

'Your mum and dad are here.'

I nodded.

'We didn't know how long you'd be so I've made them tea.'

'And the police?' I asked.

She managed a small apologetic smile. 'Them too. I'm sorry. Matt called them.'

I glanced at my watch. It was past eight o'clock and I had no idea where the time had gone.

'Are the children in bed?'

'Don't worry,' she said, 'they're awake but their doors are shut. They won't bother us.'

My parents and the two policemen all sat around the coffee table. They had drinks but all the mugs stood untouched. Somehow the awkwardness of the silence made the people look too big for the room and the scene would have been slightly ridiculous if it hadn't been that they were waiting for me.

'Can we go up to my flat?' I asked and I mouthed 'I'm sorry' at Joanne. I really didn't want to sit there and do this; I didn't need my only friend to find out about my screwed-up life. Not yet, anyway.

'I do need to talk to you,' she whispered quickly to me as I followed my parents into the hallway. I tried to read her expression to find out whether time was up on our friendship after all.

'It's about Matt,' she said.

'Not now. I need to talk to you, too. I didn't mean to cause trouble,' I breathed, 'but there are things you need to know.'

She shook her head and echoed my words. 'Not now, not now.'

I let the two policemen usher me up the stairs, my parents followed and the five of us went into my flat.

They wanted a statement from me. They asked me what happened and used the word 'harassment'.

'I haven't been harassing anyone. What I want to know is how I can find out if someone has convictions?'

One of the policemen looked a few years younger than me. I didn't catch his name. He made exhaustive notes and pressed his lips tightly whenever he appeared to be thinking. He said little.

His colleague was in his forties. Sergeant Maldon, a round-faced man, too stocky to be healthy, I thought. His voice was calm, matter of fact, like he'd heard it all before and nothing was going to surprise him.

'So, you went to Cambridge today with the intention of what, Miss Jenkins?'

'Finding out about Matt Edwards.'

'Why?'

'He's dating my friend and I'm not convinced he's being honest with her.'

'And this friend is Joanne Carter, your neighbour?'

'That's correct.'

'And it's your business because?'

'Because she's my friend, of course.'

'And what exactly is it that you think this Mr Edwards is about to do?'

'I don't know that he's about to *do* anything.'

Maldon pursed his lips as he listened to my reply and it had the effect of making his face look fatter.

'Okay. What makes you think that he's a concern? Are you aware of any violence towards your friend or her children? Has he threatened her in any way? Has he threatened you?'

'He told me to keep away.' I knew it sounded lame. 'I felt threatened,' I added.

'He claims that you've been following him.' I glanced across at my parents and it was my dad's expression that stalled me. He looked helpless. Stricken.

I didn't reply.

'Have you?'

Dad hissed my name under his breath. Mum's right hand was pressed to her face.

'Yes, I wanted to find out where he was going when he left here each night.'

'So, you followed him to Cambridge?'

I nodded.

'How many times?'

'I don't know.'

'But more than once?'

'Yes.'

'Twice? Three times? Five? More.'

'Maybe.'

'Maybe what?'

'Maybe more than five.' My dad shook his head and Mum closed her eyes. The policeman did neither.

'And one of these occasions involved an altercation between you and Mr Edwards. Is that correct?'

'Yes.'

'Do you have a reasonable explanation for your behaviour, Miss Jenkins?'

I looked at them all looking at me, the unimpressed expressions. I gave up then and that was exactly what I hoped they would do. But of course they didn't: they waited for my *reasonable explanation*.

'I was just worried about my friend and her children.' I drew a slow breath, wanting the deliberate pause to seem as though I was carefully considering the situation. 'It's not my business who she dates, I know that. I'm sorry.'

'Hmm. Sorry doesn't fix this.' Maldon looked up from his notes, one eyebrow raised. 'Mr Edwards and his sister have made a serious allegation. Miss Edwards felt threatened by you.'

'I never threatened her. I'm sorry if I upset her, but I never threatened her.'

Dad's jaw was set hard and Mum's hand was now clasped in his on his lap. Her face was pale and I noticed for the first time that she'd lost a great deal of weight since the trial. I took a new breath and tried my best to sound contrite.

'I really am sorry,' I told the older officer. The words were genuine, but only for Mum.

'Well,' he feigned reluctance, 'we have details of what occurred today and on this occasion, we won't take it any further, but I need your assurance that it won't happen again.'

'It won't, I promise.'

'Right then.'

And thankfully that seemed to be enough.

The two large men in their bulky uniforms left and the flat immediately felt bigger without them. I expected Dad to shout at me as soon as the door was shut, but it seemed he had nothing to say. Neither of them did, and in so many ways that was worse than them saying too much. When I suggested they leave, Mum finally spoke.

'I want you to go back to Dr Lahiri. He needs to adjust your dose of those anti-depressants.'

'I'm not depressed.'

'You're not thinking straight. What do you do all day? Just sit in here?' The worry was written on her face but her tone remained firm and determined.

'No.'

'Then what *do* you do? You don't have a job. You have too much time to dwell on things, to make trouble for other people. It's obvious you're depressed. Or worse. Go back and see him.'

'I'm not depressed. And I'm not making this up.'

'Are you sure?' Mum leant towards me. 'Are you sure you're not trying to find fault with this Matt for other reasons?'

'Like what?'

Finally, Dad spoke.

'Because it's a repeat of Jess and Andy. Because you're jealous. Because you've made a friend and you can't stand sharing her.'

It wasn't so much that he'd said it that rankled. It was that he wasn't the first. But I wasn't prepared to back down. 'I think he's after her for her money,' I replied.

Mum grabbed my hand then and pulled me closer.

'So what if he is? It's not any of your business. Joanne's down there and she's scared about what she needs to tell you. She wants your friendship but you have to let her get on with her life and I'm going to come straight out and say it. She and Matt are getting married.'

I drew a breath like the news had hit me in the stomach.

'They can't.'

Mum gripped my hand tighter. 'They can and if they don't it can't be because you tried to stop it or wrecked things for them. Let this go and you might save your friendship. She cares about you but if she wants to marry him . . .' She didn't finish her sentence. 'Just go and see Dr Lahiri.'

MONDAY 11 SEPTEMBER, 2017

I unpacked the tablets. The pharmacy had put them in an oversized paper bag but there were just three small packets. I stacked them on the windowsill. Mum had gone with me. She didn't say a word but I knew she'd been ready to jump in if I had been anything less than open with what I told Dr Lahiri.

I obviously said what Mum needed to hear. He listened and he didn't judge but, because he said nothing, I ended up churning over everything he might have been thinking and the least insulting of those was that I had been stupid and that I'd brought it on myself.

I'd seen no one since I'd been back. The car park was empty and, as far as I was aware, I was the only person in the building. I regretted paying the rent so far ahead. I couldn't afford to just move out.

In the end, I made a mug of tea and I took the narrow servants' stairs down to the garden and stood in the doorway, knowing that if anyone came home, I could disappear back into my flat without the need for any awkward small talk.

There wasn't much to see out there and I sat on the back step and stared at the patchy grass and the row of leylandii. That part of the garden remained sunless in the afternoon and I understood why all of Frank's efforts went elsewhere.

I expected to hear if any other car arrived but I didn't. The first I knew was when Molly came running around the corner. She wasn't looking for me, of course, and I startled her when I spoke. 'Molly?'

She seemed more hesitant than usual. Coy. She came near me but not quite within touching distance. She still wore her school uniform, a little grey pinafore with a white blouse underneath and stood with her feet together, her black Mary-Janes perfectly level with one another.

'How was school?'

'Good, thank you.' She tilted her head to one side. 'Why are you here?'

'I wanted some fresh air. I thought I'd sit in the garden.'

'But you're not. You're sitting on the step.'

'I know, but most of me is in the garden.'

'You should come to the front. Me and Luke like the front best because it's sunny and there's more space. I hid in one of those bushes. Then I itched afterwards.'

'What are you playing now?'

'Oh, I'm hiding, but I don't think he's looking for me. He's boring.'

'Not always.'

'Yes, he is. I love him because he's my brother, but he is boring. But if I could swap him, I think I'd swap him for my friend Elouise. She's never boring.'

'No?'

'Never.'

Even when Molly stood still, she continued to fidget. Like watching a butterfly on a leaf when it's trying to be motionless but the edges of its wings still flicker.

'Your mum will be wondering where you are.'

'No, she won't. She knows I'm in the garden.'

'Okay. Well, I think your mum's cross with me at the moment.'

'Why?'

'Grown-up stuff.'

'Because you fell asleep on our sofa?'

I smiled at that one. 'No. Because I was cross about something.'

'About Mummy's boyfriend?'

'That's right.'

'Is that why the police were here?'

'I thought you were asleep?'

210

'I don't like to go to sleep,' she whispered, 'that really is the boring bit.'

'Do you know you grow when you're asleep?'

'Yeah. But nobody stays this size. I'm going to grow even if I don't sleep, aren't I?'

'But you'll grow more if you do.'

'I asked Mummy if you'd been naughty.'

'What did she say?'

'She said sometimes people do bad things because they're sad.'

'Oh.'

'Are you sad?'

'Sometimes.'

Molly frowned then turned away. She walked in circles on the grass for a few seconds, studying the grass, then bent down and came back to me. She held out her hand. It was a clover leaf.

'I couldn't find one with four, but I tried.'

She dropped it into the palm of my hand and I picked it up again, holding it between my forefinger and thumb, twirling the stem so the clover-head span. 'Thank you.'

She reached forward, hugged me quickly and then ran away.

I took the three-leafed clover, laid it out in the light of the kitchen window sill and photographed it. I made it the wallpaper on my phone, then pressed the head between the pages of a book.

It is funny how the little things in life are the ones that bridge the biggest divides. I didn't want to lose Joanne as my friend, but more than that, I didn't want to have to say goodbye to Molly and Luke.

Each time I unlocked my phone, there was her clover with its little green face staring out at me.

My parents often said they didn't have technology when they were growing, so they wouldn't miss twenty-four hours without communication the way I would. They were right: I would struggle without it. I checked my texts and emails regularly. I wasn't expecting anybody to get in touch. I just hoped somebody would, but it would have been more sensible to switch the thing off.

At five past ten in the evening, it bleeped. I thought it would be Mum, but it was Joanne.

Can we talk?

The answer was easy. *Yes. Of course.* But my finger hovered over the reply. I typed it then deleted. I wanted to say more than that. To explain myself a little while I knew she was listening. But those were the things I needed to say to her, face-to-face. So in the end I replied: *When?*

And she replied: *Now?*

I pulled my old college hoodie over my pyjamas and was about to go down to her when there was a quiet knock at the door. She pre-empted my first question.

'It's fine. They're asleep.' And she came in through the doorway, giving me a slightly wide berth.

We sat and I began to say something, but she held up her hand.

'I need to go first here. Matt and I are getting married.'

I nodded. 'I know, my mum told me.'

'Okay. We're going to live here to begin with and I don't want things to be awkward. No, more than that. I want things to be good.'

'I don't see how . . .' I began.

She didn't reply immediately, and then said, 'Neither do I, not yet anyway. But let's face it, Matt is often out. I thought perhaps I could separate our friendship and my marriage. You know, keep the two things apart so you and he won't have to cross paths.'

'But why would you do that?'

'Because you are a genuine friend and, if I'm honest, I do understand.'

'My behaviour?'

'No, your worries. He's . . .' She searched for the word, her gaze roving the room as if an honest insult might be hanging on a picture hook. 'He has a bit of a chequered past, put it that way. But don't we all? I mean who makes it to thirty or older without a whole load of baggage? Look at me. He's taken me on with two kids in tow.'

'That's not a disadvantage,' I argued.

'Are you kidding? I love them but I feel like I'm lucky to have met somebody.'

Joanne was a long way beyond pretty. She would still be turning heads when she was fifty. 'You'd have met somebody,' I told her.

She cocked her head to one side. 'But that's what I have done.'

'How sure are you, Jo?'

She spread out her fingers and gazed at her engagement ring. It was the first time I'd seen it but I couldn't bring myself to ask for a closer look. I could see it was a solitaire, a square cut diamond set in white gold. I hoped it was cubic zirconia and stainless steel.

'I'm sure.' But her reply is too slow to convince me. 'Look, we are just going ahead with it.'

'When?'

'This weekend. I don't see any point in holding back.'

I was stunned and I don't think I hid it either. 'But you hardly know him.'

'We've been together four months.'

'Get a prenup,' I blurted.

Joanne's laugh tinkled. 'I thought they were an American invention? We've made wills but not a prenup. It's not a business arrangement, Emily, this is the real thing. For life.'

'You hope, like everyone does when they marry.' And then her words sunk in. 'Wait, you've made your wills?'

She shrugged, 'It's important when you have children, I've learnt that much.'

'So it was your idea?'

'Emily, it doesn't matter. There's nothing to worry about. I know I can trust him, and don't forget, I already knew him.'

'Yeah, at school.' I sounded dubious as I didn't see what difference that made, but I could also see that Joanne wasn't the tiniest bit perturbed by my concerns.

'Underneath his attitude he's a really decent guy.' Then without warning she became serious. 'Come to the wedding?' she asked.

I frowned and shook my head, bewildered now. 'Are you kidding?'

'No, please. I'm not telling my family. And I want somebody there.'

'The police have just visited because of the way I've behaved towards him; he won't want me there.'

'It's a wedding. It's the bride's big day, isn't it? And you should be there for Molly and Luke. They love you.'

It was the first time I had smiled for a while and I felt my cheeks flush. 'I love them too. They're brilliant kids.'

'Well, then. Decision made.' She hugged me, holding me tightly. 'I know you don't like him but I love him, Emily – try to be pleased for me.' I nodded and reminded myself that the marriage would inevitably fail and I would be there then.

TUESDAY 12 SEPTEMBER, 2017

I had set my alarm early for the next morning. I rose quickly, I rinsed my face and then, as I dried it, I caught sight of myself in the mirror. If I was brutally honest, I knew I could look attractive on a good day. But not like Joanne.

When I look back at my wedding photos, I realise that I didn't have to worry as much as I thought I did. Ben and I were a good match. If I didn't know Matt and just saw a photograph, I would have said the same about him and Joanne. Yeah, he was good looking, but so was she and not in a tarty, head-turning way like his sister.

Joanne had class and strength too. But last night she'd had doubts: if they hadn't been there in what she'd said, I'd definitely felt them. She had made it clear that she needed me and she didn't have to worry; I would be there for her and the children.

I leant closer to the mirror. My skin looked pale and there were dark shadows around my eyes. I stopped long enough to apply some make-up and then I headed to Cambridge. I wanted to be there at the police station when he arrived. I made sure I dressed warmly and prepared myself to wait for as long as it took. In the end though, I arrived just twenty minutes before him and fell into step with DI Briggs as he walked up East Road.

'Can I talk to you for a minute?' My voice sounded thin and too uncertain.

He didn't miss a step and kept moving at exactly the same pace. 'You can speak to me at the station if you need to.'

'It's really important.'

'About what?'

He glanced at me but immediately averted his gaze again.

'I want to know how I can find out about someone's criminal record, or whether they've been in trouble but not actually charged.'

'Like you, you mean?'

I took no notice. I wasn't sure whether it was his way of trying to stir up a bit of banter between us, although I didn't think so. I think he wanted me to walk away.

'My friend's getting married and the man she's marrying, he's . . . trouble.'

'Trouble?'

'He's using her, I can feel it.'

'And what do you know about him?'

'He's a property developer. That's how he earns his money. And he hit his ex-girlfriend and he was done for drunk driving and cautioned for anti-social behaviour.'

Finally, he slowed. 'So, you know all those things already? What more do you expect to find?'

'I don't know what else there is.'

'People with criminal records get married all the time, Emily.'

'I know that.'

'What proof do you have that he's actually a danger to your friend? And even if he is, isn't that her decision?'

'I know all that, but . . .' I ran out of words. I stopped walking and he stopped too.

'But nothing. Let it go, Emily.'

He frowned as he studied me. He seemed to think for several seconds before he spoke.

'I get the feeling that you've changed since the trial.'

I nodded, mute.

'Back then, you were in shock, but now . . . Are you working?'

'No.'

'Do you have support from your family? Your friends?'

'I see my mum sometimes.' I wanted to explain more but it seemed impossible to condense it all down to a couple of sentences. I shrugged.

'But you have this one friend?'

'That's right.'

I saw where this was going.

'You can't stop people from taking risks or doing things you feel are a bad idea, even if it is someone you care about. I have teenage kids. Don't you think every single week I'm thinking, *Please don't do that*? But I can't make their choices for them. Find yourself a job, Emily. Any job. Make yourself stay busy and I really do hope things work out for you.' He reached out, shook my hand and said good-bye. He left me on the corner by the fire station with pedestrians and people moving in all directions and me, the only one standing still.

That afternoon I visited Mum. Matt and Joanne were finalising plans for the wedding. The ceremony itself had been booked for Saturday at the registry office in Cambridge and I didn't see how they had much to plan for that; it would be one of those in-and-out affairs. But they were going over everything in detail.

Joanne had hoped I would occupy the children once they came out of school but I went to Mum's instead and apologised because I wouldn't be back in time. Dad was out at work. All in all, everything was for the best.

Mum made lunch. Just jacket potato, oven-baked, but she'd bought in fresh salmon and fussed around with a salad, arranging it in a pretty arc on the side of the plate. I hadn't wanted her to make a fuss; I just wanted her to treat it like any other time. Just to throw something together and hope for the best. But she'd tidied the kitchen for me too and it left me feeling like a distant relative who had stopped by for a visit. I didn't mean that as criticism, but that was how it was.

As we ate she ran through a chronology of the things they'd done since I'd last seen her. 'We're thinking about Crete,' she told me.

I couldn't think of the appropriate reply and I found myself fighting an urge to cry. 'Mum, I don't like this. I just want to be normal with you. I just want to talk about things that don't matter and I want to feel like I can come home without being the sort of visitor that you have to tidy up for or cook something special for.'

'It's not like that,' she said, even though the evidence was right in front of me.

I point my knife at the spiralled carrot, 'Whatever.'

'So how are things?' she asked quietly.

'Fucked up.'

'Emily.'

'You asked.'

'Well, how fucked up are we talking?'

That made me smile. 'The wedding's this Saturday.'

'Yes, I know. I thought perhaps you could stay here for the weekend? Or a bit longer if you like?'

'No, no. I'm going to it.'

She had been about to take a mouthful of salmon but she lowered her fork again, 'Why?'

'For Joanne. She wants me there.' I rushed straight into a longer explanation. 'Molly's dead excited about her dress. She looks so cute in it. It's pale blue and Luke has a shirt in the same shade and he's wearing it with a waistcoat over the top.'

'And you're going?'

'Yes.'

'How's that going to work?'

'Well, I won't be throwing any confetti, put it that way.' I meant it as a joke but even to my ears it sounded bitter.

'Emily.'

'Look, I get it. It's what Joanne wants and I'm happy to go along for her. But I can't run around pretending to be over the moon, can I?'

Mum shook her head, 'No, I don't suppose you can but perhaps you should come here for the weekend. Or even today, you could come today and stay. Just go back home next week when it's all over and done with?'

'No, Mum. That's not going to help anything. Never mind what Dad would say if I came back.'

'He wouldn't mind.'

I raised an eyebrow. No matter what she thought, I knew he would have.

'How's Charlie?' I asked her.

'The same, of course, the same. You know, every year he moves onto something new, something harder. But he's still like the same five-year-old starting school, surprised that he's expected to do any work in his own time and disproportionately pleased when he manages to get a good grade. He's a good lad, though.'

I wasn't blind and I could see the wistful look in her expression. Or maybe I couldn't and I was just picturing it there. I wasn't trouble free like Charlie, nor was I in the right frame of mind to spend a week at Mum and Dad's and enjoy myself.

'How about the others?' I asked casually and I didn't use their names. I just assumed she knew I meant Ben and Jess.

She chewed her lip for a second and I realised she didn't want to start talking about them if I meant somebody else, so she scratched around, hoping that I didn't mean them and that the answer would come to her.

'I mean Ben and Jess,' I confirmed, because I didn't want the awkward silence dragging out any longer. 'Have you seen either of them?'

She nodded slowly. 'Both actually. Jess in passing. We were both at the petrol station at the same time. I was trying to decide whether to pretend that I hadn't seen her and I think she was doing the same, because when we did catch each other's eye, we had that same startled moment of pretending we hadn't realised the other one was there.'

'How did she seem?'

'Fine, fine.'

Mum's eye contact was a little too steady and I knew she was holding something back.

'Was she with someone?'

'She and Andy are still together.' I didn't miss the evasiveness of her answer but right then I decided to let it go.

'And Ben?' I asked, changing the subject.

'Ben's fine. He came here actually.'

I hadn't expected that. She raised her hand slightly to stop me asking any more.

'He brought some things round. Things that you'd left at the house.'

I didn't ask how he was or whether he looked happy. It wouldn't have been right, even though part of me wished I was still with him.

'Is he still with Shannon?' I made myself say her name.

Mum nodded slowly. 'The baby's due at the end of January.' She blinked a couple of times and stood up. 'I'll go and fetch the things he brought round.'

She left the room and I was glad she'd gone. I'm sure I was looking calm again by the time she returned a few minutes later with a pile of clothes. 'I didn't know whether you wanted them or whether just to give them to the charity shop. What do you reckon?'

I didn't pick them up, I just glanced down at the pile.

The clothes were good items but ones that, for various reasons, I'd barely worn. A dress that I'd chosen for a wedding, a top that seemed a good idea but never felt right on, a jumper with stripes that was supposed to be an attempt at being adventurous. I put it on once for a night out with Jess but it had never made it past the front door. 'I feel stupid,' I'd said and she'd tried to say something diplomatic and then owned up that she didn't like it either. I'd flung it across the back of the sofa, swapping it for my 'wear anywhere' black cardigan. That would have been the second anniversary of working together. Damn. That was a few months before I'd married Ben but it felt like forever.

I pulled a grey dress from the pile. It was only two shades off black and I'd worn it to a funeral.

'Perhaps I should wear this on Saturday?' I joked.

Mum didn't look pleased that I'd brought the topic right back around to where it had been minutes earlier. She reached out and pressed her hand on top of the pile of clothes, stopping me from fiddling with anything else.

'Why the vendetta against him?'

'Vendetta's a bit strong, isn't it?'

'It is a vendetta. What evidence do you actually have?'

'I told you before what he's done, what's in his past.'

'Okay. And look what happened to you in that courtroom. It didn't matter whether or not Andy was guilty, did it? Not in the end? Because whether you were telling the truth or not, it came down to what you'd done in your previous life. And that's what you are doing to him.'

'Of course it's not.'

'Look Emily, you've scratched around at his background and you've found a few things that together draw a picture of somebody who isn't particularly decent. I understand that. But it doesn't give any indication that he's about to do anything untoward and I don't even know what it is that you suspect him of.'

'It's just wrong between them, Mum. I can feel it in my gut. It's not something I'm making up, it's a physical reaction.' I pressed my palm against my stomach as though that might convince her. 'I just know.'

'You don't know anything. This has grown in your head and you've let that overtake everything else. It's obsessive and, Emily, there's nothing I want to do more than to back you up, but . . .'

'But. Yeah, I understand. Why does there have to be a *but*?'

'Because you're wrong. Please don't go to the wedding. Just leave it all alone. Stay away from them.'

'And lose a decent friend because of *him*?'

'Emily, listen to me. Stay away from them. Take these clothes and sort them out. I don't want them here, but I want you to be okay and if that means you don't go until Sunday, then move back in, have your old room. And do you know what I think?'

Her expression softened. She pressed her lips together for a second and I thought she was about to cry.

'I'm so sorry about you and Ben. I always thought that you were perfect for each other and I think it's seeing your own marriage go so wrong that's at the heart of all of this. You know I love you.'

Maybe something she said hit home, because I started to cry then. I picked up the pile of clothes but I didn't make it out of the kitchen. I just stood there, clutching them to my chest and sobbing on her shoulder.

I stayed later than I'd planned and, when I arrived home, Joanne's flat was in darkness. I left the unwanted clothes on the front seat of my car, went indoors and fell asleep without even getting undressed.

WEDNESDAY 13 SEPTEMBER, 2017

It had been a long time since my sleep had consisted of going to bed at one reasonable hour and waking up at another with nothing in between but darkness. Sleep had come in snatches for months now, interspersed with the occasional complete blackout.

This time when I awoke, I had no idea whether it was last thing at night or first thing in the morning, or even if it was 11 a.m. and I'd totally overslept. The curtains were drawn and all the lights were on in the room.

I wasn't sure why I'd woken but I knew there was something. My clothes felt limp and grubby against my skin. I stood up and walked around the flat, looking for anything, any incidental item, that would trigger my thoughts. Something had been going on in my head.

I checked my watch. It was quarter past eight in the morning. I hadn't heard a thing from downstairs, nothing of the preparation for the school run. No noise from anyone else leaving the building either. I wandered into the kitchen and glanced out of the window. The driveway was deserted. No sign of Frank. It was the same from the side window and mine was the only car left downstairs. So, I guessed I really was alone there.

I made myself a coffee and took it down the servants' stairs to drink it by the open back door. The key was in the lock but when I tried to turn it, it wouldn't budge. I turned it the other way and it moved without resistance. It was then I realised it had already been unlocked. I wondered whether my subconscious had been reminding me that I hadn't locked it, whether it was the niggle of unfinished business that was making me feel restless.

When I came back inside, I shut the door and noticed how locking it was second nature. I promised myself that I wouldn't overlook that again.

My empty coffee cup was still warm but I returned to the kitchen to boil the kettle again. I shut my eyes and tried to retrace my steps, rewind my brain back to the thoughts I'd been having at the time I awoke. It was something about the journey. The journey back last night from Mum's house. But as hard as I tried, I couldn't coax it to the forefront of my thoughts.

I set my new mug of coffee down on my bedside table and flopped backwards onto the bed, staring at the ceiling. As my mind drifted, it settled on the inevitable thoughts of the wedding, of Molly's dress and Luke's blue shirt, the dress I was planning to wear and the funereal one that I couldn't, simply because it would be the wrong thing to do. But wasn't it oh-so tempting to wear something as depressing as black to an event like that?

As I closed my eyes and images still floated through my mind, I saw it folded on the front seat of the car and then I saw the other items in the pile, and a moment later I knew.

There was no fast route from Wicken to Foxton as the sprawl of Cambridge lay in the middle. In the daytime, the traffic didn't move and at night there were too many speed cameras to risk driving quickly through the city. Of course, I could have skirted round the outside, but with the miles it added, I didn't know which would be faster so I just kept driving straight into town then continued out the other side.

The urgency of the journey and the slowness of the roads were making me want to scream but I honestly don't think I was fit to drive any faster. I seemed to hit every set of red lights. Twice, I crunched the gears; once, I stalled as I tried to pull away too sharply.

When I arrived up outside her house, I don't think I locked the car. I was up on to her driveway and banging at the front door before I'd thought about it. I intended to hammer on the door until she opened it and if that meant disturbing the whole street, I really didn't care.

There was a movement of curtains in the upstairs window. Then I saw her silhouette at the glass. She stood in the spare bedroom and looked down at me, probably deciding whether to try to ignore me or, better still, call the police. I stepped back so that I was totally visible.

'I know what you did, Jess.'

I'd brought the letters with me. I held them aloft and I didn't care that the graphic images were clearly on show.

'I know you wrote these. And I don't care who else knows it either. I'm not going away.'

And I wasn't planning to. I would have stayed put or followed her to work and then back again if that's what it had taken. Perhaps she heard the doggedness in my voice. A minute later, she unlatched the front door and walked away from me towards the kitchen, leaving me to follow. I closed the door behind me and found her at the kettle, spooning coffee into two mugs, calm as anything.

The adrenaline that had been pumping through me seemed to vanish then.

'Why?'

She didn't look at me, just shook her head, the teaspoon poised above one mug.

'You must have a reason.'

She muttered something quietly, almost to herself, but I caught the word *anger*.

'Because you were angry?'

She nodded.

'With what, with me? What did I actually do wrong?'

She turned then, leaning back against the worktop.

'You think you did nothing wrong? You wrecked lives, Emily. You screwed up mine. I lost most of our regular clients. It was like we were both guilty. People weren't comfortable being in the office or working with . . . well, knowing what had happened.'

'They weren't supposed to know.'

'No, but that's unrealistic, isn't it? Your friends knew, your family knew. And people love a good gossip. In the end, everybody knew but 90 per cent of them pretended they didn't. You're not exactly a person that men want to hang around with, are you? But then women don't either. I reckon a woman who cries rape and gets caught gets less forgiveness than a man who's actually done it. People make the right sympathetic noises to me, but guess what? My business was pretty much over. You left Ben devastated. And Andy's life was screwed.'

'Hang on a minute . . .'

'Hang on what? Really, hang on what?'

'I wasn't going to keep quiet after what he did.'

'What you say he did.'

We were almost toe to toe by then and I could feel her breath in my face. I stepped back and made myself lower my voice. 'Jess, he raped me.'

'Did he really?' She came back at me then, her face right up to mine, her spit hitting me. 'You were in a house full of people and I know you can make plenty of noise if you want to. And even if you didn't, Ben was right there. You're not some helpless female but you weren't even injured. Why didn't you put up a fight then? And why would you wait so long to tell Ben?'

'I've explained . . .'

'Explain it to me. Explain how you've known Andy for years and then suddenly out of the blue, "Ooh he's raped me." I'm sorry I sent the letters. I shouldn't have done it, but you hurt me so much, Emily. You were like my best friend and sister rolled into one but I suffered because of what you did and you just walked away.'

'I wouldn't have treated you like that if it had been the other way around.'

Jess had given up on making the coffees. 'So I behaved badly, but I don't have any regrets.' She turned away to face the window. Her voice was low and I only just caught the words. 'Not after what you did to Andy and Ben.'

'I'm sorry?' My dart across the room was like a reflex and I grabbed her arm at the elbow and spun her towards me before I'd even thought it through. 'It was my word against his. What are you saying now?'

'That you're not the one I believe.'

She pulled her arm free from me and I realised then how tightly I had gripped it.

'You knew, Jess. You knew how upset I was.'

'No. I knew how upset you said you were. You never liked him and at the same time you'd known him for years, and I'm supposed to believe that suddenly, out of the blue, he'd attacked you? He's never had an interest in you, Emily.'

'I think he did it to get at me.'

'Yeah, because that's what we do when we don't get on with somebody, isn't it? He wasn't bothered about your marriage to Ben. But you were bothered about Ben's friendship with him and to get rid of him you made us all suffer.'

'That wasn't my plan.'

'So you did have a plan, did you? Because it seems to me you were just spending your time not thinking about the consequence of anything. And to anyone who knows about the case you've tarred Andy with the brush of "rapist". Even if you and he had sex, which I don't think you did, there is rape and then there's rape. You weren't dragged off the street and beaten, were you?'

'What's that supposed to mean? That rape only counts if the assailant is a violent stranger? Get real, Jess!'

'I am, Emily. I've been living with this every day, fighting to stop my business from going down the pan.'

'And that's why you sent me hate mail, I suppose? Because of money?'

She released a hard, exasperated breath. 'You don't get it. We were friends. All four of us. Friends. And I thought one day I might be able to have what you had, a happy marriage. But no, you weren't content with your life so you just had to trash everybody else's. And I sent those letters because I'd loved you and I was happy before you threw away our friendship. Even after that first day in court, you could have called it off and given me any half-decent excuse and I swear I would have stood by you. Why was going after Andy more important than saving our friendship?'

'It wasn't. But telling the truth was.' I gripped the letters tightly in my hands. 'And afterwards I moved away. None of you had to see me again. Why wasn't that enough?' Before she could answer, I'd carried on. 'How did you find me anyway? Why would you spend your time tracking me down, just to execute a bit of petty revenge? What did you do, follow me or something?'

She shook her head. 'Petty revenge. No, your letting agent rang, looking for a reference. And that was my way of getting rid of my anger.' She took a breath and her voice calmed. 'I know I shouldn't have sent them. But I did it because of what you put us through. How did you work it out?'

I found the correct image and turned it towards her. 'I wouldn't have known it was you except for that photo with the stripy jumper. I only ever wore that on one evening and then I changed before we left. Do you remember?'

Jess nodded. 'Yeah, I remember. It was the night that we met with Ben and Andy, when we went to the Junction then for a meal at

Nando's. And Andy asked why you hated him.' Jess was watching for my reaction. 'You don't remember that, do you?'

She was correct, I didn't.

'I told you then how much I liked him and you told me I'd be making a mistake.'

'I said he wasn't good enough.' I hadn't remembered the conversation at all but the words slipped from my lips. 'And after that I kept quiet about him.'

She stepped towards me but this time until her face filled my field of vision. 'I knew you'd lied as soon as I heard you'd gone to the police. There'd been two days and you'd said nothing. I'd seen you the day after he supposedly attacked you. Again. Nothing. Even after you'd pressed charges . . .'

'Stop.'

She tried to keep talking but I shoved her, sending her backwards into the refrigerator. 'Stop,' I hissed. Suddenly I knew, 'It was you who found the witness, wasn't it?'

'Your one-night stand?' She tried to sound defiant but I could hear nervousness in her voice. 'Clive Kerkes. He has a name.'

'You wanted me to be humiliated.'

I had no idea how close I was to hitting her until I saw her try to pull herself from my grip. 'If you had called it off, he never would have testified. When it came to the crunch I couldn't let you go through with what you were trying to do to Andy.'

It was night-time when I headed home. The road back to Wicken made sweeping zigzags across the countryside, the same sort of trail as a snake leaves crossing the sand. It wasn't like Joanne to be in the garden but when I reached the house, she was standing there in the dark, a silhouette against the light at the main entrance.

Her arms were folded across her body like she was cold, but my car thermometer said ten degrees and she was wearing a jacket so I didn't reckon it was that. I was glad she was there, though. I'd cried too much recently and I needed a distraction from Jess.

'You here by yourself?' I asked.

She nodded. 'I'll see him tomorrow. Do you have time for a drink?'

'Depends how strong it is,' I joked, even though I knew I wouldn't be touching the alcohol. 'Your flat or mine?'

She looked amused in the way you do when you are just trying to be polite. 'Can we stay out here tonight?'

'Sure. I have some hot chocolate.'

'Thanks, Em, I'd like that.' I wondered whether I was imagining it but there seemed to be a melancholy edge to her voice.

So I went up and, while the kettle was boiling, I tried to compose myself. I wondered whether I should tell her about Jess but then dismissed the idea. Her mind would be on her wedding. Besides, I wouldn't know where to start without describing the whole, sordid mess.

The hot chocolate was the instant mix kind where you just add boiling water. It was as basic as it could be; I couldn't run to squirty cream, marshmallows or a flake but then, this wasn't exactly Starbucks, was it? I carried the mugs down in one hand and a couple of travelling rugs in the other. I knew it was corny, but figured that we could sit on one and have the other over our laps and, as it turned out, she didn't mind at all.

So, there we were, side by side, the rug over our knees, mugs of hot chocolate balanced on them. We didn't move for several minutes and then it occurred to me how ridiculous it was that we were sharing the same pointless view: a rectangle of gravel illuminated by the doorway and beyond it everything was just one step from blackness.

'Good day?' she asked at last.

'No.' There was no point dressing it up. 'Shit, actually. And you?'

'Well, could be worse. Where did yours go wrong?'

'I'm not even going there.'

'Come on. I'd like to hear from someone who's had a worse day than mine.'

I tipped my head to one side, so that it rested on her shoulder for a second. 'Are we about to have a comparing-crap-day competition? I think I have it nailed.'

'Really? Mine's fairly shit. Okay, tell me then.'

'Oh, my mum thinks I'm nuts and I've been screwed over and royally dumped by my best friend. Crap enough?'

'Yeah, that's fairly crap.' It took me a few seconds to realise her voice sounded odd, kind of thicker than normal. The light was behind us so I leant back and she had to turn her head to see my face. I still couldn't fully see her but I was pretty sure her eyes were puffy. 'Have you been crying?'

'Nothing. It's stupid,' she said.

'Of course it's not stupid. Please tell me what's wrong.'

She didn't say anything at first. She sagged towards me, buried her face in my shoulder and it seemed the most natural thing to wrap my arms around her, my face pressed into her hair. She'd been using a coconut shampoo and I let myself breathe a little deeper.

'What's happened?' I whispered.

She shook her head and didn't reply, but I could tell from her breathing that she was fighting back tears. 'Is it Molly or Luke?' I asked but again she shook her head. Of course, I'd already suspected that it was him but I hadn't wanted that to be the first suggestion that I jumped upon. 'Is it the wedding? Or Matt?' I asked.

And when she didn't confirm or deny it, I knew that he was the cause; if he hadn't been, she'd have rushed to his defence.

'What's happened, Joanne?' I decided to press her then. 'Tell me what's happened.' I wasn't prepared to let her keep whatever this was to herself. I turned and held her away from me, not at arm's length but with enough distance between us so that we weren't completely in each other's shadows. Gently, I touched her cheek. I couldn't feel the wetness of her tears but I could feel the heat from her face.

'Tell me what happened, Jo.'

'I don't know,' she whispered. 'It's the stress of the wedding, I'm sure. Molly was trying on her dress again. You know how she loves it and she made Luke put on his pageboy outfit. The two of them, they looked so sweet. I turned to Matt and I expected him to be, I don't know, bubbling, like I was, but he just sat there stony-faced. I don't know what got into him.'

'Perhaps he feels it's all too rushed?'

'Well, I asked him that and he said *nothing*. But from then to when the kids went to bed, you could have sliced the atmosphere. Luckily, I don't think they picked up on it. Bless them, they're so excited. I thought he liked them.'

I knew I needed to be careful about what I said next. 'He doesn't seem to have too much of an idea about children. Perhaps he's not had much contact with kids?'

'Maybe.'

All I wanted to do was scream at her, *Don't go through with it. Don't go through with it*, but it wasn't the approach that would work.

'He's probably scared. It's a big responsibility taking on a whole family,' and I immediately realised that it was the wrong thing to say.

'That's why I'm so lucky to have him.'

I silently cursed myself; that was the last thing I was trying to point out to her. 'No, Joanne. That's not the case. If he, Molly and Luke don't get on, that's a serious problem.'

This time she stayed quiet and I hoped I was making progress. She was looking down into her lap and I instinctively knew there was more that she hadn't told me.

'So, what else happened?'

Again, she shook her head. 'It's not Molly and Luke. He doesn't find it easy to know what to say to them but he's trying. And he wants to be there for them.'

'Come on, Joanne. You're not the crying type. You're not like me, blubbing at every small setback. Something has happened, hasn't it?'

'Maybe it's cold feet.'

'From you or from him?'

'Both, perhaps.'

'You could postpone.'

'Oh, for God's sake, Emily. It's on Saturday. He has family coming.'

'Family would get over it.'

'He'd go mad if I backed out now.'

Her hands had been restless. Now she pressed them together and slid them between her knees as though it was the only way to stop them fidgeting.

'He lost his temper, earlier I mean. It came out of nowhere. The kids had gone to bed and I was just trying to talk to him, to relieve that horrible tension that was hanging in the air.'

'And what happened?'

'I don't know.'

'What do you mean you don't know?'

'I don't *know*. One minute I'm trying to fix things and the next, I couldn't stop him.'

I felt tightness starting to form in my chest.

'What do you mean, you couldn't stop him?' I reached out, stroked her arm, tried to encourage her to look at me. But she couldn't. Her head hung. 'Joanne. What happened?'

She unclasped her hands and lifted her T-shirt.

I grabbed my phone and found the flashlight but, by then, she was trying to cover it up again. I grabbed her hand, lifted her T-shirt and I heard myself gasp. Across the right side of her chest her skin was an angry red and bruising was already forming along her ribs.

'He did this?'

She nodded. 'It's so out of character.'

I wanted to scream at her, *How would you know it's out of*

character when you've been together no time at all? But I didn't. I didn't say that.

'You can't marry him, Joanne.'

'I can't back out now.'

'You don't have any choice.'

The old me would have told her to go straight to the police, to report it immediately. This me didn't bother.

'Not just for your sake, Jo, but for the children too. Please don't go through with it.'

'I don't know what to think. He was distraught.'

'Right. Where is he now?'

'He's gone to talk to his sister. Honestly, he's beside himself.'

'Honestly?' Joanne didn't notice the sarcasm in my voice.

'He said nothing like this has ever happened before.'

'Well, he's lying. I told you he's been charged in the past.'

I don't even know if she listened. She stared at me for a few minutes longer, her expression frozen, her eyes puffy but inert.

'I just need to go to bed,' she said. She hugged me goodnight then left me standing in the dark.

THURSDAY 14 SEPTEMBER, 2017

I pulled on jeans and a T-shirt, slipped my feet into trainers and hurried downstairs. I had no idea what I planned to say to him but knew I had to try. It was 5 a.m. and the engine of my car sounded loud in the stillness. I pulled forward very slowly and hoped that the gravel under the wheels was muted enough not to wake anybody. I found his Tesla parked up near King's Parade. He didn't have a resident's permit on the vehicle so he would have to move it quite early if he wanted to avoid a ticket. I just sat and waited until five-to-seven when I saw him turn the corner, keys in hand. I didn't know he'd seen me but he didn't pause at his vehicle, and instead walked straight up to mine. He gestured for me to step out. I simply wound down the window.

'I want to talk to you,' I said.

'And finally, we have something in common,' he replied.

'I know why you're marrying her,' I said, jumping in before he could speak again.

He leaned his head to one side and waited.

'It's because of the money. I'm not stupid.'

'It's because of the money,' he repeated.

'What is it you think you're doing and, more to the point, what gives you the right? She told me what you did.'

'Oh really, and what did I do?'

'I saw the bruises.'

He pressed his lips into a bitter and humourless smile. 'You're crazy.' He shook his head. 'You don't know anything about me and that's not just a clichéd line I'm throwing at you, you really don't.'

'I know you don't love her.'

'You think I don't love Joanne? Or do you know I do and you can't take it?' He placed both his hands on the roof of my car and leant down and forwards so his face was as close to mine as it could be without actually poking his head through the window. 'The thing is, I really do love her and I can see that you have an issue with that. It is a problem but it's not my problem. Yeah, you've probably gathered bits and pieces of information about me, there are people here or there who'll say bad things, but isn't that the same with all of us?' He seemed to wait for an answer.

I began to wonder whether or not the question was rhetorical and if it wasn't, whether that was because he already knew too much about me. 'I don't know why Joanne can't see you for what you are.'

'Yeah, well touché.'

I looked up at him through narrowed eyes. 'Why are you even considering marrying someone with kids? That's not your thing. You're going to get bored with her and bored with them, or do you know that already? Are you just in it for what you can get out?'

'Which is what exactly?'

'Her money for one.'

'Emily . . .' His voice sounded patient, the type of forced patience that was crushing something else. 'I'm only having this conversation because you mean something to Joanne. Though fuck knows why. She needs to learn when to drop hangers-on like you, but she's too good to do that, so I'll make sure it happens.' I heard his fingers strum on the roof of my car. 'Come to the wedding, by all means, but don't you try and screw it up for us. And I promise you something else: as soon as I can convince her, we're going to be out of that place. When she gets some distance from you she will start to see sense.'

'I won't let it be that easy.' I ran my hands across the top of my steering wheel. 'When it all turns to shit, and it will, I'll be there for her; I'll be the one ready to pick up the pieces, I'll be her shoulder to cry on, any of those phrases you want to throw at it.' I made my hands stop fidgeting and gripped the wheel instead. 'I'll be all of those things but if you have one ounce of integrity you won't go through with it.'

'Because?'

'Because you don't love her. She doesn't need somebody like you leeching off her.'

He pushed himself back from the car and stood three or four feet away from me. He looked down on me, his eyes like slits. 'That's enough now,' he said quietly. 'I've been more than patient and you can be there on Saturday, but not beyond then.' He began to move away, pointing at me as he walked backwards towards his car. 'I've had it with you.' He raised his voice. 'I'm going to dig into your background, the way you've dug into mine. You're toxic and I'm going to make sure that Joanne knows it.'

He opened his door and dropped into the driver's seat in what looked like a continuation of the same move. He started the engine and accelerated away from me before I'd even had time to turn the key in the ignition.

Whatever I'd intended that encounter to be had failed, he'd won the moment. I pulled out my phone, tempted to call Joanne, but what would I say? I didn't want her poisoned against me. Had anyone ever warned a friend about an unsuitable lover and found that they'd listened?

I tossed my mobile onto the passenger seat and drove towards home but never caught sight of anything that might have been his taillights.

I didn't hurry back to Wicken. I drove at a steady pace; I couldn't have caught Matt's Tesla even if I'd tried, but that wasn't the point anyway. I don't know if I'd expected him to back away when I confronted him. I briefly wondered whether I had made things worse but I pushed the thought out of my mind. All that mattered was Joanne seeing the truth. I ran over the previous night's conversation and I was sure she had begun to see sense, she just hadn't been ready to make a decision.

But then I'd had friends in the past who hadn't been treated well by their boyfriends and they'd swung backwards and forwards between reality and being loyal. Then there was Joanne's illogical self-doubt.

I'd seen it a few times, although I still found it hard to believe that she couldn't see how beautiful she was. How beguiling.

The route to Wicken wasn't congested, I was driving against the notorious flow of traffic into the city and before long the rhythmic swoosh of cars travelling in the opposite direction was enough for me to relax and my mind to wander.

It didn't travel far.

I thought a little about Ben and Shannon and I reckoned that she must have been about five months pregnant by then. Instead of thinking about my own yearning for a baby, I began to think about Molly and Luke. I wondered whether, if the wedding did go ahead, maybe they could stay with me while Matt and Emily went on honeymoon.

I jerked my attention back onto the road. I was passing a transport depot and that made me about three miles from home. I'd shocked myself. Had I really just crossed a line where I thought that spending time with Molly and Luke would mean enough for me to accept the idea that those two might get married? Well, it didn't, not at all.

I'd rather never see those children again and know they were happy and safe.

I turned out along the bypass and I could still picture the view: the low verges, the wide sky, the high clouds and the vast nothingness I was driving towards. And it was at that moment I realised something that until then had only been a shadow at the back of my mind; I was starting to twist into a person that I didn't want to be. I knew then that I had to hold onto a better part of me.

I had less than a mile to go and, instead of speeding up, I slowed. Somewhere a while back, I'd taken a wrong path. DI Briggs had seen it. He had told me I'd changed and he'd been right.

I arrived home and pulled into the car park, then sat for a minute.

It was still early, too early for school, and Joanne's car was still there alongside the Tesla. I twisted the rear-view mirror round so I could see my face, I looked myself in the eye, allowing my vision to go slightly out of focus. I held my own gaze and I made myself a promise. Then I locked the car and walked towards the house.

I could hear the sound of their voices as I walked alongside her flat.

The door was already ajar when I reached it. I knocked then pushed it gently with the tips of my fingers, just so it opened a couple more inches. I heard him first. 'Why do you keep making excuses for her?' He sounded as though he was just a few feet inside the door. 'Fuck it, Joanne.'

'Matt,' she snapped.

They sounded as though they were both in the same vicinity. Perhaps it was just my imagination but I pictured them glaring at one another. It was Joanne who opened the door properly.

'Hi,' she said. I could see the awkwardness on her face.

'About last night,' I began.

Her eyes widened and she gave me the tiniest shake of her head.

'Would you mind doing me a favour?' She looked at me urgently. 'Take Molly and Luke out in the garden, would you? Just for fifteen minutes. Matt and I have things to talk about.'

I looked from one to the other and the tension between them was beyond brittle. I hoped so much that this meant what I thought it might.

Joanne called her children and Molly came through first, wearing her school uniform but with her bridesmaid's dress on its hanger. She held it up at head height.

'Can I try it on? I want to show Emily.'

'No, no, no.' Joanne took the hanger from her. 'I want you and your brother to go out in the garden. Go with Emily, just for ten minutes. Matt and I need to have a chat.'

Molly's smile had become uncertain and she looked at each of us in turn as though someone was about to give her the answer to a question she hadn't yet asked. Joanne called Luke again. When he appeared, he was still wearing his pyjamas. His hair was tousled and he clasped a small Lego car in his hand.

'Come on, Luke. You and Molly are going outside in the garden.'

'Don't want to,' he said flatly.

'Come on, off you go. Ten minutes, that's all.'

He moved too slowly. She hurried him on again and I heard the strain in her voice.

'Come on, Luke,' I said. I helped him put on his shoes and herded them both out on to the lawn. 'Find a football and we can play.'

Luke told me it was in the hedge, forgot his previous reluctance and ran off to find it.

'Do you actually like football?' Molly asked me.

'I don't like watching it,' I said. 'Do you?'

'No. My dad used to watch rugby. That's what they have in Australia. Well that's what he liked anyway. My brother liked it too.'

'You mean Luke?'

'No,' she said, 'Connor.'

'Ah. Do you miss him?' I asked the question but she looked past me and ran towards her brother. Kicking the ball around only lasted for a minute or two and then it turned into a game of catch, the kind where if you miss, you must drop down on one knee. On Luke's first miss, he demanded a second chance.

'That's not fair,' said Molly. 'I didn't have a second chance.'

I said, 'Well you have a second chance too then.'

'Perhaps I shouldn't. I'm a whole year older.'

I said, 'No, it's only for fun.'

So, Molly took another go and then Luke claimed it wasn't fair.

'Perhaps we should play something else?'

'I like catch,' said Luke. 'But it should be harder for Molly because she's bigger.'

'Luke,' Molly complained, 'she's trying to make it fair. She can't have favourites, can you, Emily?'

Luke's face puckered into a scowl.

'Connor was Dad's favourite.'

'Luke,' Molly hissed.

'Well, he was,' said Luke.

'You don't even remember him properly,' Molly shouted back.

'Hey, hey, hey. I'm sure your dad didn't have favourites,' I tell them. 'Look, let's just play something else.'

Molly was standing closer to me than Luke.

'He did have favourites,' she said to me quietly. 'That's why he went to heaven with Connor and that's why me and Luke are Mummy's favourites.'

'So that it all evens out?' I asked.

'Uh-huh,' she said.

The ball rolled towards her and she kicked it hard towards the bushes. Luke sighed and ran after it. Molly drew a little closer. She didn't look at me. She watched her brother and then, just as he was almost back, she spoke in a voice almost too quiet to hear.

'Emily?'

'Yes?'

'You wouldn't hurt me, would you?'

The question stole my breath. I squatted beside her.

'Of course not. Why would you say that?'

I'd heard nothing from the house but just then I heard a car door slam and the sound of the Tesla as its wheels spun on the gravel. Then Joanne called out to the children. Molly looked at Joanne and then back towards me. Luke was already running towards his mum.

'Why did you ask that?' I whispered and she looked back at me with the barest of smiles.

'Because I needed to know,' she said, then ran after her brother.

I took one look at Joanne's expression and I knew she hadn't done it. Matt had driven off in a hurry, not a temper, and the day hadn't been cancelled or even postponed. I asked her why but she shook her head.

'He doesn't want you there,' she said. 'But he's agreed for my sake.'

I was standing in the doorway. Molly and Luke had run in ahead and now they were nowhere to be seen. I didn't know whether to step inside or just back away. Joanne hurried across to me and took my hand. 'I want you there,' she said, 'but I don't want to make things difficult for you. And his family will be there . . . his sister.'

I squeezed her hand. 'Don't worry. I'll be there for you and the children and I won't make a scene.' I already knew I'd be dreading it on the day. Not just because of Matt either. It would be an official building. With rules. And protocol. Not like the court but, at the same time, not so different. It was going to be tough but then, from behind Joanne, I saw Molly appear in her bedroom doorway.

'Do I look like a princess?' she asked and turned slowly round to show us all 360 degrees of her bridesmaid's dress. She did look like a princess, the kind that seven-year-old girls imagine. Or like a Victorian Valentine's card perhaps. I swear it was the most beautiful I'd ever seen her look.

I slipped past Joanne. 'You look amazing, Molly. Can you show me your shoes?' I followed her into her room, aware that I'd left Joanne in the hallway. 'We need to be quick, you have school.'

Molly picked up a white shoebox and tipped the contents onto her bed then pulled the shoes clear of several sheets of tissue paper. 'They're white, not blue, but I like them.'

'They're so pretty.'

Molly beamed up at me, her smile only faltering as she heard Joanne's voice, 'Molly, Luke. Time for breakfast. And find your uniform, Luke.'

'I need to get changed.' She stepped out of the dress and passed it to me before pulling her school blouse over her head.

'Go and have breakfast then and I'll hang it up again.'

'And put my shoes away?'

'Of course.'

She left the room still fiddling with the buttons on her gingham blouse. Molly often kept her curtains closed and, as soon as she had gone, I reached behind them and released the catch, pushing the window just enough so that, from the outside, it would stand a couple of millimetres proud of the frame. Her room was at the rear of the house and it could only be seen from the garden. I hadn't left an obvious gap between the window and the frame but I held my hand to it to make sure there was no draught. Then I took out my phone and snapped a photo of the ornaments on her windowsill: a hand-painted moneybox in the shape of a flower, two Barbie dolls and a collection of Schleich ponies trotting from left to right. I needed to return them to exactly the right position. I rewrapped the shoes in the tissue and was replacing the lid on the box as Joanne came in.

'Okay?'

'Just putting Molly's things away.' I patted the box. 'I'm done. I'll say goodbye to the kids and leave you to it.'

She followed me to the kitchen and I was sure I moved in a manner that was unnatural and too self-aware. I glanced over to the furthest corner, confirming what I'd already known; that the keys hung in the corner. 'I'll see you two later then.' Then to Joanne as we reached the front door, 'If there's any help you need for the wedding, just ask.'

She leant in towards me, not quite a hug, but she rested her head on my shoulder for a couple of seconds and whispered, 'Thank you.'

'But you know this isn't how a wedding is supposed to be?' I whispered back.

'It's going to be fine,' she replied and I think she meant it, but all I heard was doubt in her voice. 'And there's one more thing,' she said. 'Would you take them on Sunday so Matt and I can go and have breakfast together? I know it's not much of a honeymoon, but our first date was to go on this walk together and we'd like to do it again. First thing in the morning. I thought perhaps you could take the kids onto the Fen. I'd give you the money for the coffee shop and the three of you could have breakfast together.'

I relaxed. That sounded like a perfect morning, just me, Molly and Luke, trying to catch sight of the wild ponies. 'I'd love to.'

She tipped her head towards the open door. 'Okay.' Her smile wasn't convincing but I reckoned it was the best that she could manage. She took a breath and managed to muster the necessary levels of brightness. She closed the door and I turned to find Frank standing halfway up the stairs.

'I was going to invite myself into yours,' Frank said, 'but I've decided that I'm making the coffee.'

It wasn't a question and he didn't wait for me to make an excuse. He came down the rest of the flight and crossed the hallway towards his front door. I had no plans beyond returning to my own flat so I followed him dutifully. His kitchen faced out the front, the same as mine. He boiled the kettle and I stood in the doorway just within sight of the window. He glanced at me now and again, and still said nothing until the kettle had boiled and he'd loaded a tray with everything we needed.

'Do you need to stand there until you watch them go to school?' he asked.

I shook my head and retreated into the sitting room. We sat on two identical wing-chairs with a coffee table between us. He hadn't actually made coffee, he'd made a pot of tea and everything he did was very deliberate.

'Milk?' he asked and I nodded.

He used a strainer and had sugar lumps with those little tongs. Everything about him that morning seemed precise. 'It's an interesting view from here, and sometimes I can hear things, voices and noises from elsewhere in the building. Other times I just watch with the sound off, like having the TV on mute.' He pressed his tongue against his teeth. 'It's none of my business but I'd like to make a comment, do you mind?'

'Of course not.' I shook my head but then braced myself for something unpleasant.

'You don't want to become too attached to them,' he said. 'The children I mean.'

I faked my easy-going response.

'Again . . .' he said, 'it's none of my business, but three people in a relationship never works.'

This time it was a struggle not to snap back at him, I chewed on my bottom lip instead and tried to look pensive.

'Matt goes in his flat sometimes, sits there quietly as far as I can work out. I don't hear him moving around. I wonder if he will live there afterwards or they'll all live there or maybe move somewhere bigger for both of them. Do you know what they have planned?'

'Is that what you wanted to know, Frank? If you were gonna have peace and quiet again with a half-empty house?'

He shook his head. 'I've been thinking about you, actually.' He took a breath as if it was the final jumping off point but he had already decided that he was going to say whatever was coming next. 'It just seemed to me that maybe I have a different perspective on this, being on the outside, being here and being able to see what goes on from a different angle, sometimes being in the garden and hearing what goes on up close. I thought perhaps I could share it with you.'

I could feel my cheeks beginning to flush. I didn't think I did want to hear whatever it was he was going to say but on the other hand, when you are about to see footage of something terrible, it can be hard to press the pause button, so I let him carry on.

'Your friendship with Joanne, it means a lot to you and I get that. You've grown attached to the children and I understand that too but from what I see and what I hear, Matt and Joanne are in love and it strikes me that you're sharp, you're smart, so I'm thinking maybe a decent friend would tell you that you ought to back off a little, give them some space.'

I placed the cup and saucer carefully back on the tray. 'I'm not doing anything wrong, Frank, but I really don't like him. No, that's the wrong thing to say. There's something wrong there. She's in danger or the kids are or all of them, I don't know, but you can't talk me out of that. How could I live with myself if something happened to one of them and I hadn't done enough to prevent it?'

He leant forward and slid his cup and saucer alongside mine. 'Don't try and stop the wedding. There'll be no proof, no proof of how it's going turn out. Sometimes you have to step back. Let it run its course, Emily. And if it's hard at first, if you need someone to talk to, I'm old but haven't lost my marbles.'

I tried a polite smile.

'Remove yourself from the picture, Emily.'

The advice was no better from Frank than it had been from my mum. I felt my expression darken. 'I'll be going then,' I told him and suddenly he seemed to lose interest in me.

He nodded absentmindedly, didn't stand or show me to the door and as I left I glanced back to see him with the strainer in one hand, carefully pouring another cup of tea.

FRIDAY 15 SEPTEMBER, 2017

I kept a low profile throughout Friday. Frank's conversation with me hadn't changed my view; it had reinforced it.

I knew the movements of everybody in the building. I knew how they varied for each day of the week; the only unpredictable one among them was Matt, but Joanne had already told me that he wouldn't be back again before the wedding so, as far as taking him into account was concerned, Friday was mine.

As far as everyone else was concerned, my window narrowed and there was only a one-hour opportunity where the building would be completely unoccupied. Most people were out for the full day, Frank for the afternoon and Joanne from when she drove away at approximately quarter to three until she returned at approximately quarter to four.

I hadn't measured distances or rehearsed or anything like that, but I did have it planned. I had wanted to unclip the bathroom window too, just to increase my chances of being able to access her flat, but there had been no opportunity.

I walked round to the back of the house and found that Molly's window had remained undisturbed. I used my fingertips to push between the window and the frame. There was nothing to restrict it from opening as wide as I needed. I reached in and shuffled the ornaments to either side, then slithered through, belly first. It was a clumsy entrance and I was glad to have her bed to cushion my landing.

I closed the window and then used the photo I'd taken to reorganise the ornaments, leaving them as I had found them. I glanced at my watch. Five minutes had gone already but that was okay. I only needed to be in this building for about another 90 seconds.

I went straight to the kitchen and took Matt's spare set of keys from the hook by the window. I opened Joanne's front door carefully and left it on the latch. I made sure no one was around before slipping into the hallway. I began a quiet climb up to the first floor before realising halfway up that, because my flat was up there too, I would have had no need to creep around even if there had been people in the building.

I told myself that, but it didn't stop the feeling of unease that was starting to buzz in the pit of my stomach.

What if I was wrong?

I slid his key into the lock, closed my eyes and took another couple of deep breaths as I pondered another few what-ifs. What if there was an alarm?

What if it was silent? What if there was CCTV?

I decided not to think about that. Instead I thought of the smoking gun and I told myself that it had to be here.

I turned the key gently and gave the door a firm push. I expected the dry smell of dust and the look of an unloved property but I could see immediately that there was no sense of this flat having been forgotten or abandoned; the surfaces were dust free and the sun slid in from outside through clean, unmarked windows. I'd only previously been in my flat, Joanne's and briefly Frank's, but this was like none of those; this felt as though it belonged to the original house, as if all the other refurbishments hadn't touched upon these rooms. The carpet, the curtains, the furniture, all of it looked to me as though it could have been a hundred years old but without a hint of the museum or the gothic. I began to wonder if the flat was his at all, then spotted a Tesla book on the floor by the armchair and one of his jackets draped over the arm. Frames hung on the walls: black-and-white family photos, a couple of portraits of pets and then a selection of modern snapshots, lined up across the mantelpiece. Gemma was there and so was Joanne, both staring out at me.

I checked my watch. Somehow fifteen minutes had gone already and for the last few I'd forgotten my plan and I'd just been standing like an idiot, gaping round the room when I needed to find something – anything – that I might be able to use to stop the wedding.

I began with the writing desk. It was heavy oak. The front was closed and I half expected it to be locked but I guess when you live alone, you are relaxed about things like that. I folded it open. There were a dozen little drawers inside but none of them held anything more excit-ing than paper clips and rubber bands. I found one pen and no paper; I didn't think he was much of a writer somehow. There was a series of drawers down the side on the outside, and one of those had a pack of printer paper. That's when I realised there didn't seem to be any electronic equipment in the flat, in any case, certainly not a printer. I checked the rest of the room; he didn't even have a television.

My gaze strayed a few feet further and I spotted a picture frame standing in the shadows of the hallway. I knelt down next to it and angled it up to face me: Gemma's graduation. She and Matt stood between an older couple. I guessed they were their parents. I set it back down again and from that angle I glanced across and saw a pile of post, stacked in the gap between another armchair and a small drinks cabinet.

I glanced at the time again. I reckoned I could spend another ten minutes on this and still have another twenty for the rest of the place. I knelt on the floor next to the pile of mostly opened mail and slid it out gently, trying to keep it in the same shape and the same order. I was careful at first, lifting each item so I could look behind it to view the next.

About a third of the way through, I forgot my caution and the next thing I knew I was sitting with the pile split into two and an item from the midst of it open across my lap. It was a brochure from a boarding school.

I read the date on the covering letter. It was six weeks old.

Maybe it wasn't a sin to send children away for education, but it wasn't what Molly and Luke needed. No wonder the children weren't such an obstacle for him: he planned to cut them off and forget about them while he played newlyweds with Joanne until her money ran dry. After that, I found another brochure, and a third. Good local schools, but they would be boarding.

I could feel my concentration slipping, I moved on further through the stack of post, then went back and photographed the letters, making sure I'd still have the names of the places he had in mind for them. I continued swiftly through the rest of the pile. There were several unopened envelopes and I ignored them at first. I just flicked past them because I didn't think I should open his post. Ironic when I'd broken into his flat to nose around. I went back, tore one of them along the short edge and slid out the folded sheet. It was a bank statement, not a business account, but a personal one. At first glance, the figures were unremarkable but the bank balance surprised me; it was more than healthy. It showed just a few lines of expenditure, large transfers out to other accounts, against a credit of just over £6,000. I found two other statements from earlier in the year and each showed similar amounts of income and expenditure, and a balance that swelled by over a thousand a month.

I had fifteen minutes left, no more.

I hesitated at the door of Matt's bedroom. But I had come this far, and I just needed to be swift. I pushed it open and stepped inside.

It was a long way from what I would have expected of him but not like the rest of the flat either. It was modern but with a nod to the traditional. The furniture was solid wood, all pale oak, and the rest of the décor was muted and low key. It was a double-aspect room overlooking the side and rear gardens. The curtains were partially closed and the rich autumnal sunlight made a panel of gold on the facing wall; mellow and warm.

So, this had been where he'd met with Mrs BMW for his dirty assignations.

I'd have expected black wallpaper and a leather headboard at the very least.

I moved quickly, checking the bedside cabinets and then the chest of drawers. The wardrobe had shelves inside and it was at the bottom of these that I spotted a small pile of papers. I tugged them free, knelt in front of the open cupboard and spread them in a small arc on the carpet. There were brochures and tickets for the south Pacific. Then an itinerary with flight tickets to Canada, America and finally Bali. An envelope with hotel reservations and another with car hire details. I read the names on the booking and felt a wave of nausea; he had arranged a honeymoon, but it was for all of them. Molly and Luke would be going too.

For a month.

That's what he'd meant about getting rid of me after the wedding. And I was sure he'd be able to force me out of my flat during that time too. What chance would I have of keeping my friendship with Joanne then? Or of staying close to the children?

Even the fact that he had hit Joanne hadn't been enough to dissuade her from the marriage, and breaking in to his flat had proved nothing that I'd hoped. He wasn't unsentimental or thoughtless or even on the edge of bankruptcy. His ex, Melissa, had claimed he wasn't the family type but he'd just booked a month away for himself, Joanne and both her children. I couldn't grasp what this added up to, so I just stared at the paperwork, trying to reorientate myself.

There was a note with the tickets beginning 'Please find enclosed'. I turned the envelope over and saw that it bore his name at his sister's address. They were insignificant details but made perfect sense. I turned to look in the direction of my own flat, as though I would be able to stare through the walls and across the landing and see the answer.

I moved quickly then, closing the wardrobe and checking each room to make sure nothing looked obviously disturbed. I hurried out of Matt's flat and into my own. I checked through every window to make sure that no one had returned.

I took the envelope containing the vibrator from my underwear drawer. Just like the later letters, it hadn't been redirected. I held it up to the light but there was no sign of my mum's relabelling. Then I double-checked inside and, as I remembered, there was no note or receipt.

I barred my outgoing number and called Jess. She sounded suspicious as she answered the phone, probably thinking I was a cold caller. 'I have one question,' I told her, hoping to catch her attention before she slammed the phone down on me.

She sounded weary. 'Go on.'

'Was there anything you sent me apart from the letters?'

'Like what?'

'A package. It was sent to me and I assumed it came from the same source as the letters.'

'There was nothing apart from them.'

'You didn't send me a vibrator?'

'A vibrator? Are you being serious?' It was easy to hear the dismissal in her voice.

'Someone sent it in the post about two weeks ago, after the other letters.'

'Well, it wasn't me.'

'Did you give anyone my address?'

She gave a snort. 'Are you kidding? No one would want it.'

I dialled Mum's number next and, when she answered, I cut her short. 'Mum, there was nothing that came for me where you typed a label, was there?'

'I redirected your post.'

'Yes, but every time you've done it, you've stuck a new label over the top, haven't you?' I picked at the edge of the address label with my thumb nail. 'Has there ever been a time when you've pulled off the label and replaced it with a new one?'

'No, why would I?'

'And you've given my address to no one?'

I turned the envelope over.

'I already told you, and neither has your dad. I checked with him. Why?'

'It doesn't matter,' I told her and as I said it I ran my fingers along the strip of Sellotape that sealed the end of the package. 'Thanks, Mum,' I murmured and hung up. I had originally torn open the envelope at the opposite end from the tape, so the end I was looking at had remained just as it was when it had been sent. Beneath the tape I could see a thin line where the envelope had been sliced by a fine blade. The cut ran neatly alongside the sealed edge. It was close to invisible.

The package hadn't been redirected by Mum or come from Jess.

No one else knew my address apart from the letting agent and the people in this building. And this package had arrived by Special Delivery, guaranteed to come in the morning's post, with Gerald as regular as clockwork at the precise time of the school run.

My phone fell from my hand. It bounced onto the ground. It didn't break, just fell flat onto its back and slid a couple of feet across the floor. I watched its descent and in that second and a half, or however long it took, I saw my life unravel. I saw the picture swirl and spread out and finally reveal itself to me.

Matt and Joanne were wrong together, I'd seen it from the start but I'd been standing in the wrong position at the wrong angle with too many shadows distorting my view. They were wrong together but not because of him. He was like me: the chequered past, the unwise decisions, the catalogue of small wrongdoings. I looked down at the phone and then across to the top of the chest of drawers where I'd left his door key, then slowly my gaze swung towards the window.

The house was still empty but time was running out.

I reacted faster than my thoughts; it was a reflex that sent me to the stairs and rushing down to her flat. I had time to replace the key, time to get out, to lock the door, but did I have time to look in her flat? To look for anything that would give me proof?

The front door was as I'd left it. I slipped inside, into the kitchen and I returned Matt's keys to the hook. From my flat to that moment had felt like one fluid move. Then I stopped, my hand still raised in the direction of the keys. My breath had caught in my chest and I knew she was standing behind me.

The way I remember it was that I saw her face before I even turned. My words were rushed. 'I just wanted to find something to prove to you that you shouldn't marry him.'

She was biting her bottom lip but her expression remained opaque.

I knew I wasn't fooling either of us but I kept trying. 'You're too good for him, Joanne.' I reached out for her hand but my fingers were trembling. 'I was worried about you, I knew as soon as I saw you together it wasn't right and I'm sorry I broke in here and took the key, but I did it for you.' My heart was thumping, my voice sounded unnatural. 'I did it for us.' I could hear my words, I could hear myself trying to convince her that I was still her blindly loyal friend.

There had been times over the years when I had told lies but it was obvious to me then that I was no good at it.

She studied me, unblinking. 'There is no "us", Emily.'

And we stayed like that for several seconds longer. I wanted to push past her to get out of the flat. I wanted to run but, instead, I didn't move. I stood there by the sink, immobile. And I realised that was who I was: one of those people who can think in a crisis but just can't move.

And then I heard myself say, 'Where are the children?'

'They're at a friend's.'

I'd never heard her mention another friend and I realised that I'd never heard the children mention friends either. 'I don't believe you.'

'I knew you left her window open last night,' she said. 'So I left and came straight back on foot.'

'Where are the children?' I persisted.

'I'll be a little late collecting them from school. So what? It's a small inconvenience. And while they wait for me they'll have time to think about how much they need me.' She raised her chin and studied me through half-closed eyes. 'I'm the only parent they have.'

'I know,' I whispered.

'It wouldn't be fair to expect them to manage without me, would it?'

I shook my head. 'No, it wouldn't.' It took me a moment to grasp what she was implying. What it seemed she wanted. 'I can go,' I told her. 'I'll leave, I'll move out and whatever you do is your business.' Suddenly I was speaking too quickly. I forced myself to pause. 'I won't come to the wedding and I'll be gone by Sunday. I'll move back with my parents.'

'You would do that?'

'Yes, because Molly and Luke need their mum, they need you. I was wrong about Matt. You have your reasons for wanting to marry him and that's up to you.' I slowed myself further and tried to sound sincere. 'Joanne, I really shouldn't have tried to stand in the way. I can see that now.'

253

She nodded, 'Okay. But I really do want you gone.'

I nodded too. She stepped back from the doorway and I hurried past her. At least I started to.

But that was the last thing I remembered.

SATURDAY 16 SEPTEMBER, 2017

When I woke up I was in my own bed. I could tell from the angle of the sunlight that it was still morning. I turned towards the window and an immediate bolt of pain shot through my head, surging from behind my eye sockets. It was followed by an almost overpowering urge to vomit. I froze and lay completely still until both sensations had subsided. I could hear the blood pumping steadily through my veins and I focused on that, counting my heartbeats until I felt safe to try to move again.

It was then I became aware that my clothes were wet, I moved my hand a little and felt the mattress. 'For fuck's sake.' I'd wet myself. This time when I tried I opened my eyes just a couple of millimetres and the first thing I saw was Joanne.

She was standing next to me, looking down on me with her head tilted to one side as though she was curious. 'Here's what's going to happen,' she said.

Her visit was brief and efficient. She dropped a tablet onto my tongue then pressed her hands over my mouth and nose until I had no choice but to swallow. I tensed my diaphragm and heaved my chest a few times hoping I'd be able to make myself vomit. I tried lifting my hands up to my mouth but they were just too heavy and unwilling.

She didn't speak to me after that, not a word.

She was wearing jeans and a man's shirt untucked and open at the neck; her clothes might have been casual but her hair and make-up were immaculate and she smelt of a floral perfume. I guessed to the rest of the world she still looked beautiful but I couldn't see it anymore, although as I drifted back into unconsciousness one part of me was still looking for an excuse for her, trying to argue how it was all a mistake. The rest of my mind knew what a fool I'd been and succumbed to the darkness.

Joanne tried to wake me. She touched me gently on my cheek with her index finger.

'Emily,' she said. 'Try this.'

She held a glass to my lips. I couldn't coordinate enough to tip my head the right way but I knew that water would help me. Then, through the haze I reminded myself that I hadn't been drinking. I'd been dreaming, though. Nightmares filled with disturbing images and my own inability to take control.

I still thought water would help. That it would clear my mind.

She tipped my head back just a little and I swigged.

The heat of neat Jack Daniel's hit the back of my throat and I gagged from the shock of it. But she was fast and jerked my head back, again covering my mouth with her hands and I swallowed. My coordination was off, I could feel it. Anyone should be able to spit something back out. But not me. My brain remained out of step, at odds with my muscles and the alarm that was ringing in my head was barely sounding anywhere else. It was like the emergency was beyond a thick sheet of glass, like it was happening to somebody else and I couldn't hear a single word of explanation.

I told myself that I hadn't been dreaming. All of it was real.

I managed to lift my head but my cry for help emerged as nothing louder than a whimper.

She was holding a syringe now. Not the vaccination kind. It was the kind for dosing animals, for shooting the medication straight down their throats. I managed to grit my teeth but she squeezed her thumb into the back of my jaw, pressing hard in the gap between my upper and lower teeth. My mouth snapped open and it was involuntary. She didn't release her grip and I tried to push her off with my hands but they were heavy and clumsy.

257

I still gagged the next time too but whatever she'd shoved down my throat was immediately hitting my stomach. It only took a few minutes. I knew what it was like to feel this drunk. In my past life, this had probably been a weekly occurrence. But it had been many months since I'd had any amount of alcohol.

It was a shock to feel so intoxicated and a shock to register what a shambolic stagger I'd taken through my years with Ben.

Joanne stayed for a little while. I didn't see her leave but I heard her downstairs laughing with the children. She put on a CD, turned it up, making the walls vibrate with love songs.

Her wedding mix.

I felt for the piped edge of the mattress through the sheet and managed to grip it. I pulled myself to the side of the bed. I knew I couldn't sit, so still holding on I rolled gently, hoping to find the floor and stand or at least manoeuvre myself onto my knees. For one moment, I seemed to be in control but in the next I toppled, my shoulder hit the floor and my head crashed into the gap between the bed and the nightstand. I listened, hoping to hear footsteps, hoping they wouldn't be Joanne's, but there was nothing apart from the music and the incessant pumping of blood in my ears.

The once familiar sensation of the floor rocking was the next thing to hit me. I managed to raise my cheek an inch or two from the carpet as I vomited. I let it dribble clear of my mouth before slumping back down.

I don't know how long it took me to pass out but I was glad when I felt it coming. The room was swaying and all I could think of was going to sleep.

The next sound I heard was banging on the fire escape, the sound of boots on metal as footsteps rattled down beside my window. A man was shouting. I couldn't make out the words. I wasn't sure I knew the voices and for a moment I couldn't place where I was. It took several seconds before I remembered enough to convince myself that I was home.

That this was my own room.

I was lying face down and the carpet beneath my fingers had a stubbly pile, a bit like bristle but not quite that harsh.

It was then I first noticed the smell of smoke. I hadn't moved at all but suddenly I registered the fumes and I realised they had been there all along, that I just hadn't paid any attention.

Now though, the smell was becoming stronger. My left hand was buried under my body and too numb to feel. I tried to push myself up with my right but I couldn't find the strength. I reached up to the bedside table and found the switch for the bedside lamp. It was nothing more than a reading light but I turned my head and saw the room through its weak yellow glow. Smoke hung like wisps of stratus cloud near the doorway.

I closed my eyes for a moment and felt myself drift back towards unconsciousness. 'No, no,' I muttered.

The bottle of Jack Daniel's was above me on the bedside table. I reached up, knocked it onto its side then rolled it onto the floor next to me. I walked my fingers across the bottle neck and one handed, unscrewed the cap. It contained little more than fumes but I splashed what there was into my face. It hit my eyes and I yelped. I screwed my eyes shut against the stinging. 'Shit,' I gasped but felt my head clear just a little.

I heard more screaming then. The voice was distorted but I knew it was Molly.

I kept my eyes pressed shut, waiting for the tear ducts to start washing the alcohol out of my eyes. I struggled to raise myself onto one forearm and pushed myself clear of the furniture. I could taste the bitterness of the smoke and pulled the neck of my shirt over my mouth. I extricated my left hand from under my body but the circulation was still gone so I inched forward, alternating my moves between elbow and shuffling body.

The smoke had become dense. I kept my face low and fought the urge to gag. Visibility was limited but I followed the hardest worn track in the carpet and felt my way past familiar items of furniture. I didn't have a fire escape, but I had the second set of stairs.

I found my way to the top and hauled myself over the edge until I was head first, facing downwards.

Gravity did the rest.

I reached out to try and steady myself but, instead, just slid head first, belly down towards the door at the bottom. I knew right away I'd been bruised. My chin, my chest, my knees, my hips all hit the lip of each step as I slid. My thumb bent back against the wall and I was aware of the warmth of blood on my knuckles.

I didn't have time to think beyond that. I lay at the bottom, clear of the smoke, and didn't attempt to move until I heard the crack of glass and the sound of the key being turned in the lock. Then I felt a cold draught as the door opened and Frank's bony fingers reached under my arms, hauling me outside.

'Come on Emily,' he whispered urgently. 'You have to wake up. Emily, wake up.'

He should have put me in the recovery position and left me there until help arrived. But, in his opinion, I needed to be up on my feet and walking it off. So, when I tried to stand, he helped pull me up.

I swayed momentarily then, seconds later, stumbled free of his grip. I staggered down the side of the house towards the sound of frantic shouts and breaking glass. The first person I saw was Luke, being held in the arms of the golf woman, Maureen, and then, as the front of the house came into view, I saw Dan Watts hanging on to Joanne as she screamed at the fire.

'Molly?' It was the first word I'd managed to say aloud and it slurred from me. I repeated myself, more coherently this time. 'Molly.' Then louder, 'Molly!'

And as Joanne turned towards me I saw Sally Watts with Molly next to her.

I hurried towards Molly but never made it. Dan Watts stepped into my path, he caught me and pushed me back. 'No,' his face was in my line of vision. 'Stay here.' His hands were clamped around my arms, gripping me at the elbows. 'You have to wait.'

I didn't have the strength to fight him. I barely had the strength to stand. I tried to explain but could only manage guttural sobs punctuated by one coherent name.

'Joanne. Joanne.'

Over and over until the first blue lights appeared and the sirens drowned me out.

I've seen photos of what they call the thousand-yard stare. Somewhere in between being tugged and led and directed and seated and propped up and being breathalysed and giving blood samples, I found out what it meant to be the person behind those eyes. People moved around me, even held on to me and made me move but I was separated from it all, with my eyes focused somewhere in the middle-distance, into the blackness that was beyond flashing lights and streaks of smoke.

'Miss Jenkins? Emily. Emily, can you hear me? I'm DS Simon Lomax. Emily?'

His voice pulled me back far enough so that my gaze briefly settled on his face. He was older than me with dark hair and dark brows and a bit too much of a tan for this time of year. My focus slipped away again. I was finding it hard to concentrate, to stay awake.

'What day is it?'

'Saturday.'

Tiredness kept lapping over me in waves and although I told myself the urgency of the situation, at that moment, I didn't feel the panic the way I ought. 'Is it after the wedding?'

Then the second voice started.

'I'm DC Zoe Anderson.' This one had a harder edge. She said my name once then grabbed my face and held it straight so that I couldn't help but look straight at her.

'What have you taken?' she said. She jiggled the flats of her fingertips against my cheek and I stirred enough to find it annoying. Apparently, according to her anyway, I needed the paramedics. According to her, I'd taken an overdose.

'Is it after the wedding?' I repeated.

And then her face was in mine and I could read the names on her lips. Matt. Joanne. And the sound followed afterwards and then, through the confusion, I heard my own garbled words. 'I wanted to stop the wedding.'

Something was happening, I couldn't focus on what exactly but DC Anderson wanted me to say more. I could see the exaggeration of her lips as they formed my name. My brief lucidity faded and it was a relief to feel nothing again. To watch the uproar fading into silence. Anderson didn't want me to go to sleep but I kept my eyes open just long enough to see them carry Matt's body out of the house.

I remember snatches of the next few hours. Something of the ambulance journey, of the ride to hospital, the speed bumps and the way gravity tugged at me as we took the corners. I remember staring up towards the ceiling and faces staring down at me. Overhead lights and people talking about me, their voices batting backwards and forwards across my body, as though I was a child or a puppy or a corpse, where it was okay to talk about me in my presence and with the assumption that I couldn't understand.

I remember my bed being wheeled into an empty bay and lying there, just waking up now and again, and the only thing changing about the view was the progression of the clock, as one hour clawed its way into the next.

I don't know how long I was like that but I know that at one point it was light outside and, by the time I heard the voice of DC Anderson again, the day had gone. I'd been asleep again and as I regained consciousness I was suddenly aware of her standing nearby. It wasn't that I remembered everything at once, not the details, but in that instant my memory returned like one ugly composite picture.

I opened my eyes and shuffled up into my pillow, trying to push myself into a sitting position. I succeeded enough to make it to forty-five degrees.

'Are you aware,' she said, 'that you've been cautioned?'

I shook my head and it hurt still but my thoughts were clear. 'No.'

So, she told me again. Under arrest on suspicion of murder.

'Matt?' I queried and she nodded.

'Who else?'

'No one. Mr Edwards was the only casualty. Do you have legal representation?' she asked.

I shook my head. 'I never hurt him.'

Anderson didn't respond.

'I believe the hospital is happy to discharge you. You are lucky we brought you here so quickly. You could have died.'

'I'm sorry, am I supposed to be thanking you or something?'

'I'm not a fan of suicide,' she said, 'and you have too much to answer for. We couldn't let *you* go.'

'I didn't do it . . .' I began.

She was close to my bed so that when she looked me in the face she was looking straight down on me. 'We'll get you in an interview room and we'll do this there. I'm comfortable with that if you are?'

Her mouth tightened into a fake smile. She left the room without waiting for me to reply and I wasn't surprised. I don't think it was meant to be a question, in any case.

A nurse made me a cup of tea while I was waiting to be discharged but once I arrived at Parkside Police Station, I was just supplied with water in weak-sided plastic cups. Two mouthfuls and it was gone and, as thirsty as I was, I didn't feel comfortable asking for more.

The room we were in was small. Not windowless exactly, but with the glass set high so that it would have taken a chair to be able to see outside. The air smelt of cleaning products. Not the fragrant ones you use in the home, but the germ-killing kind. The sort they use in schools and old people's homes.

There wasn't much furniture either, just a table and three chairs. It was all mass-produced, government issue. Everything about the place was as anonymous as it possibly could be and I got it. They didn't want a person in my position taking comfort or inspiration from anything. But when I was there the last time, when I made the rape statement, the room had been warmer and the chairs softer. There were hot drinks, leaflets on the table and a box of tissues next to the chair. I found it hard to believe I'd actually come down in the world since then, but there you go.

DC Zoe Anderson had small dark eyes and an unnervingly steady gaze. I knew what she wanted but she wasn't getting it from me.

'I didn't do it,' I told her repeatedly.

'So, Miss Jenkins, when did you first meet Mr Edwards?'

'When I moved into my flat.'

'After you split up with your husband?'

'Yes, of course.'

'Of course? Do you mean you never meet a new man until you're done with the last?'

'I didn't move to the flat until I'd separated from Ben.' I felt myself redden. 'That's all I meant.'

'Were you having an affair with Mr Edwards?'

'No.'

'Have you had sexual relations with him?'

'No.'

'Did he specifically request that you weren't to attend his wedding?'

I knew she wouldn't move on to the next question until I'd answered that. I hesitated before I replied. 'I knew he didn't want me there.'

'But?'

'But he agreed I could attend.'

'Why?'

'For Joanne.'

'I see.' Anderson looked down at her notes, she seemed to spend an inordinate length of time studying very few words. 'Actually,' she said at last, 'I don't see. According to Mrs Edwards, you planned to come to the wedding but didn't arrive?'

'Yes, because she drugged me.'

'But you were going to the wedding as her guest?'

'Yes . . .'

'To support her? We have other witnesses who say you'd expressed concern for her safety, that you accused Mr Edwards of assaulting her.'

'That was before . . .'

Anderson leant on her elbow, her chin resting in the palm of her hand, and pretended to listen to me. Her pen was in her other hand and she wrote every time I spoke. 'Before what exactly?'

'Before I realised it was her, not him.'

'It was *her* not *him*. A revelation that you shared with . . . who exactly?'

'No one. I had it all back to front.'

'All what exactly?'

'Everything.'

Anderson waited for more but I didn't know where to begin. The silence dragged until I became aware that I'd stayed too quiet for too long and I rushed to answer. 'He'd assaulted his previous girlfriend and when he hit Joanne it confirmed what I already suspected.' Anderson looked dubious. 'He punched her in the ribs, she has bruises.'

'You saw them?'

I thought back. 'Wednesday evening, she showed me. So I thought he was dangerous, and I was scared for her, and for the children.'

'And you wanted her to call off the wedding?'

'Of course.'

'And you felt like this until when?'

'Friday?'

'Two days ago?'

'Yes. When I realised that she'd been manipulating me. And him.'

Anderson shook her head then leant back in her chair. She chewed on her lip and studied her notes again. 'So you claim that Mrs Edwards attacked you?'

'She drugged me.'

'Uh-huh.'

Anderson made far more notes than it would have taken to write down what I had just said. Then she set down her pen.

'You must be aware of how this looks? Tell me again, this time in order.'

So, I started to run through the story again and I couldn't help watching to see when she made notes and when she didn't.

As she listened I watched her sketch two stick figures on the page, one male, one female. 'Tell me about the children. About Molly and Luke Edwards.'

'Carter,' I reply, 'their surname's Carter.'

'How would you describe your feelings towards them?'

'I'm fond of them.'

'Would you say you feel attached? Maternal perhaps?'

'I've become attached,' I admit. 'They're lovely children.'

'You must have been concerned that Joanne's marriage would have meant losing them. They were considering boarding school for them. Did you know that?'

I nodded. 'I just found out.' And I realised as soon as I said it that I'd made a mistake. Nothing I was saying was helping me. 'I think I should have a solicitor with me.'

'Of course, if you feel you need one . . .' She began gathering her notes.

'Not because I'm guilty,' I added. 'Because I'm not.'

'And what evidence do you have?' she asked finally. 'Evidence that Joanne Edwards has done the things you claim?'

And, of course, the answer was *none*.

SUNDAY 17 SEPTEMBER, 2017

When you are being held for questioning the hours move slowly. And not knowing if or when I might be released made them even slower. They arranged a lawyer for me. A thin and nervy looking man named Nick Forde. He too made notes and warned me about saying anything. I found myself with the same feelings of depressed inevitability that had smothered me in court. But my own head was clearer this time and I overrode Forde's reluctance as I spoke to Anderson and Lomax.

I sat straight in my chair and spent most of my time staring directly at Anderson. 'I believe she manipulated me throughout. She exploited my vulnerabilities.'

Anderson smiled; she seemed to enjoy making her blatantly fake expressions. 'And by that you mean your previous experience with the law?'

'The fact that I'd suffered sexual assault and had moved away to start again.'

'And how do you think Mrs Edwards discovered about this alleged incident?'

'I think she looked at everyone in the building and picked me as the target.'

Forde muttered my name, then, when I didn't respond, spoke directly to the two detectives. 'Miss Jenkins is hypothesising.'

Lomax ignored him. 'What makes you feel you were picked as a target? That sounds rather paranoid.'

'It's no different to the way Matt was picked as a target.'

Anderson ignored both men. 'Tell me again why you decided against attending the wedding?'

'As I said, I was incapacitated.'

'By?'

'Joanne disabled me and drugged me. I have the head injury.'

'You have a head injury consistent with a fall and you had ingested both drugs and alcohol. But you were capable of visiting Mr and Mrs Edwards in the hours after their return?'

'I didn't, she visited me.'

'According to Mrs Edwards you brought alcohol with you, apologised for missing the wedding and suggested a toast. You all drank together before you returned to your flat.'

'Why would Matt share a toast with me? He hated me.'

'He was prepared to have you at the wedding. You said so yourself.'

Forde tried to interrupt again but I raised my hand to silence him.

'I never visited Joanne's flat after the wedding.'

'We recovered a bottle of Malbec. It's being analysed but we know the bottle had been tampered with.'

'It's nothing to do with me.'

'Your fingerprints were on it. Did you think the fire would destroy them?'

'No. I bought Malbec weeks ago when we had dinner together.'

Anderson smiled coldly. 'So you knew which wine he liked to drink?'

MONDAY 18 SEPTEMBER, 2017

The hours pushed on and Anderson and Lomax were constants. Forde stayed too but eventually became silent. I regretted asking for him. Most times when he intervened I ignored him and each time I turned to him for advice he seemed to draw a blank. I was sure he didn't believe me any more than the other two did. Anderson led the questioning and each time they re-entered the room and restarted the recording she would start from a fresh angle. This time she'd come in holding an envelope.

'Mr Edwards was rescued from the building but despite the efforts of the fire crew and the paramedics, he never regained consciousness and was declared dead on arrival at Addenbrooke's. Smoke inhalation.'

I nodded.

'The fire was intense. It started just inside the front door. Preliminary reports suggest something was posted through the letter box. The fire damage in the hallway is extensive but, unfortunately for you, the whole building didn't catch light. Flames are good at destroying evidence. Smoke, not so much.'

'I didn't start the fire.'

Anderson sighed slowly and patiently. She seemed on surer footing than last time and that unnerved me a little. 'We've conducted a thorough search of your flat.' She turned back to an earlier page in her notebook and read a list to me.

'We found petrol in a can, half empty, concealed in the cupboard under your stairs. Your car is a diesel, isn't it?'

I nodded.

'I will tell you now, we'll be able to tell whether it is the same kind of accelerant that was used to start the fire.'

She reached for the envelope and slid out the contents. I could see that they were photographs but she held them at an angle so all I could see was the backs. She took the first one, dropped it on to the table then spun it with the tips of her fingers through 180 degrees. I recognised my under-stairs cupboard. A green petrol can that I had never seen before was poking out from behind the vacuum cleaner.

'That's not mine,' I told her.

There was no response and Lomax kept his gaze firmly on the photographs. The next one hit the table.

The second photo was of my kitchen cupboard. The photographer had obviously stood on something, my high stool maybe, and I could imagine his or her head bending over under the ceiling to get the angle right.

The picture showed the tops of jars – jams and a few bottles of spices. The things I had bought when I first moved in, the ones that I purchased, optimistically thinking that I might encourage myself to cook. Most of them have never been opened and behind them there was another jar. It was the kind that contains vitamins from a health-food shop. But it wasn't a jar I recognised. The next photo was of the same jar but in close up.

'It's flunitrazepam,' she tells me.

I shrug and look blank. 'I don't know what that is.'

'Commercially sold in many countries as Rohypnol.'

'The date-rape drug?'

'It is used to treat insomnia but you're correct, it is also known as a date-rape drug. It's a strong sedative. It dissolves in liquid.'

'And?'

'Mr Edwards hadn't moved out of his bed. It seems he made no effort to escape, so we're working on the principle that he may have been sedated. We'll have to wait for toxicology on that one, but drugs leave very specific traces, like fingerprints. If he was sedated and it was by this, we will know.'

I shook my head. 'I don't know why that's in my flat. It isn't mine.'

'So you say.' Anderson's eyes narrow slightly. I was sure where this was heading but I knew there was more to come. 'We have an IT forensics team. They have your computer now. But even the first hour brought some interesting results. Like this . . .'

And the next sheet turned out not to be a photograph but a printout of an invoice.

'You ordered these drugs. We have the receipt. Paid for from your PayPal account and it was delivered to this address.' She pointed to where it listed my flat.

'I didn't.'

'And then we have your search history.'

Another sheet was placed on the table and she tapped on three different lines. 'How to sedate someone without them knowing', 'Will fingerprints survive a fire?' and 'Is flunitrazepam detectable post-mortem?'

Joanne had spent around fifteen minutes on my computer. Had that been long enough to do all those things? 'You can tell the date and time of each of those. I can work out the day when Joanne used my computer and if they match . . .'

'They won't. There are various dates . . .'

'And I found the door to my flat unlocked.'

Anderson looked resigned. 'Well, that is convenient.'

I shut my eyes then and responded to nothing else. Eventually they returned me to a cell.

In the afternoon they took me back to the interview room, put me in a chair, brought me a glass of water and left me to wait. By the time the door opened again, I expected more of the same. But instead of Anderson and Lomax, there was DI Briggs wearing the kind of crumpled weariness that came at the end of a shift. He handed me an apple then took the chair across from mine.

It was a Braeburn and I polished it against my jeans. 'From my mum?'

He nodded. 'Your parents have been here in rotation. Your brother too.'

'My dad has?'

'Yes, parents plural.'

'I had no idea.' I stared at the apple, wanting to eat it but fighting the lump in my throat. It wasn't fair on them. None of it was. 'I'm so sorry for what I've put them through.'

'There's always fallout, but you know that already, don't you?'

Briggs wasn't holding the obligatory notebook, or carrying anything else that might be aimed at making me incriminate myself. 'Are you working on this case now?' I asked him.

He shook his head. 'No, not exactly. But Lomax came to me. We've worked together a lot over the years and he knew of my involvement on the Tyler case . . .' Briggs leant both elbows on the table and interlocked his fingers. For one moment, I wondered if he was about to pray for me.

It felt as though someone needed to.

'Lomax is decent. And by that I mean he's unbiased. He wants everything to be solid.'

'And how's it looking?'

Briggs shrugged. 'Charges have been brought for less. But he wants me to talk to you, to see whether I can find an angle that they've missed. To make it clear, he doesn't want me to find a way out for you, he'd be just as happy if I find more that will convict you. It's the glimpses of grey he doesn't like.' *Glimpses of grey.* I turned the phrase over in my head and, as if he'd heard me, he added, 'They're his words, not mine. They're the points that make a case collapse in court.'

'And Detective Constable Anderson?' I wondered.

'This *is* official but I'll fill Anderson in after the event.' The corner of his mouth flickered, 'Smoother that way,' he muttered. 'So why did you break into Matt Edward's flat?'

'I entered with a key actually. I wanted last-minute proof of what he was like. I wanted to convince Joanne to call off the wedding.'

'And that was on Friday?'

'Yes, in the afternoon when I knew the building would be empty.'

'So you planned it?'

I was beyond being evasive. 'Yes, the night before. I wasn't getting through to her and I was desperate.'

'Why desperate?'

'I thought she was in danger, I thought the children might be too.'

He frowned and his forehead puckered with impatience. 'That's not what I'm asking, Emily. I want to know how you came to be so emotionally involved. What made you cross the line from concerned to desperate?'

'What makes me tick?'

I didn't hurry to answer and this time the silence didn't feel pressured. Facing Briggs made it easy to go right back to the trial; he and I were the link between my old life and this one. 'I misjudged Andy Tyler, but I misjudged Jess and Ben even more.' I paused to gather my thoughts.

'And that means?'

'That I can't rely on myself.' I pursed my lips. 'But then I met Joanne and I felt as though she needed me. As though I had something to give. I suppose I felt in control. I admired her luck for having children and I empathised with her loss. To wave your child off and never see him again . . .'

'And his dad?'

'Yes, in the same accident . . . maybe it's enough to screw with anyone's mind.'

'That fire wasn't the result of a moment of madness on anyone's part.' Briggs removed his glasses and wiped the lenses.

He was right. It was either Joanne's premeditation or my own. Repeating that I hadn't done it had already become the most redundant of sentences. I didn't waste it on Briggs. 'We seemed alike. She was easy to talk to and she was starting again too. Neither of us was working and she was the only person in the building who was close to my age. It felt like serendipity.'

There was nothing in Briggs's expression that told me that he believed me but I still told him everything I could remember. I went back to the beginning and recounted all the details I'd already given Anderson and Lomax. Briggs left the room once and returned with Kit Kats and coffee and never rushed. I saw how tired he looked and wondered whether he would call a halt but two hours stretched into three and his attention never faltered.

But whatever eureka moment he'd wanted simply hadn't materialised.

'Could I see my parents soon?' I asked when I finally ran out of words.

'Not yet.' Briggs tucked his glasses into his top pocket. He squinted without them. 'But I can pass them a message.'

'Tell them I'm sorry. That I love them.'

He stood up and I followed although I had no idea whether I was going to be leaving the room. 'I reckon they know that too. And Mr Emmerson stopped by.'

'Who?'

'Frank. Your gentleman friend.'

And for that I managed a smile. 'You know, Joanne said that falling in love was 50 per cent admiration, 50 per cent sympathy. I've thought about that a lot since. And I think friendships come about that way too. Like with Frank; he seems to have purpose but he's lonely too.'

Briggs took his glasses back out of his pocket and peered at them before returning them to his nose. 'When did Joanne tell you about her son's death?'

'Early on . . .' I thought back. 'When I found out that my ex and his girlfriend were having a baby. But Molly told me first.' I saw her clearly then, her limpid brown eyes watching me. 'She told me that they'd died and that her mum was sad.'

'Do you think Molly was scared of you?'

'No.' My answer was instant but then I felt a shadow of doubt. I was beyond holding back by then. 'There was once when she wanted reassurance, she said, "You wouldn't hurt me, would you?"'

'Those exact words?'

'I wouldn't forget. I didn't understand.'

'Perhaps Joanne had said something to scare her?'

'I would never hurt those children.'

'But the fire could have done.'

I levelled my gaze at Briggs. 'Then Joanne is a danger to them, isn't she?'

Briggs didn't reply and this time didn't delay leaving. I called out to him when the door had almost closed. 'What happens now?'

He stopped the door with the toe of his shoe. 'They'll hold you as long as they can. They'll rush through test results and look for enough to charge you.'

And it closed behind him before I had the chance to reply.

I had done nothing but move between the interview room and the custody suite and here I was, back again, facing Anderson and Lomax. This time Anderson didn't have photos. She just had sheets of paper.

'This is a statement made by your neighbour. I would like to read it to you. Or perhaps you would prefer to read it yourself.'

I held out my hand.

'Please answer for the recording.'

'I'll read it myself, please.' My voice sounded hoarse.

She slid the sheets across to me and for the first time I realised there were multiple copies and she and Lomax read silently as I read.

My name is Joanne Felicity Edwards. I live at the address overleaf. I'm making this statement following the death of my husband, Matthew James Edwards. I'm a white female, aged thirty-four, height five feet seven, weight nine stone eleven pounds, with blonde hair and brown eyes. On the evening of Saturday 16 September, 2017, my husband Matthew Edwards died as a result of a fire at our home address and I believe Emily Laurel Jenkins is responsible for his death. I first met Emily Jenkins when I moved back to the United Kingdom from Australia with my two children Molly Rose Carter, aged seven, and Luke Ross Carter, aged six. They are the children of my first husband, Grant Allan Carter.

Emily introduced herself to us shortly after her arrival and I initially felt that she was someone with whom I could strike up a friendship. We spent some time getting to know one another and I would have classed her as a close friend, even though only a few weeks had passed.

I initially had no misgivings about Emily. I knew nothing

of her background, only what she had told me, which was that she had been recently separated from her husband and had decided to move to Wicken. My first concerns were raised with her behaviour towards my children. Initially, she respected the boundaries that I set and checked with me before buying them sweets or toys. But she very quickly began to encourage friendships with them by buying gifts and spending time with them without my full approval. When I suggested that her behaviour was a little inappropriate I felt that she became slightly possessive with the children. I put this down to loneliness and at that point did not feel that she was a danger to me or my family.

I believe the turning point in my relationship with Emily was when she first met my then boyfriend, Matt Edwards. Emily made it clear from the outset that she was not happy with this relationship and I think she felt our friendship was threatened because I had a boyfriend. This sense of threat increased when I became engaged to him. I noticed that Emily's behaviour became more erratic and she'd turn up at my flat at various hours, sometimes uninvited. I did my best to reassure her and to maintain our relationship, which I then valued.

With hindsight, there are several incidences that are now of concern to me. One of those was when Emily came to us for dinner. We attempted to make the evening an opportunity for her and Matt to smooth out some of the tensions that lay between them but throughout the evening, Emily seemed on edge and occasionally argumentative with Matt. Matt eventually went home and the following morning I woke up with symptoms of nausea; headache and disorientation. The food I had eaten had not been different to anyone else's meals. At the time, Emily and the children were both well so I asked Emily to take the children to school for me. She had picked up the children and dropped them off on a number of occasions and I have no complaints about the way she had looked after them.

On this particular occasion, however, I woke up to find that Emily had spent the night asleep on the sofa in my flat and she seemed unsurprised that I was unwell. I do now believe that she had administered some kind of sedative with the aim of manipulating me and spending more time with my children. There have been a number of occasions when I have felt incapacitated through tiredness; I have felt lethargic and generally run down and the responsibility of the children has fallen to Emily.

As a result of these concerns, I have requested extensive blood tests with the aim of trying to prove whether or not I have been drugged. On the day after the meal in question, when I woke up ill, I was at home alone when the post arrived. The parcel that was delivered was a package which required a signature and I signed for this on Emily's behalf. Emily returned home within five minutes of this delivery and I was with her when she opened the parcel. It contained a bottle of pills. The bottle was about 4 inches, 10 centimetres high, and dark blue but I did not see the label and did not recognise the bottle, nor have I seen it since.

Emily's statement that she unwrapped a vibrator in front of me is absolutely not true and it is something that I would not have forgotten witnessing.

I tried to step back slightly from my friendship with Emily but only after encouraging her to get on better with Matt. I felt that cutting her off just before the wedding would be inappropriate and although my husband did not want her present he agreed for my sake. A couple of days before the wedding she confronted my husband and accused him of beating me around the chest and stomach. This was a complete fabrication and the police surgeon has confirmed that there is no evidence of any such injuries.

It felt to me to be a sign that her mental state was becoming erratic and I was surprised but relieved when she did not attend the wedding.

I did not feel any ill will towards her at that point. The wedding was small with just a few members of my husband's family present so we arrived home in mid-evening. Later that same evening, she knocked at the flat. I answered the door and she apologised for missing the wedding; she brought a bottle of wine and asked if we could have a drink together to celebrate. Matt and I agreed. She also wanted the opportunity to say goodbye to the children before we left for our honeymoon the following day, but they had already gone to bed. It seemed as though it might be a positive way to settle things with Emily.

The wine she brought was Matt's favourite, a Malbec, and he drank more than I did. I had a single glass and he had at least two. Matt and I had already drunk alcohol at the wedding breakfast and it took me a little while to realise that Emily was also drunk. I don't remember what triggered it but it became apparent that she was angry and when she called him a 'lying bastard' I asked her to leave.

She didn't openly threaten us, but I felt threatened by the situation.

I'm not aware of her actions between then and when the fire started.

Shortly after she had gone I thought that my husband had just drunk too much so I helped him into bed and then went to see my children who were still awake. It was while I was in my daughter's room that I smelt smoke, I opened the hall door to see flames in the hallway. These were coming from burning papers directly under the letterbox and it was clear to me that the fire had been started deliberately.

Fortunately, both children were with me and we were able to leave through Molly's bedroom window. If my son had been in his own room at that time I do not know that I would have had time to help both my children escape.

I believe that Emily Jenkins became obsessed with my family. That she murdered my husband and intended to murder me. I believe that she deliberately endangered the lives of my children.

Anderson and Lomax had already finished reading and were both watching me as I put the pages back on the table. I expected Anderson to speak but it was Lomax. 'We have proof you bought the flunitrazepam, evidence that you drugged the wine, and the accelerant was in your possession. Your story doesn't add up. Mrs Edwards's statement, on the other hand . . .'

Anderson took over, 'Now would be the right time to amend yours, Miss Jenkins.'

The police had permission to hold me for a further forty-eight hours and when I returned to the custody suite and lay back on that thin plastic mattress, I closed my eyes and thought of my parents. Wondering whether they were still in the building. Still taking shifts to wait for me. Wondering why they bothered. I'd come full circle. I was back in the hands of the police but this time was far worse than the last.

I curled up more tightly and tried to find thoughts that would take up my concentration and allow me to have respite from the gnawing emptiness that was eating into me. I tried to remember how I'd felt at my happiest, to pick individual days that should have been easy to revisit, but they were all out of reach.

There had been other moments in the previous months when I'd been filled with despair but this time I just wanted to give up.

Eventually I sat up again. I looked around the room and I understood why these places were designed without breakable bulbs or moveable furniture.

I was too confined to pace. I had no view, nothing to read or listen to. No one to watch or talk to. I would have left my name on the wall if I'd had something sharp. Others had done so and I wondered how. And perhaps if I had had something sharp that wouldn't have been how I would have used it.

I'll never know what I would have done if I'd had the opportunity to end it there and then. But I fell asleep admiring the ingenuity of the ones that had the balls and the resourcefulness to carry it off.

TUESDAY 19 SEPTEMBER, 2017

It was 6 a.m. when I found myself back in the interview room. I'd had a single slice of toast, which I'd eaten slowly and washed down with a mug of stewed tea. They'd offered me more but I had no appetite. I was exhausted and overwhelmed by inertia. My clothes were grubby and my skin felt thick with dried sweat and the dirtiness which had built up as I'd moved from ambulance to ward to cell to interview room. All without washing. Maybe those things should have been a sign that my resolve was close to breaking, that giving in and making a full confession was on the cards but, instead, I sat opposite Anderson and Lomax feeling calm.

Zoe Anderson was unhurried. 'Can you confirm that you requested that we continue the interview without the presence of your lawyer, Mr Nicholas Forde?'

'That is correct.'

'Why was that, Miss Jenkins?'

'I disagreed with his advice.'

'Which was?'

'To admit my guilt.'

'That is also our advice.'

'You're all wrong then.' I crossed my arms and leant back in my chair. 'I have told you everything. I have been honest and accurate, and now I have nothing to add.'

Anderson unfolded a sheet of paper, turned it over and spread it face up on the table. 'I have a checklist of all the things we can prove. Some you know and some where the evidence has now come in. I'm going to read them to you and I want you to consider your situation.'

'They don't matter.'

'These are the facts that will form our case against you.'

'I have nothing to add.'

Suddenly Lomax leant forward, reached across the table and slapped his hand down in front of me, 'Miss Jenkins, this is serious. It isn't the time to play games with us.'

'I'm not.'

'What is this then?'

I gave the tiniest shake of my head and didn't answer. I'd stayed awake for much of the previous night feeling that my life was over. And then realising that I'd spent the previous months slipping towards this point. Now I was somewhere near the bottom of the slope and all I had was the truth and it was falling on deaf ears.

I lowered my eyes and watched Lomax's hands. I repeated silently, *I didn't kill Matt. I didn't lie about Andy.*

I guess my lips must have moved. 'What did you say?' Lomax asked.

I glanced at him and then turned my head to meet Anderson's gaze. 'I didn't kill Matt Edwards. I didn't lie about Andy Tyler.'

'We're not here to discuss your case against Mr Tyler.' She spoke for the benefit of the recording. 'Miss Jenkins appears in a fit state to continue.' And then to me, 'We have evidence that you purchased a sedative, namely flunitrazepam, from an online retailer; that you also purchased a bottle of Malbec wine.'

'The wine, not the sedative.'

'That you added the sedative to the wine and administered it to both Mr and Mrs Edwards without their permission.'

'No.'

'That you stored petrol in your flat and used this to start a fire at your neighbour's flat. That you searched the internet for advice on arson, administering flunitrazepam and hiding evidence.'

'I did neither.'

'That you had followed and assaulted Mr Edwards in the weeks

284

leading up to the fire. That you behaved in a threatening manner towards his sister as well as towards your estranged husband Mr Ben Stirling, his new partner Miss Shannon Bridges and your former business partner Miss Jessica Foley.'

She paused to see whether I planned to respond. I stared back. 'I didn't kill Matt Edwards. I didn't lie about Andy Tyler.'

'You entered the separate properties of both Mrs Edwards and Mr Edwards without their permission and your parents were so concerned by your increasingly erratic behaviour that they encouraged you to see your GP, Dr Lahiri, who prescribed anti-depressants.' She held up the sheet of paper. She wasn't at the bottom of the list. 'The accelerant was on your clothes, your fingerprints were on the wine glasses, your DNA . . .' Her flow was broken by a sharp knock on the door. 'Interview paused at 07.23.'

Lomax left the room but returned just a few seconds later. He leant close to Anderson and murmured in her ear. 'Fuck,' she muttered and her expression darkened. She stood abruptly and jerked the door closed when she left the room. I could see her shadow moving behind the frosted glass panel and hear the rise and fall of her muffled words.

She pushed open the door and snapped at Lomax, 'Just wait here.'

It was almost twenty minutes later when she returned with her mobile phone clenched tightly in her hand. She glared at Lomax. 'Shades of grey, Simon? I'm only seeing red right now.' She jerked her head in the direction of the corridor, 'Come with me, Miss Jenkins. Someone else wants to speak to you.'

'Who?'

'Someone who shouldn't.'

Anderson walked half a pace ahead of me for the short walk between rooms. She made no attempt to speak. But neither did I. We made a final turn and it was only then that I recognised the corridor. DI Briggs stood outside a familiar door. I searched his face for an explanation but found nothing.

'Thank you, Zoe.' He acknowledged Anderson but said nothing more until she'd walked away.

I nodded towards the room behind him, 'So we've come full circle?'

'It's the best room we have for this kind of thing.' He opened the door by an inch and I saw Molly through the gap. 'She asked for you.'

He pushed the door wider. Molly sat alongside a heavily built woman, and they had a book spread on the table in front of them. They looked up simultaneously and I took a tentative step forwards. Briggs stepped between us. 'Molly, you can talk to Emily in a minute as soon as June's spoken to her. Is that okay?' Molly nodded. Her fingers tightened around the book and she watched me as 'June' took me to one side.

She spoke in a low tone. 'I'm DC June Leonard, with the Cambridgeshire safeguarding unit. This is an unusual situation where Molly has repeatedly asked to see you. We understand that she has an attachment to you and in normal circumstances we would not entertain a meeting such as this without parental consent. However, DI Briggs has provided information . . .' She broke off in the middle of her sentence. 'You may speak to Molly for a few minutes only. You are not to ask her direct questions that relate to our current investigation. The idea is that you give her space to talk if she still wants to. Do you understand?'

I nodded, 'Of course.'

'Briggs and I will remain in the room and the conversation is being recorded.'

'I understand.'

Molly hugged me and I hugged her back. I expected either Leonard or Briggs to break it up but they seemed to want to stay invisible. I sat back on the settee and Molly slid alongside me and tucked her hand inside mine. 'How have you been?' I asked.

'I miss you.'

'I miss you too. How's Luke?'

'He's got wobbly teeth.'

'So do you.'

'I lost one last week. Look.' She pulled her bottom lip to one side to show off the gap in the gum and the second tooth breaking through. 'The tooth fairy didn't come though. Mum said it was because we were in the wrong house. We don't live in our flat any more. It stinks of smoke. So we're in a hotel.'

'Is it a good hotel?'

Molly shrugged. 'There's no swimming pool and Mum says you burnt our house down. Did you?'

I glanced across at Briggs. He raised a cautionary finger.

'Well, I'm not allowed to talk about the fire.' I squeezed her hand. 'But fire is dangerous and I'd never hurt you or Luke.'

She squeezed back again.

'You know that don't you, Molly?'

She pressed her cheek against my arm.

I point in the direction of the others, 'June says you wanted to talk to me?'

'I wanted to see you again.' She wrapped her other hand over the top of mine, 'We were always safe with you, weren't we?

'Of course you were.'

'Do you remember I asked you if you would ever hurt me?'

I nodded. Mute.

'That's not everything I wanted to say and now this is my only chance.'

I slipped from my seat and knelt on the floor. Our heads were

287

almost at the same height and I could look at her face. I stroked my hand against her cheek. 'What's wrong, Molly?' I whispered.

'I wanted to tell you that my mum would.'

'Would what?'

'Hurt me. Hurt Luke.'

I felt the colour wash from my face. 'How Molly? Did she hit you?'

In the edge of my vision I saw June shake her head urgently. I looked across at her. 'Don't lead,' she breathed in a stage whisper.

It was as though Molly had noticed the others for the first time and I felt her hand pull free. 'Molly?'

'Are you in trouble?' she asked.

'Not really. It's you I'm here to see. Will you tell me about your mum now?'

She leant closer again until our foreheads were almost touching. 'She doesn't hit us. She scares us.'

'How?'

'When we're naughty she says, "You know what happened to Connor."'

Despite everything I knew of Joanne, I was sure that Molly must have misunderstood. 'But that doesn't mean . . .'

Her eyes widened and her voice became more urgent. 'He went to sleep and didn't wake up, Emily. She makes us go to sleep and sometimes I go in Luke's room to make sure he's still breathing.' She was searching my face and I knew she wanted to know whether I believed her.

'I do, Molly, I do believe you. But why would she do that?'

'She likes us quiet. She likes to go out without us.'

'And leave you home alone?'

Molly nodded.

I was careful then. I'd never seen any sign that she'd left the children unattended but I didn't want Molly to think I doubted her. 'When was the last time?'

'I don't know.'

'Since I've known you?'

She shook her head, 'She has been good since we came here but she's started being angry again.'

'Angry about what?'

'She says we're in the way. She put it in the orange juice and I told Luke not to drink it.'

'How do you know it was in your drink?'

'I saw her. And if she was really angry we had to swallow tablets.' Molly brought her thumb and forefinger together as if holding something tiny. 'Sometimes I hid them and we'd be home all night on our own.'

'You hid them? Where?'

'Connor painted me a moneybox.'

'The one with a flower on your windowsill?'

She nodded. 'It's where I save important things.'

I heard the door close and Briggs had already gone. I wrapped my arms around her and hugged her tight. 'You are so brave, Molly.'

DC June Leonard joined us then.

'How did you know?' I asked.

'It was Briggs. He has an ear for the truth.'

I spent the rest of the afternoon in that room. I sat with Molly until Luke arrived and then the three of us and DC Leonard were given a tray of sandwiches. Luke ate, Molly didn't. Instead she curled up against me and fell asleep.

It seemed hard to believe that it was the same room that I'd sat in when I'd made my statement against Andy Tyler all those months ago.

I stayed with Molly until she woke, then I spoke to DC Leonard. 'June? Please could I see my parents now?'

MONDAY 25 SEPTEMBER, 2017

It had been several days since Joanne had been formally charged with Matt Edwards's murder. Briggs and I sat on the bench closest to Cambridge's Parkside Station. Molly and Luke had brought a sponge football with them and kicked it around on the grass. It was an unorthodox way to meet but none of us was complaining.

'Do you want to know the great thing about the internet?' Briggs said.

'Go on.'

'Sometimes people forget what they've saved to the cloud. They delete their hard disc, bin it even, and don't notice what they can't see.'

'Such as?'

'Research on Matt and everyone in your building. She studied you all, then picked you to take the blame for his death before she'd even met you in person.'

'So,' I asked, 'how did you know it wasn't me?'

'There were inconsistencies in your story, and the source was always the same: Joanne. Connor was her stepson, not her son. He and his dad Grant died in a boat, but not in an accident. It was ruled as suicide and murder. The boat had a small sleeping area and a motor. Grant Carter had supposedly given his son sedatives, dosed himself up, then fed the exhaust into the cabin. They died from carbon monoxide poisoning.'

'But I didn't say anything to disprove any of that.'

'You said enough for me to know that one of you was, at very least, a small-scale liar. And yes, it could have been you, but sedatives were used in Matt Edward's death and Grant Carter's; that alone warranted further inspection.' He gave a snort of disgust. 'All the circumstantial against you was clouding the picture for some. Anderson was convinced it was you. But the best lessons in this job are the ones that can't be taught.'

'Such as?'

'Knowing in your gut when a child's asking for help. Molly wasn't asking whether you would hurt her, she was checking you were safe.'

'Poor kids.'

'Molly's a clever girl. We found seventeen Hypnovodram tablets in her moneybox. The tablets were manufactured in Australia to a formulation that was discontinued four years ago. The same batch was used to drug Joanne's husband and stepson.'

'She killed them?'

Briggs and I were both watching the children but from the corner of my eye I saw him nod. 'Joanne and Grant weren't happily married. They'd been separated for several months and she didn't want him to have custody. He didn't have much money and she inherited debt she wouldn't have had if she'd simply divorced him.'

'So much for her being able to buy a house outright.'

'I reckon the debt was a shock to her. I'm sure if Grant and Connor hadn't died a two-hour drive away from where she was living with two small children she might have been under greater scrutiny.'

'She never was?'

'Not really. A woman had been sighted at the boat but there was no clear description. Being at home with the children was Joanne's alibi. It would have taken a minimum of four hours to get to the boat and back and that was without convincing her husband to share a drink and waiting for the sedatives to kick in. Who leaves a two-year-old and a four-year-old unattended for that length of time? But now we know that the children could have been drugged while she left them, her movements become a lot easier to piece together.'

'That's still not proof.'

291

'No, it's not.' A small smile played on his lips. 'She confessed this morning.'

'To killing her husband and his son? Why would she?'

'Matt Edwards was her meal ticket and she worked on him; she knows we have more than enough for a guilty verdict in his case so she's confessed to the other deaths in return for the agreement that we won't extradite her to Australia. She won't be tried for killing a child.'

'She should be.'

'It will be better for Luke and Molly this way.'

'Shit,' I muttered. I watched Luke dribble the ball around Molly then pass it to her.

Briggs nudged my arm. 'They'll be okay.'

'I hope so.'

A moment later his phone buzzed and he flashed it towards me as he relayed the message. 'Five minutes.'

'Good,' I replied, but I was unprepared for the sudden rush of tears that filled my eyes. I wiped them away.

'And you'll be okay too,' he assured me. 'And just so you know, I've always believed you.'

Their names were Penny and Ron Carter. They looked about the same age as my own parents. Ron greeted me warmly, Penny was more hesitant.

'Molly, Luke,' I called. The children stopped playing and studied the group of adults from fifty yards away. 'Will they remember you?'

Ron nodded, 'Of course.'

Penny stared back at the children, 'Maybe not. We never saw them after Grant's death, you know. We tried, but she moved away.'

'And it's a big country,' Ron added.

I waved at the children to come over and they made an unhurried approach.

'She didn't just take these two from us, she took Grant and Connor too,' he continued.

I nodded. 'I know.'

'We had to accept that our son had killed our grandson and taken

292

his own life. And poor Penny . . .' He reached for his wife. 'You love them no matter what they've done, but it crippled us.'

Tears rolled down Penny's cheek and she fought to dry her eyes before Molly and Luke came too close. She stepped forward and spread her arms wide to greet them.

Ron leant closer to me. 'You'll never understand what you've given our family, Emily.'

They were just yards away when Molly grabbed her brother's hand and led him closer. 'Luke, it's Nanna.'

ACKNOWLEDGEMENTS

I must begin by thanking Little, Brown and, in particular, Krystyna Green, Amanda Keats, Rebecca Sheppard, Ellie Russell, Tara Loder, Jess Gulliver, Amy Donegan and Beth Wright. And special thanks to Howard Watson, who is an absolute pleasure to work with, and to Sean Garrehy for the fabulous cover design.

I also want to say a huge thank you to my excellent agent Broo Doherty and to the team at DHH, particularly for their inspirational Crime in the Court event, and to Emily Glenister for lending her name to a character.

Thank you to the Royal Literary Fund for their ongoing support.

And thank you to Lisa Faratro and all at CPI Books, Chatham for a wonderful visit.

Writing the acknowledgements gives me the perfect opportunity to thank those who have shared their expertise and given me their time. In no particular order, thank you to Liz Bradbury, Yvette Smith, Lisa Sanford, Genevieve Pease, Jane Martin, Lynn Fraser, Charlotte Hockin, Jenna Hawkins, Dr William Holstein, Claire Tombs and Christine Bartram. I also greatly appreciate the generosity of writers Sophie Hannah and Amanda Jennings.

Finally, love and thanks to my wonderful family for all their support and encouragement: to Jacen, Lana, Dean, Natalie and my sister Stella.